# FROM THE RIVER TO THE SEA
## A Novel of Love and Conflict on an Elite College Campus

LAWRENCE MARTIN

This is a work of fiction. All characters portrayed herein with spoken dialogue are created by the author, and any resemblance to living persons is purely coincidental. All faculty and student names associated with fictional Great Lakes University are also fictional, as are book citations attributed to these characters.

Book and article citations not attributable to fictional characters, or about the works of fictional characters, are real and searchable on the internet. Film documentaries cited in the book are also real, and can be downloaded on streaming services.

Lawrence Martin
drlarry437@gmail.com
January 2024

# Acknowledgments

I received valuable feedback from my writing critique group Wannabe Writers, from my wife Ruth, and from beta-reader Paul Rothberg.

# Source of pictures in Chapter 7

**<u>Amin Husseini meets with Hitler</u>**

https://www.timesofisrael.com/full-official-record-what-the-mufti-said-to-hitler/

From Ullstein Bild/The Granger Collection

**<u>Attacks on Israel May 1948</u>**

https://en.wikipedia.org/wiki/1948_Arab%E2%80%93Israeli_War

**<u>Camp David Summit 2000</u>**

https://en.wikipedia.org/wiki/2000_Camp_David_Summit

**<u>Golda Meir</u>**

https://en.wikipedia.org/wiki/Golda_Meir

\* \* \*

Cover design by Dan Traynor, danieltraynor66@yahoo.com

# Contents

# Preface

## October 7, 2023

'We Are at War,' Netanyahu Says After Hamas Attacks Israel

## October 14, 2023
### College Students Protest Israel-Hamas War
News Reports

At colleges across the country, students marched in pro-Palestinian demonstrations, disrupting campus life. Supporters of Palestinians, many of whom wore face masks to hide their identities, held signs that read "Free Palestine" and "From the River to Sea, Palestine Will be Free."

After the Palestinian militant group Hamas' weekend attack

on Israel October 7, Israel has bombarded and laid siege to the Gaza Strip, controlled by Hamas, and plans a ground invasion. The Israel death toll had risen to more than 1300...

Amid the growing conflict, tensions between students on opposite sides of the issue have boiled over on some U.S. college campuses.

Statements by student groups supporting Palestinians have prompted outrage and fear among Jews and, in some cases, wider rebuke from public officials and corporations. There have been reports of harassment and assaults of both pro-Israel and pro-Palestinian students, deepening grief and putting students of all political stripes on high alert.

Several masked speakers at the pro-Palestine rally declined to reveal their full names, with one saying they did not feel safe enough on campus to disclose their identity. Many faulted the university for not expressing more support for Palestinian students and the people of Gaza.

The campus climate may only become more tense in coming days. Israel has vowed to annihilate Hamas in retribution for the deadliest attack by Palestinian militants in Israeli history.

Meanwhile, college administrators are grappling with how to keep campuses secure and denounce the violence in the Middle East without wading too deeply into a supercharged political and historical dispute that affects Jewish and Palestinian students personally.

# ONE

## Shabbat Shalom [Peaceful Sabbath]

### ONE YEAR EARLIER...

### Hillel House [Jewish campus organization], Great Lakes University, October 2022

Near the end of Hillel's large Shabbat dinner, with dessert on the table, faculty advisor Adele Birnbaum stood and clinked her glass with a spoon. After several clinks the room's conversation subsided, then she spoke. "Another great meal. We'll start our weekly meeting across the hall in ten minutes. It should be a short meeting, no more than half an hour. David Applebaum has prepared a very interesting topic for discussion, about a new movie on campus. See you over there."

David Applebaum, Hillel's student leader, sat next to Adele at one of the large round tables. "I'll keep my remarks short, Adele. Doubt we'll have many questions. I counted thirty-five students. Several new faces."

"I hope we're not opening up a can of worms here."

"Can of worms?" asked David.

"What I told you when you proposed Hillel get involved with this movie. Other Hillel chapters have said, 'leave it alone, let it be,' when the movie was shown on their campus. I did not agree, and have given you full support. I just hope we know what we're doing. Nothing is predictable in this business of fighting anti-Semitism."

"If Hillel doesn't fight it on campus, who will? I was hoping for more than thirty-five, considering we have over a thousand undergraduate and graduate Jewish students. But thirty-five is better than nothing. Well, let's get over there."

* * *

In the conference room, Ms. Birnbaum went to the podium, checked the mike and began speaking.

"Welcome once again to Hillel. Hope you all had a nice dinner. The main topic this evening is about a campus showing of the film 'Boycott,' this Sunday at the Student Union. It's free and begins at 2 pm. I'm sure most, if not all of you, have seen the ads in the campus newspaper. Let me see a show of hands. How many are *not* familiar with this film?"

Nearly every student raised a hand.

"Good. Then you've come to the right place. Your student leader David Applebaum has seen the film, and will be there during the discussion phase that follows on Sunday. Our hope is that you can attend, and be able to offer some comment during the discussion. David will explain more, then answer your questions. David?"

Applebaum got up and walked to stand behind the podium. He wore a baseball cap with "Hillel" stitched on the front.

"Shabbat shalom."

"Shabbat shalom," came several replies, albeit without much enthusiasm.

"The movie Adele mentioned, 'Boycott,' is a 2021 documentary available on Amazon Prime about one hour twenty minutes long. If you subscribe to Prime, it's only four dollars to watch.

Get a group of four together and it's a buck each. Not too bad. Anyway, as Adele said, the movie is showing this Sunday at the Union, and of course it's free to all students. So if you don't see it before then, try to make it at two pm. If you do see it ahead of time, just come at three fifteen and you'll be in time for the discussion that follows the film."

"What's it about, already?" someone shouted from the back of the room.

"Right," said David. "Basically, it's about one aspect of the Boycott, Divestment, Sanction movement against Israel, or BDS for short. I suspect most of you are at least somewhat familiar with BDS, since we've discussed it in previous Shabbat meetings, and in the Hillel newsletter. BDS is designed to influence – pressure would be a better word – people around the world to stop doing business with Israel unless and until Israel treats Palestinians in a manner more to the movement's liking. I'm being a little vague here by the term 'the movement's liking' because you'll never get a straight answer about the ultimate BDS goal, which is really only one thing. That is, the destruction of Israel.

"But I'm getting ahead of myself. As I said, the documentary is only about one aspect of the BDS movement. As you may know, many states have passed laws making it illegal for state-run or state-funded businesses to participate in BDS. Well, three different people in three different states sued, arguing that the state law as written against BDS violated their First Amendment rights. Arizona, Arkansas, and Texas were the three states. Each individual plaintiff refused to sign an agreement not to support BDS, and as a result they were cut off from receiving state funds. Then they sued, citing the First Amendment.

"So, the basic theme of the movie is the legal argument in these three states. Can they compel people who receive state money to sign a document pledging they won't boycott Israel. The movie was made a few years ago, so it's kind of dated in that respect."

"David, can I make a comment here?" asked one of the students.

"Uh, sure, Don, what is it? Please stand so people can see you and hear you better."

After standing, the student spoke. "For those of you who don't know me, I'm Don Ensley, a second-year law student. I wrote a paper on these cases, and have an update. As of now, thirty-five states have bills or executive orders to discourage boycotts of Israel. The three lawsuits portrayed in this movie have not erased the anti-BDS laws in those states, only led to modification in two. As David said, the basic argument by the plaintiffs is that the state laws requiring them to sign an agreement not to boycott Israel violate their First Amendment right to freedom of speech.

"The states have argued that the laws have nothing to do with prohibiting freedom of speech, and that they only specify what you must agree to if you work for the state, or provide services for payment. One of the plaintiffs ran a travel magazine with ads from a state travel bureau. Another plaintiff did counseling work for state prisoners, and the third, a Muslim woman, worked as a speech therapist under a state contract. I know David has more to tell you about the movie. Just keep in mind that the producers have tried to frame the documentary as basically about First Amendment rights, and there are good legal arguments on both sides. But let David tell you more."

David resumed his explanation. "Thanks, Don. Yes, that's right. The movie starts out as a pretty good documentary about whether these three states' anti-BDS laws infringe on freedom of speech, that is, whether or not they violate the First Amendment of the US Constitution. Had the movie kept this focus, as I said, it would be pretty reasonable. But as you'll see, it really has a much wider focus. It uses these lawsuits to unfairly malign Israel, and toward the end degenerates into a hate-filled anti-Semitic work of pure propaganda, comparing Israel to the apartheid regime of South Africa. The comparison of Israel to South Africa's apartheid is a lie, and designed to appeal to the ignorant students who watch this."

"Ignorant students? At Great Lakes University?" someone yelled from back of the room, affecting an air of disbelief.

Laughter ensued.

"Yes," replied David, "in this narrow sense. Look, I know students admitted to Great Lakes are all pretty much from the top ten percent of their high school class. But, sad to say, that doesn't mean every student has an open mind or cares to do research to uncover facts about controversial areas. For the current situation in Israel, there is no similarity whatsoever to South Africa's apartheid history. Yet that ends up being the major theme of the movie – that Israel treats the Palestinians like the white supremacists treated Blacks during apartheid.

"Students ignorant of Israel's history are apt to believe this," he continued, "but unfortunately that's the target audience. When you watch the movie, pay particular attention to the last scene, when pro-Palestinians are marching in a parade, carrying signs. Look carefully at what's written on those signs. That is the BDS message. Now, I'll open this to any more questions."

One student called out, "Who made this movie, and why is it being shown on our campus?"

"It was made by a pro-Palestinian group, Friends of Palestine, and is distributed by another group, World Without War. It's being shown because the campus is the home of free speech, and there's no reason to block it. It starts off as a reasonable documentary. It lulls you in. Only if you know the true history and the reality of Israel today does it become clear that it segues into anti-Israel propaganda. To have tried to block it from being shown would have been a big mistake."

"Let me rephrase my question," asked the inquisitor, a young woman. "Which group arranged for this showing on our campus?"

5

"BDS for Justice, which is an authorized campus club," replied Applebaum. "It's my understanding the club was contacted by World Without War, which distributes the film to campuses under license from the producers. Again, if you check the internet for reviews, you'll find little mention of the film's overt anti-Semitism. It's billed and promoted as a documentary about the First Amendment, and does start out that way. But as the film progresses, its intent becomes apparent."

A young man raised his hand and was called on. "Well, I'm Jewish and a member of BDS for Justice. And I know several Jews in the club. We do promote peace, and I haven't heard anything overtly anti-Semitic since joining. We just think Israel could do a better job in the way it treats Palestinians, and that a better job would ease the Israeli-Palestinian conflict."

"Thanks," said David. "Yes, I'm aware that several Jewish students are supporters of the BDS movement on campus. There are also national Jewish organizations who support BDS, or at least what they think BDS is all about. I'm not here to debate that, at least not now. If there are others here who support BDS, all I ask is for you to do some basic research on the internet. By the way, what year are you?"

"I'm a sophomore."

"Well, I hope you can come Sunday, and feel free to offer your comments after the movie."

There were no more questions. David took his seat in the front row and Adele resumed the podium. "Thanks, David," she said. "Now I'll go over Hillel's campus activities leading up to and including Thanksgiving."

Fifteen minutes later the meeting ended. On the way out another student, Steve Mandelbaum, walked up beside David and caught his attention. He and David had roomed together as freshmen. With different majors, they'd had only intermittent contact in the ensuing years. Like David, Steve now lived off campus.

"Hi, Steve, glad you could come. I almost didn't recognize you with that goatee."

Steve did not return the greeting, stating only, "You're wasting your time. You know that."

"What do you mean?" David looked around. Wishing to distance any discussion from other students, he stopped walking, and the two seniors were soon alone in the aisle.

"All this bullshit about fighting BDS, speaking out after the movie, doing research on the internet."

"What do you suggest? You're certainly aware of the anti-Semitism of BDS."

"And look who joins. Jews! Morons. You think you can change them? Fucking waste of time. That kid who spoke up? Oh, yeah: 'A better job would ease the Israeli-Palestinian conflict.' Bullshit. You're not going to fix that nonsense."

They resumed walking to Hillel's foyer. "And what do you suggest?" asked David.

"You want to help Israel fight BDS?"

"I'm listening."

"Follow me. Make Aliyah, move to Israel. I'm moving right after graduation, joining the IDF. That's how you fight BDS and anti-Semitism. Not with namby-pamby discussion groups."

"Steve, I hear what you're saying, but I disagree. We've got to fight here in the United States. These young Jews who join BDS are not morons, they're just misguided, willfully ignorant."

"Bunch of crap," Steve snapped. "I've talked to some of them. You can't get through their progressive bullshit. I've pointed out founder Omar Barghouti's comments, I've shown them the true goals of BDS. They don't believe it. It's all about "fairness" and "equality" to these morons. You want to help? Move to Israel, make Aliyah. Defend Israel where it will mean something."

"How do you know the Israeli army is going to accept you?"

"Any healthy young Jew can join. You move, you get Israeli

citizenship, you sign up. Then you can fight this garbage where it counts. Over there, where you belong. Not here."

"Steve, I don't remember you feeling this way when we roomed together. When did you change? When you decided to grow a beard?"

"Long before that. It took a while. I decided last year, during an extended trip to Israel. I almost quit college and joined then, but realized I'll be more useful with my engineering degree."

"Do you speak Hebrew?"

"A little. I'm learning."

"Let's stay in touch. I plan to return to Israel next summer, not for Aliyah, but to tour the country and see an old friend in Beersheba. If you're not hidden away in some army camp, I'll look you up."

"Yeah, that's fine. Maybe by then you'll see the light. Wasting your passion at Great Lakes University. Which I now refer to as Great Lakes Stupidity."

"What a strange comment, Steve. Last I checked, we are ranked among the top ten universities."

"Yeah, I know. And in the other nine are several Ivies. Even stupider. Don't get me started."

# TWO

## "Boycott" - the Movie

David arrived at the Student Union theater a half hour early and deposited 150 copies of a reading list on a table inside, near the entrance. The table served as a distribution site for flyers about upcoming movies and other events, but you could place just about anything there except for-profit ads.

Of the theater's three hundred cushioned seats, two hundred were on the lower level and another hundred in the balcony. It was rare for any event to fill all seats, and David did not think more than a hundred students would attend this one – several, he hoped, from Hillel. By 2 p.m. the lower level was about three-quarters filled. As he expected, there was no pre-show announcement. Also, thankfully, no coming attractions, and no ads. The lights went out and the movie began.

David did not relish viewing the film again, but figured he might pick up some things missed the first time, though there were really no subtleties in the story. The movie explained that it was about a First Amendment issue in three specific states: Arizona, Arkansas, and Texas. These three passed anti-BDS laws, stating that if you do business with the state, you must agree to abide by the law: not to participate in any boycott, divestment, or sanctions against Israel. If you didn't sign, you risked losing whatever payment – or job – you had with the state.

The movie covered three plaintiffs, one from each state, their legal arguments and the three states' counterarguments. But it covered more than the three legal battles. Interspersed were scenes from Israel, edited to show a cruel and discriminatory country. Not a word about the unprovoked attacks from Gaza and the West Bank, or the Arabs' repeated promises to destroy the country and remove all the Jews.

Throughout the movie he occasionally turned around to see if any more people were coming in. A few minutes before the movie ended, he saw a cadre of seven or eight students enter the theater and take seats toward the back. He could not make out faces but assumed they were from Hillel, coming as a group.

At 3:20 the movie ended, lights went on, and a man in his mid-thirties, dressed in a suit and with a microphone in hand, stood in front of the audience.

"Great movie, wasn't it? I'm Brian D'Haviland, from World without Borders. We sponsored this movie and I'll be opening up for discussion in a minute. Let me just add that a representative from Hillel has placed a flyer on the front table, with a list of references about BDS. I noticed a few people came in late. If BDS is new to you, in a nutshell it stands for Boycott, Divestment, Sanction—basically a grass roots movement to persuade Israel to deal fairly with the Palestinians in the Holy Land.

"The Hillel flyer is fine, and you should read as much as you care to. However, his list omits some very important references, many by Jewish authors, both from the United States and Israel. So, next to Hillel's list you'll find a one-page list of *Jewish* authors that World Without Borders has assembled. Their books will give you a more accurate picture of the Israeli-Palestinian conflict and the goals of BDS. I'm not going to make any speech, just ask you to pick up both flyers, do your research. See what Jewish authors think about how Palestinians are treated by Israelis. Okay, any questions, comments?"

David raised his hand and was called on. He stood to speak. "Can everyone hear me?"

"No," came several replies. D'Haviland rushed over to hand David the microphone.

"Thanks. I'm David Applebaum and I placed Hillel's list of recommended books on the table. Do pick one up on your way out, then go to Amazon, look up the books, and download or order one or two. There you'll see the truth about BDS. Israel is not anything like the apartheid of South Africa years ago, which is what this movie tries to claim. To state so is pure propaganda, nothing more. The goal of BDS *is* the destruction of Israel. But don't just take my word for it. Do some reading, investigating. On that point I agree with Mr. D'Haviland. Yes, there are some prominent Jews who support BDS – academics and intellectuals – and I hesitate to call them anti-Semitic. They have peculiar motives, which vary, but the more prominent ones have been debunked by Alan Dershowitz and other writers listed in the Hillel handout. So please read and come to your own conclusions. I'll stop there."

There was scattered applause, with students from the back of the room clapping in unison – the late-to-arrive Hillel group. Amidst the clapping another hand went up, and the student stood to speak, someone David knew well, at least his views. He waited for quiet, then began.

"I'm Gordon Geddy, head of BDS for Justice here on campus, so many of you know me. David and I have sparred on this issue before, and I respect his opinions, though very much disagree. When you see just how Palestinians are being treated by Israelis, you can't help but conclude that in many ways it's worse than South Africa years ago. Israel calls itself a democracy, something the old South Africa never claimed. Israel claims to respect all religions and races, another aspect South Africa made no pretense about, unlike Israel.

"South Africa was open about its apartheid. The separation practiced between Blacks and Whites was never denied. In Israel, apartheid is hidden behind barriers, unwritten laws and rules, and the always-spouted claim of anti-Semitism when criticized. I am not anti-Semitic. It's a cliché, I know, but some of my good friends are Jewish. So yes, do your reading, your investigation. Better yet, if you can, travel to Israel, to the West Bank, and see for yourself how the Palestinian refugees are being treated. Then you will come to understand why the world considers Israel an apartheid state. Thank you."

Applause came, from perhaps a third of the audience.

A young woman raised her hand, just two rows behind David, and was called on. "Please state your name and student status," requested D'Haviland, who brought her the microphone as she stood.

"Rebecca Goldman. I'm a freshman. My grandparents survived the holocaust. They barely made it out alive, liberated from Auschwitz as kids in 1945. Luckily, they were able to come to America. They married over here in their early twenties, gave birth to my mother. I was raised Jewish and am a member of BDS for Justice. I know from my own history what discrimination can do. BDS aims to have all people treated fairly, not shoved into refugee camps. I want Israel to thrive, but I also want justice for the Palestinians. That's why I support BDS."

Some applause, and she sat down. David stared at the girl. *Holocaust survivors? My grandparents lost relatives in the holocaust. Who is she?*

He did not hear the next speaker. Something about this Rebecca Goldman took hold of his brain – her background for sure, but more so just the way she looked, her flowing light brown hair, sensuous lips, nice-sized breasts accentuated by a tight sweater, even the way she spoke. Not the opinion she offered – words of just another ignorant freshman – but her voice and her bearing. *A beautiful Jewish girl.* He could not stop staring.

She caught his glance and smiled. He turned around to take his seat. *I'll meet her.*

Another student was called on and David re-focused. She was one of the Hillel group to enter late. Microphone in hand, she spoke in a clear, loud voice.

"I'm Sadie Myofsky. I agree with David Applebaum. I saw the movie on Amazon Prime and found it very biased, really one-sided. David remarked that the true goal of BDS is the destruction of Israel, which is well-known to anyone who has studied the movement. Why wasn't this mentioned in the movie? Oh, wait a minute it was – but by a far-right religious zealot, who is portrayed as unhinged. Having that guy being the main mouthpiece speaking the full truth against BDS is subtle propaganda. Makes it seem like both sides are being presented. So throughout the movie we have sane, educated, smooth-talking people supporting BDS. Then, almost for comic relief, the few anti-BDS people are portrayed as nut jobs or far-right extremists. As I said, movie propaganda. Many more people, people not far right, not unhinged, will tell you the truth about BDS, and quote sources to prove it. My god, fellow students, please, do your homework!"

"Damn right!" yelled one member of her group.

"One more comment, if I may," offered Ms. Myofsky. "When you go to Amazon Prime, look for another movie titled 'Boycott This!' It gives a true picture of the BDS movement. It's a little older than the movie we just saw, so has nothing about the lawsuits, but does go into the history of BDS. And it tells the story with a bit of humor. So watch 'Boycott This!' on Amazon Prime."

There was further back and forth among the students, more

pro and con about the movie. David could hardly wait for the end, to meet the young woman just two rows back.

Finally, at four p.m. the session ended. The last words from D'Haviland were, "Remember, pick up the list of Jewish authors as you leave the theater. See what they write."

David walked to the aisle beside Rebecca's row and waited. *Don't blow this.*

Once Rebecca reached the aisle, he said, "Hi. I just wanted to meet you. We have something in common. My ancestors were also from Europe, caught up in the Holocaust.

"Oh?" she replied, "That's interesting."

"Yes. Could we talk just for a few minutes, maybe in the lobby? It's a little chilly outside."

"Sure."

They reached the lobby and David spoke first. "I see we have different views about BDS, but I'd like to learn a bit more about your views, how you arrived at them." *I want this girl, not her views.*

"What do you want to know?"

He looked around. Students were milling about and talking. "This isn't the best place to discuss anything. How about we go for a cup of coffee at the Union Deli? It's pretty quiet in there, we can talk."

She looked at her watch, waited a moment, then said. "I'm okay with that."

# THREE

# Coffee, Key Lime Pie, and Talk

Inside the Student Union Deli, adjacent to the theater, they found a booth and sat facing each other. Waiters and waitresses no longer served customers at tables; everything was ordered by tablet, and David picked up the attached device. "I'll have coffee, how about you?"

"Same, that'll be fine."

"How about key lime pie? Don't know why they serve it up here, but I've had it before. It's good."

"Oh, not a whole slice. How about we split a piece?"

"No problem. He pressed a few buttons on the tablet, placing the order. "What'd you think of the movie? Have you seen it before? It's on Amazon Prime."

"Never before. Our club told us about it, but I also read the ads in the *Daily Laker*. I liked it. I agree with some of the discussion. Israel's not comparable to South Africa, but I see many of the criticisms as justified."

*Go slow. Don't argue. She is not stupid. Just a bit ignorant. Well, a lot ignorant.* "So, where are you from?"

"Palo Alto."

"Palo Alto?" replied David, with genuine surprise. "California?"

She nodded.

"How'd you end up in Great Lakes University?"

"I wanted a top school not in California. My father's a professor at Stanford. I applied there, but along the way decided it best if I go elsewhere. Also got into Berkley, but still too close to home."

"Well, why not Harvard, Yale, Penn?"

"The East Coast was a bit too far from home. So, I applied and here I am."

"Happy with the choice?"

"Very. A little worried about the winters, but I've seen snow."

"In Palo Alto?"

"Sure. Maybe a few days a year, not much. We don't have snowplows. It melts quickly."

"What does your father teach at Stanford?"

"He's a law professor."

"And let me guess. You're pre-law."

"Very good. But no intention of being a law professor."

"I know, I see your future gig. Corporate attorney, defending wealthy business execs. Fits in with your concern for the oppressed of the Earth."

"Funny you are."

They both laughed.

*I'm hitting it off with her. This is good.*

"If I end up a corporate lawyer, shoot me now," she replied.

"When did you learn about your grandparents? In the camps."

"One camp. Auschwitz. Something I really don't feel like discussing now. I'm sure we both have stories to tell about the Holocaust. But not now. Instead, what about your career goal? Let me guess. College professor, of Middle East studies."

"No way. I'm headed to medical school. Just finished my applications."

"Fooled me. Where do you want to go?"

"It doesn't matter much. It's very different from law school, where the school's ranking is important for a future career. Not so in medicine. Do you know what they call the person last in class in med school?"

"Dumb?"

"Now *you're* being funny. I like that. No, one more guess."

She shook her head.

"Doctor," he replied with authority.

"Got me. I haven't heard that one before. No doctor jokes at home. My mother's a physician."

"Oh? What's her specialty?"

"Pediatrics. She works in a clinic now, only forty hours a week."

"Your family impresses me more by the minute. What about siblings?"

A serving robot rolled up to their booth and announced, in the voice of a young woman, "Your order is ready. Please transfer dishes to your tabletop. Thank you." David removed the two coffee cups and a plate of pie and two forks. The robot rolled away.

"Amazing," he said. "These bots solve the staffing shortage. Taste the pie. It's good."

Rebecca scooped up a slice. "Not bad. I don't know if they even have this in California. It's a Florida dish, isn't it?"

"Key West. That's one of the things Key West is famous for. Do you know what else?"

"Not really."

"The Hemingway House. He lived there in the 1930s. And kept six-toed cats. It's a popular tourist attraction, and these cats roam all over the place. Hemingway's gone but the cats – or their great- great- great- grandchildren – live on."

"Interesting."

"Yeah, you can google it. 'Hemingway six-toed cats.' Now, what was I saying? Oh, yeah, any siblings?"

"I have an older sister, married, with one child."

"Let me guess. She's a nuclear physicist."

"Not quite. She went to nursing school. Her husband's a software engineer with Apple. Highly paid, from what I hear. I think you've about used up your twenty questions. More about you. Where from? Parents? Siblings?"

"*Borr*ring. Rebecca, do you read Wikipedia?"

"You have a Wikipedia page?"

"Not yet. That was a joke."

"Really? Want some advice? Don't do standup."

They laughed again.

*I'm falling in love with this girl.* "Okay, I'll be serious. I'm from Cleveland. Not so far away, compared to California. My mother's an attorney, dad's a lung doctor." *Stop, see if she reacts.*

Rebecca took a sip of coffee, made no comment.

"I thought you'd jump on the sort of mirror image of our parents. You know. Lawyer-doctor, doctor-lawyer. And we both plan to follow our father's profession. That sort of thing."

"Is your mother a law professor? That would help solidify the mirror image thing."

"No, she's a federal public defender."

"I'm impressed," she said. "That may also be my career path. As for medicine, my Jewish mother always told me, like all Jewish mothers, don't ever marry a doctor."

"I think you've altered your mother's words. The clue is when you said, "like all Jewish mothers."

"Right. I misspoke. The exact quote: "Try not to marry a doctor.""

"Why so, if I may ask?"

"She was being a bit flippant. She thinks they sometimes work too hard, to the detriment of their children. One colleague in particular had a messy divorce, kids got caught in the middle, and that bothered her."

"True, some doctors do bury themselves in their profession, their kids hardly see them. Not me. I'm not going to work more than eighty hours a week."

She laughed. "Second City, here you come."

"You know about Chicago's Second City?"

"Yeah, the birthplace of many comedians. Read about it."

"Have you been to downtown Chicago since coming to Great Lakes?"

"Nah, too busy. And I hear the traffic is horrendous."

"I assume you don't have a car. If you drive it's only about forty-five minutes due east of the campus, via the interstates. Probably longer during rush hour. But you could take the train; Metra will get you there in half an hour. And the station's only a short walk from here."

"What's to see?"

"Just the birthplace of modern American architecture. Architecture was my first career choice. At least in high school."

"What happened?"

"Couldn't draw. And if I couldn't be Frank Lloyd Wright, I lost interest."

"He did the Guggenheim Museum in New York, right?"

"Right you are! About Wright."

She smiled. "You're getting better. For now, though, stick with medicine."

*She is fun to talk to, but I can't stop fantasizing about her body, those mounds under her sweater. Need to stay focused, keep talking.*

"Yeah, medicine as a career. But I'm a nerd on Wright's architecture. At some point we should drive up to Taliesin in southern Wisconsin, his summer home for many years."

"Tally what?"

"Taliesin. It's a Welsh term for 'shining brow.' How Wright envisioned the setting for his home. On a hillside."

"Tell me, will I get this smart when I'm a senior?"

"You're smart now. Everyone here is smart. What you learn over the next four years is up to you."

"Do you give graduation speeches also? Sounds like one I heard in high school."

"Sorry. I can get pedantic at times. Just tell me to shut up."

"I don't want you to shut up," she replied. "Would like to hear more. Do you have brothers, sisters?"

"An older brother. Eight years older."

"What's he do?"

"He's on Wall Street. Runs a private investment fund for J.P. Morgan. Smart guy, Harvard undergraduate and business school. We're not that close."

"Why not?"

"As I said, eight years between us. I'm twenty, he's twenty-eight. Married, two kids, lives in Manhattan. Don't see him that much."

"Is he as pro-Israel as you are?"

David paused, did not answer.

"Should I repeat the question?"

"No, I heard you. It's just something that doesn't admit to an easy yes or no. Let's say we have our differences. It's nuanced. Leave it there. Maybe another time I'll bore you with how my brother and I interact."

They bantered for another twenty minutes, discussing trips taken, pets, hobbies, and food choices. Then she got up to use the restroom.

"I'll pay the bill while you're gone." He hovered his credit card over the screen total, declined a printed receipt. Alone for the moment, he thought hard about how to phrase his next question.

*We've hit it off. Maybe she'll say yes. Maybe she'll tell me to get lost. I'll never know if I don't ask.*

# FOUR

## David's Desire

Rebecca returned from the Deli restroom a few minutes later, resumed her seat opposite David. "Well, I really should get back to the dorm. I have an eight o'clock class tomorrow."

"Would you like to come to my place for a while? So we can get to know each other a little better?"

She stared at him for a few seconds, then: "That question didn't just pop into your head. How long have you been thinking to ask?"

"Oh, since I first laid eyes on you. I became attracted the minute I saw you in the theater. Can't help it."

"I've been here less than two months, and this is now the second time a first date has asked me to have sex with him that same night."

"Did I mention sex?"

"Was there something else on your mind?"

"I guess I'm like an open book. Sorry. It's true. You mentioned 'the second time.' What happened the first time?"

"It didn't happen."

"I mean, what were the circumstances, if I may ask?"

"Mundane. It wasn't even a date, just a random conversation."

"I'm all ears."

She stares for a moment, then says, "It was a social at our sorority, a few weeks ago. I had just joined, and all the new members had a meet-and-greet with some guys from TEP fraternity. They came over for an hour, for some punch and cookies. I got to talking with a nice Jewish kid from Detroit. We had some things in common, Jewish geography, that type of thing, so we hit it off pretty well. Talked to him for about twenty minutes until the social ended, and the guys had to leave. At that point, he asked, 'Hey, would you like to come to my place? I live off campus, we can drive over there.'"

"After just twenty minutes?"

"Yep. Weird, isn't it?"

"But you and I have been talking much longer. So, in my case, not weird. Normal, maybe. What'd you tell him?"

"His question was so absurd, I had to fight hard to avoid insulting him. I said, no, I had a lot of work to do, but said it in a nice way, showing I was open to seeing him again. He asked to exchange phone numbers, which we did. Then we said goodbye. His last words were, 'I'll call you.' Then the strangest thing."

"What's that?"

"He never called."

"You mean he wants to sleep with you, you give him your phone number, and he never called? Does your phone block unknown numbers?"

"Yeah, but I put his number in my phone, so that wasn't the issue. He just never called."

"I can only assume he found another girl to sleep with. And you never tried to contact him?"

"No, of course not. I thought the same thing. He found another girl."

"So, are you also fighting now to avoid insulting me?"

She laughed. "No, no. You waited an hour. Beyond the insult range."

"That's good. And your answer to my very reasonable question?"

"Why is sex on every boy's mind? Dumb question. Scratch that. I'm not naïve. There is one thing I'll tell you, and I don't know why I'm telling you, but since you've opened the door, I'll tell you anyway. I'm a virgin."

"Really? A beautiful young girl from California? How'd you get through high school not having sex? Last stat I read, 101 percent of Palo Alto seniors lost their virginity by graduation."

"Not true. It's 99 percent. I was in the one percent."

"Wait a minute. Wait a minute. This wasn't on my mind at all, but you're not, you're not…"

"A lesbian?"

"Yeah, a lesbian."

"No, no. I like boys. I just made a decision not to lose my virginity while in high school."

"Did you date?"

"Sure. I even had a steady boyfriend the last few months of high school."

"Assuming he's like any normal high school teenager, how did you keep him away from your body parts?"

"I didn't."

"Rebecca, you're getting me excited. My anatomy is changing as we sit."

She laughed. "Well, there's three feet of table between us, so I don't feel anything."

"You are cruel. Driving me crazy. Is that your intent?"

"No, I'm sorry. But you started this with your question. I guess I wanted you to know two things. I'm a virgin and I'm not sexually naïve."

"Please explain the last part. I won't ask for any details."

She paused.

"Please? Just generalities is okay."

"We – his name was Judson – had an agreement. I would satisfy him when we were close, and he wouldn't force himself on me. Inside of me. It worked fine for a while."

"Satisfy him when close? That can only mean one of two things. Your hand or your mouth."

"Use your imagination."

"Got it. Did he reciprocate?"

"Again, your imagination."

"Got it again. Right now, three feet away may not be enough. We'll have to sit here a while, maybe talk about the weather."

"No, not much longer. I really have to get back."

"You're leaving me hanging. Oh-oh, not the right word choice. I'll try again. You're leaving me curious. You said, 'It worked fine for a while.' What happened?"

"You really want to know? It's kind of seedy."

"Absolutely. Seedy is good."

"Well, okay. We had this relationship for about four months. We'd get intimate, on average, once every week to ten days. I knew it would end at graduation since he was going to UCLA, and I was coming here, but we sort of planned to stay in touch with calls, Facebook, whatever, then perhaps see each other during holidays, when we both returned to Palo Alto." She paused, to have a sip of coffee.

"Anyway, a month before graduation, I'm in class, the bell rings, and as I get up to leave, this other senior girl comes up to me and says, 'Rebecca, can I talk to you for minute?' This is a girl who hasn't said two words to me the whole year. A campus whore, with a reputation for sleeping with every football player. Twice, maybe three times."

"Not your best friend."

"Seriously, the girl is stacked, drop-dead gorgeous, with the morals of a pig. Well, at least by reputation. 'Sure,' I say to Cynthia, 'what's up?'"

"She says, 'Let's go outside where we can have a little privacy.'"

"I already have an inkling what this is about, but say nothing. We walk out to a courtyard, away from other students, and she says, her exact words: 'I know you've been having sex with Judson, and I just wanted to fill you in on what's happening.'"

"Bombshell. No surprise, though. I played dumb. I asked, innocent like, 'Oh, what's that?'"

"And she said?"

"She said, 'I've recently gotten together with him, and he just wanted you to know.'"

"I assume," said David, 'gotten together' is all-the-way-sex."

"Obviously, but I told her to just get to the point, I have another class in a few minutes. 'Well,' she says, 'he won't be seeing you again, and he wanted me to tell you.' Then she twists the knife and adds: 'I can give him something you couldn't – or wouldn't. He just wanted you to know, and thought it best if I told you. That's all. No hard feelings.'"

"Wow! How did you respond?"

"I didn't scream, but did get a little crude. I said, 'So, how long have you been fucking Judson? Just curious.' And she replied, 'It's called sexual intercourse, honey, something with which I'm told you're not familiar.'"

"Rebecca, this is fascinating stuff. I can see it streaming on Netflix. The language – my God, you can't write a better script."

"Not fiction, trust me. I should have put my cell phone on record mode, the minute she asked to speak to me."

"Did she answer your question about how long?"

"Yes. Two weeks, she said. And I had been with Judson just a week earlier. That meant I had my mouth where...I'm going to vomit."

"Please don't. I get the picture. So, you never saw Judson again?"

"Just in the hallway. Didn't make eye contact. It was over."

"Okay, but that was five months ago. No boys since? None?"

"A few dates, but nothing sexual. Virgin still."

"So, getting back to my question about tonight, the answer is no?"

"Yes, it's no. I'm not ready."

"Not even the Judson arrangement?"

"Not even. The next intimacy will be all the way or nothing. No more game playing."

"I understand. Would you promise me one thing?"

"What's that?"

"When the time comes, let me be the one?"

"I can't promise that. Maybe when the time comes, it will be my wedding night."

"I seriously doubt that. Can't imagine your fiancé would wait that long. One more question. Can we exchange phone numbers?"

"Sure."

"Great. Guaranteed you will hear from me again."

David waited a few days, then called Rebecca early Wednesday evening. "Still thinking about you," he said. "Every waking minute."

"What about medical school? Have I replaced that ambition?"

"Okay, you and med school. Anyway, I want to invite you to a talk at Hillel House on Sunday afternoon. We have a guest speaker from New York, who has written a book about the Israel-Palestinian Conflict. Fair warning, it'll be pro-Israel, but based on facts. Should be educational. Will you come?"

"Funny you should ask. I'm actually walking over to our monthly BDS for Justice club meeting, where we also have a guest speaker. It's on Zoom, though. The speaker's from Jewish Voice for Peace. You've heard of them?"

"Oh, yes. Famous for being anti-Israel. One of several Jewish organizations who lobby against Israel, but they're the most extreme. Big supporters of BDS. No surprise JVP is speaking to your group."

"David, it didn't even enter my mind to invite you to this meeting, but now that I have you on the phone, would you like to come?"

"Think I'll pass on that opportunity. Gordon Geddy would not like to see me in his meeting."

"Oh, I understand. I'm just a dumb freshman, fixed in my ideas and –"

"Rebecca, you're not dumb. Far from it. I think you know how I feel about you. I would just love for you to come Sunday, sit and listen. Will you?"

"For you, yes. But it doesn't matter what history your esteemed professor teaches. I'm not going to abandon *Tikkun olam.*"

"*Tikkun olam?*"

"Yes, you know, 'improving the world.'"

"Right, right, I forgot. Anyway, can I pick you up Sunday, and we'll walk together over to Hillel House?"

"Sure, what time?"

"The talk's at two. I'll come by at one, after lunch, and we'll have a slow walk over."

"That's fine."

"Okay, see you then. Enjoy your Zoom talk. Bye."

FIVE

# BDS for Justice

At the BDS meeting Rebecca counted twenty-five students, almost filling one of the Student Union rooms. The large screen in front showed a live feed from the JVP office in Berkeley, California. The speaker was not yet at her desk.

A few minutes after seven, Geddy stood to address the BDS group. His features suggested European stock: six feet tall and slim, blond hair, blue eyes, aquiline nose.

"Thank you all for coming to BDS for Justice. It's certainly been an interesting few days. How many were able to attend Sunday's showing of the movie 'Boycott'?"

Half the group raised a hand.

"It's unfortunate that our group is sometimes perceived as anti-Semitic, which was the opinion of some after the movie. It's just not true. We attract students of all faiths, and tonight we have a Jewish speaker, from a large national Jewish organization, Jewish Voice for Peace. Just a show of hands, how many of you are Jewish?"

Four students raised a hand, including Rebecca, who sat toward the back.

"And, how many are Christian, including Protestants and Catholics?"

More hands raised, including Geddy's.

"And I know we have several Muslim members, from Qatar and Egypt. How many are here tonight?"

Rebecca counted three students with hands raised.

"And lastly, how many of you profess no religion at all, or are atheists?"

Three hands went up.

"Did I miss anyone? Hindu, Buddhist?"

One hand raised.

"Yes?" asked Geddy of the lone student, a short, stocky man who wore a ponytail.

"Bahá'í," came the reply. Then he stood so the students could see the front of his sweatshirt, a large picture of the domed Bahá'í temple in Wilmette, IL.

"Welcome," said Geddy. "We truly have great diversity in our group. Our speaker tonight is Miriam Silverstein, communications director of Jewish Voice for Peace. JVP was founded in Berkely over two decades ago, as an organization advocating for Palestinian freedom. Since it's a Jewish organization, they can hardly be called anti-Semitic. Miss Silverstein will talk for about twenty minutes, then take your questions. So, we're ready to begin. She's just waiting for me to – oh, there she is."

The speaker, a middle-aged woman, entered the screen and sat at her desk. Behind her were two flags, one for Israel and one for the Palestinians.

"Ms. Silverstein," said Geddy, "we have over two dozen students eager to hear your talk, so please begin anytime."

"Thank you, thank you. I heard Mr. Geddy's introduction. Just a little background. Jewish Voice for Peace was founded to promote peace with the Palestinians, an organization where Jews against Israel's occupation could freely express their views without the charge of anti-Semitism. It's no secret that the U.S.

gives Israel several billion dollars a year for military spending. We lobby against this support, and work hard to convince our politicians that Israel has to treat Palestinians fairly, and the money doesn't help. We should all work to ensure a just society in the Holy Land. We believe the Palestinians have the right to a national home of their own, living side-by-side with Israel in peace and security. We believe in a two-state solution that serves Israel's and America's interests and fulfills the legitimate national aspirations of both the Jewish and Palestinian peoples."

She raised a 2 x 2-foot cardboard poster from her desk, the print easily visible on the screen.

"Let me be more specific. From our perspective, Israel has three goals, and they are not all achievable. Any two, maybe, but not all three. Here they are." She read them aloud.

The 3 Goals of Israel – Realistic?

- Remaining a Jewish homeland
- Remaining a democratic country
- Maintaining control over all the land between the Jordan River and the Mediterranean Sea.

"Israel cannot achieve all three goals. Israel can remain both Jewish and democratic only by giving up the land on which a Palestinian state can be built. That is the only path to peace. This means giving up the illegal settlements in the West Bank, opening the borders of Gaza, and working to achieve peace with the four and a half million Palestinians who live in those areas. Walls, checkpoints, borders won't work. They haven't worked."

Rebecca felt flush. *I wish David could hear this. He probably would have some rebuttal, he's so smart. But there really are two sides. He's only focused on Israel, and ignores the oppression of the Palestinians.*

Ms. Silverstein covered more points in her remaining time, then opened for questions. The Bahá'í student had the first one.

"Ms. Silverstein, thanks for your presentation. Regarding Gaza, I noticed you didn't mention Hamas. Do you think that organization would agree to peace with Israel?"

"Excellent question," she said. "By the way, what is your first name? I always like to know students' names when I answer questions."

"Michael, Michael Solomon. I was born Jewish but am now Bahá'í."

"Thanks, Michael. Hamas responds to Israel with what the United States calls terrorist acts. Then Israel responds, inflicting way more harm on the Palestinians than warranted, killing innocent women and children. It's an asymmetric response and only leads to a vicious cycle. Hamas wants the occupation to stop, borders to be removed, and people in Gaza to be free to move outside their restricted borders.

"It's our belief that if Israel made these necessary moves – removing settlements, removing borders, returning East Jerusalem to the Palestinians – in other words, working for real to establish a two-state solution, that Hamas would cease its missile attacks. So yes, it's complicated, but today Israel calls the shots and has military superiority. It's Israel who must make the critical moves to achieve peace. As long as the Palestinians feel oppressed, peace will not be possible."

Rebecca raised her hand and was called on. *I've got to ask.*

"Yes, young lady? Your name?"

"I'm Rebecca Goldman, a college freshman. I have a friend who swears that the goal of BDS is the destruction of Israel. What should I say to my friend?"

"Utter nonsense, HOGwash," replied Silverstein, eliciting a few chuckles from the students. "No, seriously," she continued.

"BDS has been around for over two decades, as long as JVP. The goal of BDS is to influence Israel to treat the Palestinians fairly, through economic boycotts and sanctions. Boycotts have worked in South Africa and other countries, and are having some influence in Israel. Student organizations like yours are an important part of the movement. They bring together a diverse group to hear speakers like myself. It's good that you have a dialogue with your friend. I encourage that. Just let him or her know about what you've heard tonight. Mr. Geddy told me earlier he's handed out a reading list, which includes Jewish authors from both the United States and Israel, who print the truth about Israel and its oppression of the Palestinians. So do some reading there, and keep up the dialogue."

The meeting continued with more Q & A, ending around 8 pm. As Rebecca stood to leave, Michael came over. "Hi, he said, I don't think we've met before. I'm Michael Solomon." He pointed to his sweatshirt.

"Yes, I see. That's the Bahá'í Temple in Wilmette, isn't it?"

"Yes. Have you seen it?"

"Driven by. Never went inside. How'd you go from Jewish to Bahá'í?"

"Interesting story. Hey, would you like to go get a cup of coffee. We can talk then?"

*This is crazy. Have coffee, and then he'll ask me to his room? Do all Great Lakes guys have the same lines?* "No, no thanks, I've got to get back to the dorm. But you can walk me back there, and tell me your story."

"Okay, that would be great. Which dorm?"

"Newell Hall. A short walk"

"No problem. Let's go."

The path from the Student Union wound through the Great Lakes quadrangle, past buildings with a variety of architectural designs, from traditional Classical Greek to modern Corbusier style.

"The cool air feels good," she said, as they began the walk. "Glad I brought a coat. So how did you convert to Bahá'í?"

"Where do you think I'm from?" he asked.

"I was wondering. You have an accent I've heard in movies. Let me guess. Boston?"

"Nah, that's a very different accent. Brooklyn."

"Brooklyn? I've never been to New York, so don't know how Brooklyn people sound. Brooklyn people? Brooklynites? What are they called?"

"New Yawkers," he said, emphasizing the 'yaw'."

"Okay, New Yorkers. And where do you think I'm from?"

"Kansas?"

She laughed. "Really. Have you ever been west of the Mississippi?"

"No, but I saw on a map there are some states on the other side."

"You're funny. All you guys are funny." *David!*

"All you guys? How many do you have?"

"Oh, it's just an expression. In class, guys make jokes all the time. I'm from California. Palo Alto."

"Never been there."

"I'm sure we have Bahá'í in California."

"Yeah, we're all over the world. Including Israel, where we have the beautiful Bahá'í Gardens in Haifa. It's on my bucket list."

"You're way too young to have a bucket list."

"Yeah, like you say, 'just an expression,' picked up from somewhere."

"So, how did a Jewish boy end up Bahá'í?

"A little complicated. Growing up in Brooklyn, I got into a lot of scuffles as a kid. Occasional anti-Semitic slurs by other kids, or just arguments over marbles. They say words will never hurt you, but they did. I fought back, physically. Learned martial arts, you know judo, taekwondo, so people wouldn't mess with me. I got a reputation as a fighter. In ninth grade, one kid started name-calling, called me a kike or something. I should have ignored him, but didn't. I tripped him, knocked him down, and when he fell he broke his arm."

"Doesn't sound Bahá'í to me."

"The boy went to the emergency room. I was sent home. The next day, I was expelled from school."

"*Oy vey*. Just for one fight with another kid? Must happen all the time."

"Well, there had been others. I always fought back, so I was on what they called 'probation' when the last one happened. You, know, the last straw."

"Double *oy vey*."

"Yeah, right. My parents didn't know what to do. They are middle class, not a lot of money. Desperate situation. Then Uncle Nat stepped in, my father's brother. A lawyer in Manhattan. He said the only solution was a private boarding school, and he would help pay the tuition."

"Why a boarding school?"

"Uncle Nat said I had to get out of Brooklyn, that it was a bad influence. He wouldn't pay for a private school in the city. My parents really had no choice. So, I was sent off to a school in Long Island, a school for boys like me who had issues in public school."

*He loves to talk.* "So tell me how you got to Bahá'í."

"A fellow student was of that faith and told me about it. They don't have churches *per se*, no sermons or any of that stuff. Just great discussions and meetings where they cite some of the founder's teachings. I went one Sunday with him to the Bahá'í Center of Nassau County, in nearby Valley Stream. I learned about their pacifist philosophy, their goals for peace, their blending of all religions. I studied the teachings on my own, and senior year decided to convert. It's that simple. I'm still Jewish, technically, I guess, but my religion is Bahá'í."

"You must have done well in boarding school, to get into Great Lakes University."

"Yeah, computer science. It's my thing. Won a gold ribbon in Nassau County's science fair my junior year. 'Artificial intelligence meets I, Robot.' Going to that school was a lucky break for me. Got me a scholarship to come here. One more year and I graduate. I may get a job in Silicon Valley, near where you're from."

"Well, there's my dorm," she said, pointing to a drab four-story building. *I know he's going to ask for my phone number. Do I like him? I think so. Do I like David? I think so. Should keep both in mind.*

"Yeah, we got here too soon, Rebecca. I really enjoyed talking to you, but didn't get a chance to learn much about you. Say, can I have your phone number?"

"Sure."

# SIX

# The FBI Visits

On Friday morning of the same week, two young men entered the university's administration building and announced to the receptionist that they had an appointment with the school president, Richard Hightower.

"Your names, please?" she asked.

"William Galston and Thomas McDowell," replied one of the men. "Mr. Hightower is expecting us." They were dressed in dark suits, not the daily dress of any faculty. And they did not smile.

The receptionist asked no more questions, swiveled in her chair and punched a few keys into her computer. "Yes, I see he is expecting you. I'll walk you over there." She led them to a locked door, held up a key fob to open it, and escorted the pair to Hightower's suite.

She introduced the two men to a secretary, who took them into Hightower's office, a large rectangular room. Bookshelves lined one wall and on another hung four framed photos of the campus quadrangle, one for each season. A large bay window overlooked part of the quadrangle. In front of the window, behind an oak desk, sat the president, a middle-aged, trim man wearing a blue blazer, no tie. Next to him stood a younger man, perhaps about forty, also dressed in sport coat and tie.

Hightower stood but did not come around to shake hands. "Come in, have a seat," he said, pointing to a comfortable couch beside one wall, then returned to his chair.

"No thanks," said one of the men, "we'll stand for now. As I explained on the phone, we're with the FBI, and the purpose of this visit is merely to obtain information and let you know about our investigation. I'm William Galston, and my partner is Thomas McDowell. I assume the other gentleman is the school attorney?"

"Yes, I'm Lester Zimmerman, head attorney for Great Lakes University. Mr. Hightower said you suggested I be here for the interview."

"Right. As is customary, we're going to record the interview, and I assume you will do the same."

"Yes, I will," said Zimmerman.

FBI agent Galston placed a recorder on the president's desk, while Zimmerman pressed a button on his smartphone and laid it next to Hightower.

"Well, let's begin, said Galston."

"Excuse me gentlemen," said Zimmerman, "but protocol does require that I see your FBI identification. I'm sure you understand."

"Of course, said Galston." Each agent took out his FBI credential folder, and handed it to the attorney. Names and pictures matched, and the folders were returned.

"Are you sure you don't want to sit down?" asked Hightower, "We have a couple of comfortable chairs next to the couch. You can bring them up to the front of the desk."

The FBI agents decided to take the offer, and once seated in front of the desk, Galston began. "We're here because our intelligence sources have information that there may be illegal foreign influence on your campus. Specifically, we have evidence of money transfers between a Middle Eastern country and this zip code. The transfers are encrypted, which strongly suggests funding something illegal, possibly even a potential terrorist act. Within Great Lakes Township, the university is the first place we would look for subversive activity. No slight against your school, Professor Hightower. We could say the same about any large American university."

Hightower gave Zimmerman a look suggesting, 'Can you believe this?'

"So, my first question," said Mr. Galston, "are you aware of any unusual activity that might raise a concern?"

Hightower shook his head.

"No, we're not," said the attorney. "Can you be more specific? Faculty? Students? There's other property in this zip code besides Great Lakes University. This is pretty vague."

"Students," said Galston. "Not faculty."

"We have a lot of foreign students, and I imagine they receive money from family all the time. So, what makes this illegal?"

FBI agent McDowell spoke up. "For starters, it's cryptocurrency, which by itself is not illegal. But that makes it unlikely to come from families just to cover a student's expenses. More concerning, the language of the communications suggests the money is part of a covert operation, designed to evade detection."

"If it's sent to evade detection, how did you detect it?" asked Zimmerman.

"Before I answer," said Galson, "and I should have mentioned this in the beginning, this conversation is confidential, and our visit must be kept a secret. Whatever internal investigation you arrange from this office, you must not mention this visit or conversation. Do you agree? We'll need you both to affirm agreement, please."

"Understandable," said Zimmerman. "I agree."

"I agree also," said Hightower. "You raise a lot of questions. So, how was all this detected?"

"The State Department received some warning from a foreign agency and confirmed the situation. Then referred it to us."

"What foreign agency, if I may ask?"

"A very reliable foreign intelligence agency. That's all we can say for now."

"Mossad?" asked Zimmerman.

The FBI agents did not respond.

"The FBI is for federal crimes," said Hightower. "How is it involved in uncovering a foreign plot? I mean, how did you even get involved?"

"The money is foreign, but the activity which it may be funding is local, and that involves us. The FBI gets involved in all terrorist activities."

"Okay, I see," said Hightower. "But if you know who received the crypto, why not arrest them?"

"We don't know exactly where the crypto ended up, but are working on it. So we have no specific target for any arrest at this point. This is a preliminary, ongoing investigation, which is why we are here."

"And what exactly do you want us to do?"

"We would like you to keep your eyes and ears open for any suspicious activity. You have student groups on campus who are vocal about issues that may not be in the best interest of the United States. These groups are certainly not unique to your school, so it's not out of the ordinary. But if you learn something that seems concerning, give us a call so we can investigate."

"Are you referring to Students for a Socialist America?" asked Zimmerman. "They're pretty active, but I don't see them as a threat."

"No particular group, but within these types of groups may

be students involved in something illegal. We are being very proactive here. I don't need to remind you of Nine-Eleven. Better intelligence back then might have prevented that tragedy. This may be a smokescreen and come to nothing, we don't know. Just want you to be aware."

"Well, thanks for the information," said Hightower. "We'll keep our eyes and ears wide open. You know the campus motto?"

"Yes," said McDowell. "*Where the truth never sleeps.* Nice words."

"We do our best to keep to that."

The agents thanked Hightower and Zimmerman, removed the recorder, and left.

"Well, that was interesting," said Hightower. "What do you suppose is going on?"

The attorney put a finger to his lips, indicating to hold speaking. He walked over to the two stuffed chairs in front of the desk and searched each crevice with his fingers. Finding nothing, he said, "Wouldn't put it past them to leave micro recorders. I'm just a little paranoid with the FBI. I don't find anything, and they didn't touch any other part of the office, so I think we're okay."

"Yeah, Lester, a little paranoid. They weren't even going to sit until I offered the chairs. So my question. What the hell is going on?"

"I don't know, Richard, but if I had to guess, the issue isn't with Students for a Socialist America, but another group."

"Oh? Which one."

"BDS for Justice."

# SEVEN

# The I-P Conflict

Sunday afternoon at Hillel House, Adele Birnbaum called the meeting to order. The room was at capacity, fifty-plus. Mostly students, with a few faculty.

"We have a guest speaker this afternoon, Aaron Peretz, a native of Israel who now lives in New York. He runs a consulting business for companies seeking to invest in Israeli technology firms. Aaron is also author of a popular book, published last year, *The Israeli-Palestinian Conflict, Why It's Not Resolvable Anytime Soon.* That is the subject of his talk this afternoon. I think you will find it very informative.

"I am also pleased to announce that Aaron has donated twenty copies of his book to Hillel, and they will be for sale after his talk, at the back table. We are discounting the retail price, so they are only fifteen dollars each. All money collected will go into Hillel's general fund. Once they sell out you can still get it online, of course, but at a higher price. So pick up your copy today. Thank you, Aaron. Now, the podium is yours."

Peretz got up from his seat, put on a baseball-style cap with "Hillel" on the front, adjusted a lapel microphone and picked up a slide clicker. The first of his PowerPoint slides was already on the screen, showing the population of the various parts of what he labeled the "Holy Land," the land between the Jordan River and the Mediterranean Sea: Israel, Gaza, and the West Bank.

"Thank you, Adele. And thank you for this cap. I'm thirty-eight, but wearing it makes me feel eighteen again. Nice to see so many young faces. I'll run through about fifty slides, with information extracted from the book, then open for questions and comments. I titled the book 'The Israeli-Palestinian Conflict,' but it's more accurately the 'Arab-Jewish conflict,' as shown on this next slide. In its modern form the conflict dates from the 1880s, when Jews began immigrating to the Holy Land from Europe. Although there were both indigenous Jews and Arabs living there at the time, the sudden influx of European Jews began to create some conflicts with the local Arabs."

Peretz proceeded to give a brief chronology, starting with Theodore Herzl's early efforts to forge a Jewish nation in the 1890s, then: the British Mandate to govern Palestine following WWI; the Arab attacks on Jews in Hebron in 1929, long before there was any nation of Israel; the repeated assaults by Arabs against the Jews throughout Palestine, 1936-1939; the failed Peel Commission plan to create two states in 1937; the role of Amin-Al Husseini, the Mufti of Jerusalem, who blocked any attempt to create a Jewish nation before WWII.

You can tell if a speaker is effective by how the audience reacts. Are they shuffling feet, looking at their phones, nodding off? None of that for this lecture. All eyes focused on the slides, all ears on Peretz's commentary. Each slide included a few words and, in most of them, a relevant picture.

The slide showing Amin-Al Husseini meeting with Hitler in Berlin during WW II, to plot the destruction of all Jews in the Middle East after Germany won the war, was particularly riveting. Few in the audience knew this history.

Amin al-Husseini, Grand Mufti of Jerusalem,
meets with Hitler in Berlin, 1941

A few more slides and Peretz came to the major wars in the Holy Land. First, the civil war after UN Resolution 181 November 29, 1947, establishing the right of the Jews to form a nation. That war – between indigenous Arabs and Jews, without invasion by other countries – lasted until May 14, 1948, when David Ben-Gurion declared the new nation-state. The next day Israel was invaded by five Arab armies, hell-bent on destroying the new nation. He showed a map, with arrows indicating attacks between May 15 and June 10, 1948.

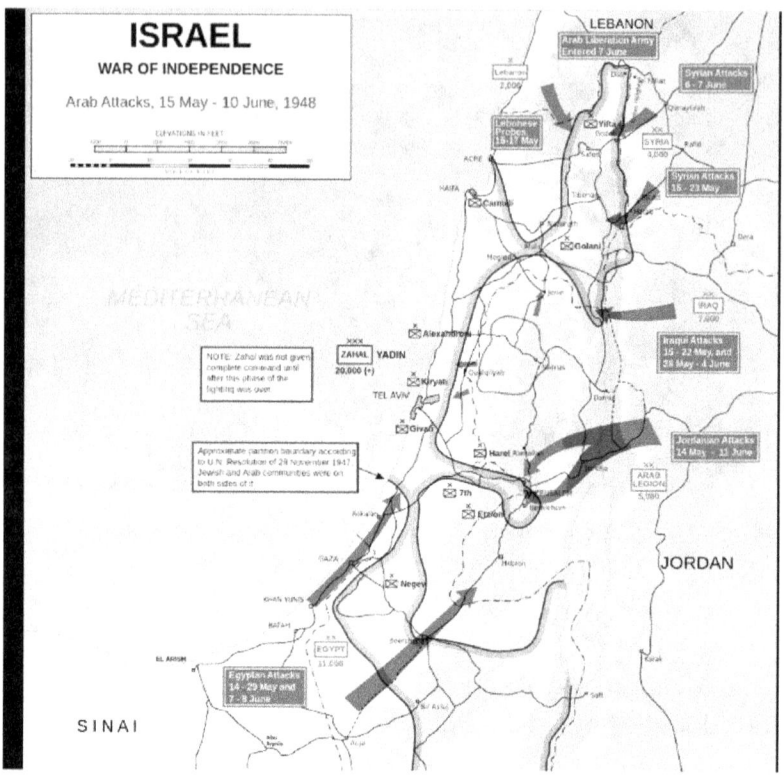

The world thought Israel had no chance against five established countries. Allowing for a few cease-fires, the War of Independence lasted ten months, and Israel prevailed, but lost the West Bank and East Jerusalem to Jordan. For the next nineteen years, Jews had no access to the Old City or the Western Wall of the ancient temple, a Jewish holy site.

"The civil war and then the full-scale War of Independence caused some 750,000 Arabs to leave Israel. They left for a variety of reasons," said Peretz, "and became refugees."

He acknowledged that "the variety of reasons" was itself highly contentious, with the Israelis claiming most Arabs left at the urging of their own leaders, who promised they could return once Israel was defeated. The Palestinians later claimed they left due to planned "ethnic cleansing" by the Jews. Never mentioned by the Palestinians is that during this same period, some 800,000 Jews were kicked out of Arab countries around the Mediterranean, and most of them migrated to Israel.

A young woman, a student, sitting toward the front of the room, shook her head. She would speak later.

Peretz continued with more history. Another war in June 1967, lasting only six days. Israel gained back East Jerusalem and the Old City, and control of the West Bank. Then another war, begun on Yom Kippur 1973, the holiest day of the year for Jews – an Arab attack that took Israel by surprise. But the country mobilized quickly and prevailed again.

"Arabs can lose every time," Peretz reminded his audience. "Israel cannot afford to lose once."

More slides: a brief profile of Yasser Arafat, the Egyptian who led the PLO until his death in 2004; the two intifadas, 1988-1993, and 2000-2005, during which over a thousand Israelis were killed by suicide bombers, Molotov cocktails, and sniper fire; the Oslo Accords in 1993-1995. So much history! How can any audience assimilate this information in one lecture? But they listened. No feet shuffling.

To this point, Peretz had only briefly mentioned the attempts at creating a two-state solution. Now he summarized the main ones, with a PowerPoint slide for each date: 1937 and the British Peel Commission; 1947 and UN Resolution 181; 1967 and Israel's offer of land for peace after the Six-Day War; 2000 with President Clinton, Yasser Arafat, and Prime Minister Ehud Barak at Camp David; 2008 with PLO leader Mahmoud Abbas and Prime Minister Ehud Olmert.

Israeli prime minister Ehud Barak, U.S. president Bill Clinton, and Palestinian leader Yasser Arafat, at Camp David, July 2000

Peretz explained how all the opportunities for a two-state solution were turned down by the Arabs: first Husseini, then Arafat, then Abbas, the latest PLO leader. And almost always, no counteroffer, no Palestinian plan for peace. When any Arab demands were made, Peretz explained, they were absurd. The demands, if accepted, were guaranteed to destroy Israel, such as the right of return of all *descendants* of *all* refugees from 1947-1948. Or, the inclusion of all Arabs in the holy land – West Bank and Gaza – with full voting rights, another obvious ploy to wipe away the Jewish state.

"Of course," Peretz continued, "the Arabs knew Israel would not, could not, accept these demands. But the point of making them was so the Arabs could claim Israel was intransigent, unreasonable, not willing to negotiate."

The young woman in the audience again shook her head.

Peretz continued, emphasizing the history as one of total Arab intransigence, refusal to negotiate in good faith with the

Jews. He showed a slide of the famous three no's arising from the pan-Arab summit in Khartoum, September 1967, in response to Israel's offer of land for peace.

```
Arab League Summit Resolution
        Khartoum, Sudan
          August, 1967


No peace with Israel
No recognition of Israel
No negotiations with Israel
```

"It needs to be pointed out that there are two ways of looking at this history," he told his audience. "Israel-haters could claim I am giving a false history, or a false interpretation of history, that I am biased. Well, yes, I am biased, but the history I have presented is not false. It is real. It shows that Israel has a right to exist as an independent Jewish nation, a democracy, and that the Israelis want nothing more than peace with their Arab neighbors."

He reminded the audience of a fact, stated earlier, that twenty-one percent of Israeli citizens are Arabs, with full voting rights. And that Arabs served in the Knesset, and in all professions. "To call Israel apartheid shows ignorance," he said. "But that's what people do. They make up lies about Israel, apartheid being just one of them. Two other obvious lies you will hear are that Israel and Zionism are like the Nazis, and that Israel practices genocide against the Palestinians. Insane, but these are all over the internet. These charges – apartheid, Nazis, genocide – are easy to refute. More complicated," he said, "is a total and purposeful misinterpretation of history." He showed the next slide, from a discussion website where the topic is often about the I-P Conflict.

From Quora.com Discussion Website

**Question:** Why is the Israeli-Palestinian conflict so difficult to resolve all these years ?

**Answer:** To be honest, it is largely due to Israel's repeated refusal to negotiate with Palestinians in good faith.

"The fact that this interpretation is truly believed, by so many, gives an indication of the conflict's intractability. We are viewing the conflict from two different and wholly incompatible perspectives. The Pro-Palestinian position is that Israel was founded illegally, and has no right to exist as an independent Jewish state. The pro-Israeli position is that Israel was founded legally, based on UN Resolution 181 in 1947, and has every right to exist as an independent Jewish state, and that it's the Arabs who have been intransigent, that their ultimate and only goal is to eliminate a Jewish state and take total control of the Holy Land."

Peretz showed a few more slides; one about the Israeli pullout of all Jews from Gaza in 2005, which led to Hamas taking over; the conflict between Hamas and the PLO, and how that would likely lead to an Arab-against-Arab war if Israel didn't exist; and about the way kids in Gaza are brought up to hate the Jews, with kindergartners given roles in skits where they kill Jews.

And then Iran. How it sponsors so much of the terrorism in the region, Hamas, Islamic Jihad, Hezbollah.

Once more the young woman shook her head. Not many noticed.

"With current Arab leaders, the conflict is not resolvable," continued Peretz. "The solution requires a change in the world order. A regime change in Iran. New Arab leaders willing to work for the Palestinians, not against them, not to keep them dependent on corrupt regimes. With current Arab leaders, and their singular goal of destroying Israel, the conflict is not resolvable. Indeed, these leaders need the conflict to stay in power, to continue receiving aid from around the world.

"Even with a change in leadership," he continued, "it will likely take another generation or two or three to raise Arabs who learn to not hate the Jews, but who yearn to be free and independent. Sadly, I don't see this happening soon. I will end by quoting Golda Meir." He showed the last slide, then remained silent while the audience read her words.

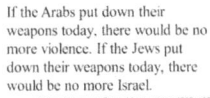

The head-shaking young woman raised her hand to speak.

EIGHT

# The Head Shaker Speaks

With the Golda Meir quote left on the screen, Peretz ended with, "Thank you. Now, I will be happy to take your questions."

Applause followed, during which the young woman kept her hand raised high. Peretz called on her and she stood, holding some papers. She was dressed in a white blouse and brown slacks, no head covering.

"An interesting talk, Mr. Peretz," she said.

"We can't hear you," came from a few people in the back of the room.

Adele went to the podium, picked up a hand mike and brought it to the woman.

With the mike close to her lips, she asked, "How about now?"

"Yes, much better," several replied.

"Okay. As you said, sir, there are two sides to the issue. I would like to speak to the Palestinian side, the side of human rights and decency."

"Name, please?" someone yelled out.

"Okay, sorry. I'm Lena Nadir, a junior. Now, Mr. Peretz, you stated that apartheid regarding Israel is an obvious lie, is that correct?"

"Yes, by the accepted definition of the term."

"I have in my hand copies of documents from Amnesty International and Human Rights Watch, documents which state, specifically, that Israel is an apartheid state. These documents result from extensive research by these world-recognized organizations, showing without doubt that Israel is an apartheid state. How can you come here and claim the opposite?"

A few people clapped at her question.

Peretz stayed calm. "Well, you bring up a very interesting point, how organizations that one would think should be interested in human rights can make such a claim. If you don't mind, I would like to ask one question about your documents."

"Sure. Go ahead."

"What are the boundaries of 'Israel' that the documents claim as an apartheid state?"

"The whole country," she shot back.

"Well, as I explained, Israel's population is twenty-one percent Arab, and they have full voting rights. In South Africa's apartheid, the majority population was black with no voting rights. How then is Israel apartheid like South Africa?"

"In the way it treats Palestinians, sir."

"But the Palestinians you refer to are not Israeli citizens. They are under the control of Hamas or the PLO, and vote in their elections, if they have any, which they rarely do. How is Israel, the country, with defined borders, apartheid?"

"Because, Sir, Israel *does* control those areas, Gaza and the West Bank. It sets the borders. It determines who can leave. And Israel controls services, utilities. The Palestinians may not live inside the borders of Israel, but they are fully controlled by Israel. That is apartheid! For you to deny this fact, is itself a lie. Have you even read these documents?" She waved a sheaf of papers above her head.

"Yes, I have," said Peretz, raising his eyes to speak to the whole audience. "We really have two definitions of apartheid. The standard definition, the one that applied to South Africa, applicable to any country where a large segment of the population essentially has no rights, cannot vote, is fully discriminated against. This young woman's definition, the one set by Amnesty International and Human Rights Watch, is a total re-definition, designed to appeal to people ignorant of the true situation. It applies to Palestinians living *outside* the country, even though those people have their own government and their own leaders. Calling this situation apartheid is just propaganda, an invented lie by agencies known for their anti-Israel bias. That is, Amnesty International and Human Rights Watch."

"Are you calling me a liar?" Nadir asked.

Rebecca, sitting next to David, asked in a whisper, "Do you know this student?"

"Later, let's listen," he replied, his voice low.

"No," answered Peretz, focusing on the student. "I am stating that the documents you wish to quote are full of anti-Israel propaganda. These two organizations, like the UN itself, started off years ago with good intentions. But over time they bought the Palestinian narrative of oppression and occupation, and now write reports *wholly biased against Israel*."

There was some applause to his statement.

"You didn't mention the UN sanctions against Israel," he continued, "which are often quoted as somehow evidence of Israel's bad deeds. In fact, the UN General Assembly repeatedly sanctions Israel more often than all other countries on the planet, *combined*. How is that? Easy. More than half the UN members are either Muslim-dominated countries, or close allies of those countries. Yet all the countries notorious for human rights violations – such as North Korea, China, Russia, Iran, Venezuela – are altogether sanctioned *less* than the single democratic nation of Israel. In regard to Israel, the UN has no credibility. None."

"I quoted Human Rights Watch."

"Okay, Human Rights Watch. Let me speak to that for a moment. Human Rights Watch was formed in the 1980s, with the focus on abuses in closed societies lacking free speech. When the organization morphed into its current anti-Israel agenda – Israel being the only country in the Middle East with free speech – the very founder of the organization, and its chairman for twenty years, wrote an op-ed in the 2009 *New York Times*. His name is Robert Bernstein. In that article Bernstein was critical of Human Rights Watch, pointing out that instead of focusing its attention on countries without freedom of speech or press, it only seemed to focus on Israel, the one Middle East country with both freedoms. And it has been that way ever since. It's a similar situation with Amnesty International. So, you can quote documents from both organizations, but I will tell you they are nothing but anti-Israel, anti-Semitic propaganda, from organizations that are not interested in human rights or personal freedoms."

"So you say!" she called out. "People should read these documents," and she again waved the sheaf of papers. "They are not propaganda. They are detailed, fact-filled. Mr. Peretz can deny all he wants. The documents speak for themselves. Israel *is* apartheid!" She sat, a heavy scowl on her face.

A Black student raised his hand and Peretz called on him. He stood as Adele came forward with the microphone.

"I won't need that," he said in a booming voice. "Can everyone hear me?"

Nods and yesses.

"Good. My name is Kwame Johnson, a junior. I'm majoring in history. I've had a chance to study South African apartheid, so would like to throw in my two cents, if I may."

"Yes, of course," replied Peretz. "This is an open forum."

"As you notice, there aren't a lot of black students here this afternoon. I see just one other. Yet about ten percent of the campus is Black, including about a hundred foreign students, from various countries, Brazil, Cameroon, Nigeria, and others. Most of the Black students have no interest in the Israeli conflict, and in fact little interest in African apartheid. They can tell you more about Selma, Alabama, than what went down in Johannesburg and Cape Town years ago. So I can't speak for them, only offer my own perspective."

"Which is?" someone snarled from the back row.

"I'm getting there. Calling the Israeli situation apartheid is an affront to language, and to history."

Brief applause, as he continued. "People who apply the term to Israel simply don't know what they're talking about. Or worse, they do know, and choose to make up their own definition which has nothing to do with the history of South African apartheid. In true apartheid, there was no right to intermix. No right to vote. Separate public facilities for eating, bathrooms, sports. And most significantly, apartheid was written into government policy. It was the *law*. Unless people who claim Israel is apartheid can show me that it is inscribed in law and actually practiced within the boundaries of Israel, the claim is absurd. It stinks of anti-Semitism."

There followed a chant by a few students looking toward the previous speaker: "Response! Response!"

"I will respond," she said, standing.

"Microphone, please" someone called out. Adele brought it to the student, who then spoke.

"I do find it ironic that a Black student, whose people have suffered from White supremacy for hundreds of years, would call Human Rights Watch and Amnesty International either ignorant or anti-Semitic. I certainly am neither ignorant nor anti-Semitic."

"The girl lies well," David whispered to Rebecca.

"You, sir," Ms. Nadir continued, looking toward Kwame, "are locked into some arbitrary definition, of your own making, to defend what is happening to the Palestinians. Do you think slavery really ended with the Thirteenth Amendment? Are you unaware of the Jim Crow era, where Blacks were treated just about the same as before the Civil War? Still slavery, but a different kind. Same with apartheid. Different flavor, but still apartheid."

A couple of people clapped as she sat down.

Kwame put in the last word. "My definition is not arbitrary. In truth, Miss, to pursue what I perceive as your anti-Semitic agenda, you've made up your own definition of terms like apartheid and slavery. Jim Crow was reprehensible but not slavery. Israel may have policies you hate but it's not apartheid. Please stop spewing out propaganda."

After a smattering of applause, Peretz nodded to Kwame and said, "Thank you." Then, speaking to the entire audience: "All of you are in an excellent position to read more, to study and come to your own conclusions. Don't just take my word for it, or Mr. Johnson's. Read the Human Rights and Amnesty documents. Google them with the qualifier 'anti-Semitism,' and see how what they write about Israel is nothing more than anti-Semitic propaganda. And go beyond them. Study South African apartheid, and see if anything in Israel today is remotely similar. If you've been to Israel, or studied the real history, you can see these claims for what they are. Lies."

Returning his gaze toward Ms. Nadir, Peretz continued. "So, Miss, let me be clear. I'm not calling *you* a liar. Far from it. From your perspective, I'm sure you feel you are telling the truth. And I thank you, in a way, because you nicely illustrate why this conflict is irresolvable. When people who hate the existence of Israel hear lies, are fed propaganda, that only reinforces their hatred. It gives no hope for compromise, for negotiation."

She did not respond except to mumble something in Arabic.

Another hand went up, from a young man in the back of the room. As he stood to speak Ms. Birnbaum brought him the microphone.

NINE

# Gordon Geddy

"Mr. Peretz, my name is Gordon Geddy, and I am president of the BDS club here on campus. To your credit, you did state that there are two ways of looking at this history, but you only presented one way, the way of the colonial Zionists. You also stated that there is some controversy about why 750,000 Arabs were expelled from Israel around the time Israel declared its illegal nation-state. Palestinians call this the "Nakba," or catastrophe, as it uprooted a whole population, who had to live as refugees, and their descendants are still refugees, aching to return to their homes and homeland."

"Refugees in name only," interrupted Peretz. "Nowhere else on the planet are descendants called refugees. Just keep that in mind."

"Allow me to continue, please," retorted Geddy. "So, you purport to give the Jewish, or Israeli, narrative of the Nakba and of the fighting that took place before and during that war. I think the audience here this afternoon, mostly students, should know that many Jews, including native Israelis, don't buy your narrative. There are Jews honest enough to seek the truth about the

Nakba and about the atrocities inflicted on Arabs during that and subsequent wars."

Peretz stared at the young man. He sensed rage, anger in Geddy's tone.

"Are you familiar with Plan Dalet?" asked Geddy. "The Israeli plan before the 1948 war began? According to Israeli author Ilan Pappe, the plan was for the expulsion of as many Palestinians as possible. Pappe wrote a book about this, called 'The Ethnic Cleansing of Palestine,' documenting the Haganah's blueprint for getting rid of the Arabs."

Peretz remained silent as Geddy continued.

"I could quote other Jews, both native Israelis and prominent U.S. Citizens, who find major fault with the colonial oppressors, the Zionists who have stolen the land from the Palestinians. Gilad Atzmon, Noam Chomsky, Richard Falk, Norman Finkelstein, Sara Roy – so many. I did not bring a handout to this meeting, but students here can just google 'Jews who condemn Israel,' to see the other side of the narrative. Or, look up Ilan Pappe – that's spelled P-A-P-P-E – who has perhaps written the most about Israeli oppression. Or google Jewish Voice for Peace, an organization that supports the Palestinians against their Jewish oppressors. So yes, Mr. Peretz, there is another side, and it highlights *your* version as nothing more than propaganda." Geddy sat, and a couple of people clapped their approval.

"Mr. Geddy has raised some interesting points, which I would like to address," replied Peretz. "Adele, how much time do we have left?"

"As much as you need. If any students have to leave, no problem. I think this is very important, and don't want to cut anyone off."

"Good, okay. First, let me acknowledge that there are indeed many Jews, including many Israelis, who find major fault with the country. It's a democracy, and like the political conflicts we have in this country, between Democrats and Republicans, you can find much more in Israel, where there are several political parties. They criticize each other, they criticize government policies, they criticize a lot. *Haaretz*, a far-left-wing Hebrew newspaper, is constantly criticizing the government. You will not find this type of criticism of Arab governments in Gaza or the West Bank. The person doing the criticism is not apt to live long."

Some snickers from the audience.

"But Mr. Geddy brings up another type of criticism by Jews – including Israelis – who choose to rewrite history, to spread misinformation, or write with serious omissions of the history. Pappe is perhaps the worst. I could spend an hour pointing out his propaganda about Israel, his misinformation. For those who don't know, he was born in Israel but lives in Great Britain."

Several students pulled out cell phones. Peretz figured they might be googling "Pappe." Or else playing Solitaire, out of boredom.

"By the way," he continued, "if anyone wants to leave, no problem. I won't be offended. I do want to respond to the question about Ilan Pappe." At that point one student stood and walked toward the front, suggesting he was going to leave the room by the front entrance near the speaker, which was a longer walk than out via the room's back door. Peretz waited a moment for the student to leave.

When the student reached the front, near the podium, he pivoted, half raised his right hand, and bellowed, "I will speak before leaving."

"Rude!" someone shouted from one of the seats. Others shouted "Sit down!" and "Wait your turn!"

Peretz did not know this student but sought to calm the crowd. The fact that the student wore a kippah reassured him somewhat. "It's okay," he said, "let him speak, then he'll leave."

"My name is Steve Mandelbaum," said the interloper, his loud voice needing no microphone. "I've been listening to this back and forth, and am fed up with Geddy's propaganda. You should know that Gordon Geddy is a rabid anti-Semite who advocates for the total destruction of Israel. Everything he says is a lie, a smokescreen, a façade for his single wish – to KILL ALL THE JEWS, including ALL OF YOU in this room. Don't be fooled by his pro-Palestinian bullshit. He wants you dead!"

Adele Birnbaum stood abruptly, yelled "That's enough! Mr. Mandelbaum. Leave now or I will call security."

"No need," replied Mandelbaum, his voice aimed at the entire audience. "Just remember one thing. Geddy is a hard-core anti-Semite and a liar. Believe anything he says at your peril." With that, Mandelbaum pivoted and left the room.

Applause ensued, but Peretz wasn't sure if the clapping was for Mandelbaum's message or for his leaving. "I apologize for the interruption," he said. "And I apologize to Mr. Geddy for the unwarranted interruption. Let's try to get on with our dialogue. Now, about that book Mr. Geddy mentioned, 'The Ethnic Cleansing of Palestine,' a well-respected Israeli historian named Benny Morris wrote, some years ago, and if my quote is not exact you can look it up. Morris wrote: 'At best, Ilan Pappe must be one of the world's sloppiest historians; at worst, one of the most dishonest.' As Morris points out, Pappe simply rewrites history to suit his motive, changes words in historic documents, or omits key facts. Anti-Semites love his stuff. Because in fact, though born Jewish in Israel, he writes as an enemy of the state."

Looking at Geddy, Peretz continued. "You mentioned other names, all of whom have been called out for their misinformation, their lies. I cannot honestly explain why Jews would resort to propaganda to smear Israel, but it happens. To see the details of this misinformation, read the several books by Alan Dershowitz, or the thoroughly documented work by Ben-Dror Yemini titled *The Industry of Lies*. These and other works are listed in my book."

A few students quietly left the room, through the rear door.

"I think we may be confusing the hell out of our audience,

and I apologize," said Peretz. "I was not planning to get into a debate with quotes or argue over what some might call minutiae. The real message for the students here today is to do your own research, look up these people, read the history, and determine for yourself. Reasons for the Arabs leaving in 1947-48 are multi-faceted, and it's easy to pick sides."

"Nakba!" someone yelled from back of the room.

"Yes, Nakba," said Peretz. "But that term, mentioned earlier by Mr. Geddy, refers to Arab refugees only. It is never applied to the 800,000 Jews who were expelled or forced to leave Arab countries after the 1948 war began. No pro-Palestinian ever mentions them. They lost homes, jobs, possessions, and had to start over. But Israel welcomed all of them who chose to come, and now their descendants are part of the Israeli fabric. Why didn't Arab nations welcome the Palestinian refugees? Good question. Do your research to see the truth of the Arab refugee situation."

"Those Jews left voluntarily," answered Geddy, his voice steely cold.

"Voluntarily?" replied Peretz. "I don't think so. How many Jews are in Egypt today? I'll tell you. Zero. How many in Libya, Morocco, Jordan? Same number. Zero. You think one hundred percent decided to leave voluntarily, to give up their homes and jobs? Of course not. They were forced out. But our students here can do their own research."

Peretz paused to let his last comment sink in, then continued.

"And one more point, Mr. Geddy, your repeated reference to colonialism is easy to refute, given the details of how Jews acquired the land before statehood, by legal purchase from the Ottomans or native Arabs."

"Geddy's a liar," yelled one of the students.

"Please," said Peretz, looking over the whole audience, "let's keep this civil. There are many, many areas of controversy, and people can easily find something to criticize about Israel and

Zionism. But always – always – keep in mind, that the driving force behind the 100-year Arab-Jewish conflict is the Arabs' singular goal of eliminating all Jews from the river to the sea. That is why they have always refused to negotiate a peace plan in good faith. They want all the land, Jew-free."

"Then you agree with Steve Mandelbaum," yelled a student. "From the river to the sea!"

Peretz ignored the comment and continued.

"And by the way, Mr. Geddy, I don't know about your BDS group here in Great Lakes University, but Jewish members, if there are any, should know that the nationwide BDS movement has one overriding goal. Not to change Israel's behavior toward the Palestinians by boycotting or sanctions, not to make nice neighbors, but to remove all the Jews. The founder of BDS, Omar Barghouti, has stated this explicitly. Look him up, too. B-A-R-G-H-O-U-T-I."

"Are you done, sir?" asked Geddy. "With your diatribe against Palestinians?"

Peretz did not answer, and Geddy continued. "I came to offer another side to your propaganda, but see that I am outnumbered. Time will tell. History will be on the side of the oppressed, the victims of Zionist colonialization. There is just so much oppression the Palestinians can tolerate, and one day they will rise up. Instead of spreading propaganda, you should be working toward a reconciliation, a peaceful solution, one that recognizes Palestinians as equal citizens, not slaves to colonial oppression. I've said my piece. Now I, too, will take my leave."

Geddy walked out of the rear door, to the sound of some applause.

"There is not much more to say," offered Peretz. "Any other comments?"

This being Hillel, most in the audience did seem to support Peretz's talk, and there were a few more speakers, all agreeing in some respect with his message. Peretz looked over at Lena Nadir, who showed no signs of wanting to speak again.

At 3:15 Adele Birnbaum ended the presentation, again thanking Peretz for his donation of books. Several students moved to the podium to engage a bit further, or to get his signature on their newly purchased book.

* * *

Rebecca and David remained seated. "Do you know Steve Mandelbaum?" she asked.

"Oh, yeah. Quite well. He was my roommate freshman year."

"He seems unhinged."

"Just very pro-Israel. Passionate you might say. And realistic, if I might add."

"That's debatable," she replied. "And the girl who spoke before Geddy. Do you know anything about her?"

"Yeah. She's Geddy's girlfriend. They've been together for about a year. Her parents are Christians from Lebanon, though she was born in the U.S. If she wasn't nutso when she entered college, she's clearly become radicalized since meeting Geddy."

"Then why wasn't he sitting with her?"

"My hunch is, he wants to make it seem like the arguments against Israel aren't coming from a single source. What did you think of Peretz's comment about BDS?"

Before Rebecca could respond, Michael Solomon walked up to speak with her. "Well, I made it," he said. "Thanks for telling me about this talk. It was interesting."

"Oh, hi," she replied. "Michael, do you know David?"

"No, don't think we've met."

David stood and they shook hands. "David Applebaum."

"Michael Solomon. Glad to meet you."

"Michael was raised Jewish but converted to Bahá'í," said Rebecca. "He also attends BDS for Justice."

"Oh, okay," replied David. "Bahá'í, that's interesting. It was originally started in Iran, if I'm not mistaken. A religion which incorporates beliefs of all religions."

"Yes," said Michael, "so it's not Muslim nor Christian. Bahá'í is its own religion, and emphasizes peace and respecting thy neighbor."

David nodded. "One of the great sites in Israel is the Bahá'í Shrine and Gardens in Haifa. Have you been?"

"Not yet. Tell him, Rebecca."

"It's on his bucket list," she said.

"That's good," replied David. "College kids can have bucket lists, too."

An awkward moment ensued. Two guys, both wanting the same girl. Only one had her, for the moment.

"Well, I've got to get back to the dorm, have a lot of studying to do," said Michael. "Nice meeting you, David. Bye, Rebecca."

"Bye."

As Michael walked ahead, up the aisle and out of earshot, David asked Rebecca: "A close friend?"

"As close as you."

"No closer?

"No closer."

"Good," he replied. "Let's go get a cup of coffee."

"Only coffee? Promise?"

"Maybe more key lime pie."

"You know what I mean."

"Okay, I promise. I won't ask. But it's on my mind."

## TEN

# Great Lakes Township

The commercial center of Great Lakes Township begins just a block from the campus. It contains a variety of coffee shops, restaurants, and retail outlets, plus several low-rise and a few high-rise rise apartment buildings where many students lived.

David and Rebecca walked there from Hillel, stopping at Mona's Coffee Bistro, a favorite student hangout. David liked Mona's because it had booths that offered a modicum of privacy, where you could drink coffee and, if alone, read a newspaper or magazine. Other students flocked there because the proprietor – Mona – made the best cream pie anywhere.

Standing in line to place their order, they read the menu items listed on the wall. "They don't have key lime pie," he said. "Something better. The best chocolate cream pie. Can you eat a whole piece?"

"No way. Let's split it."

They ordered two coffees and the pie, then waited at the end of the bar. The items came on a tray, which David picked up and took over to one of the empty booths. As before, they sat opposite one another.

They each took a bite. "Good, isn't it?" he asked.

"Yeah, glad we're splitting it. Must be a thousand calories."

"Maybe just 900. So, what do you think? Did Peretz's talk change any views?"

"You said that student is Geddy's girlfriend?"

"Yeah, why?"

"I've been to two meetings of BDS for Justice. Geddy ran both, and I don't recall seeing her. How long have they been dating?"

"At least a year, from what I know. Maybe she had other things to do during those meetings you attended. Or maybe he wants her to keep a low profile on the BDS movement, for the same reason I think he didn't sit with her this afternoon. I sound like a conspiracy theorist. Anyway, back to my original question. Did the talk change any views?"

"Maybe a little. I see there is a stridency associated with Israel, and there are probably some extremists in the BDS group, but they haven't surfaced in the two meetings I've been to. I do need to do more reading, though."

"How about those links I sent you? Read any of those?"

"Honestly, no. I'm behind on a lot of things."

"So, you plan to stay a member?"

"Yeah, why not? In fact, we have a march coming up next Saturday."

"A march?"

"Yeah, a march for freedom. BDS has arranged a demonstration right here, in downtown, that will start at the plaza across the street. Gordon said groups from other area colleges will be joining us for a short walk, on streets around the plaza, to promote BDS."

"And you're going to join them?"

"Yeah, me and Michael plan to march. Want to come with us?"

"Kill me first. I don't think you should go."

"Why not?"

"Honestly, Rebecca, as much as I like you and want to get closer...I don't think you fully understand this group. I don't want you to get hurt."

"Hurt?"

"Hurt emotionally, not physically. You never told me about your grandparents, and I imagine that was very painful for you at some point, growing up, learning about the Holocaust."

"People have to behave better," she retorted. "That's what it's all about. What happened, happened. I can't believe the plight of the Palestinians has nothing to do with Israel's policies."

"Does any of this come from your parents? Your sister? Are they all in line with you?"

"There hasn't been much discussion. Dad's a liberal of course, everyone at Stanford is. But I don't know if he has strong views one way or the other about Israel. Mom's more conservative, but doesn't push Israel on me. My sister is too caught up in motherhood to discuss anything. And by the way, you were going to tell me about your brother. Something mysterious, as I recall."

"Not mysterious. Nuanced."

"Meaning?"

"Well, I have had discussions with him, over the years."

"Over the years? How long have you been a fanatic about Israel?"

"I'm not fanatic," he replied, voicing a little irritation. "More of a mild obsession. It started in high school. I spent part of my junior year at Alexander Muss High School in Israel. Ever heard of it?"

"Nope."

"It's a program for U.S. students, to spend several months over there in a high school outside of Tel Aviv. Named after Alexander Muss, a major donor. Anyway, you get full credit for the courses taken, which are in English. When you return to the U.S., you graduate on time with your class. So, I was in Muss for four months, then spent another month touring Israel with some friends."

"As a junior? Wasn't that dangerous?"

"Not at all. We had guides for some day trips we took. But most of the time, we were on our own. One of the guys I toured with spoke Hebrew, so that was helpful."

"So that radicalized you?"

"Why do you use terms like fanatic and radical? I'm neither. What happened is, I learned about Israel, what you might call the facts on the ground. And that was five years ago. Later, when I first heard people say Israel was guilty of apartheid, I knew from firsthand experience that was a load of bullshit, pardon the expression."

"Is that what your brother said?"

"No, no. More nuanced."

"By the way, what's his name?"

"Joe. Joseph Abraham Applebaum. Nice Jewish name. Anyway, when I got back home from Israel, age sixteen, my brother was twenty-six, just out of Harvard, working on Wall Street in his first job. I went to visit him several months later, stayed in his apartment for a couple of days. We got to talking about Israel, and then I learned, much to my surprise, that he was critical of the country, had lots of negative things to say about Israel's 'occupation' and West Bank settlements. He said they were the barrier to peace. I argued, and he kept disagreeing with me, like I was an idiot."

"Did he do that high school session also?"

"No, he's never been to Israel."

"So how did he disagree with you?"

"Good question. He only knew what he read in the left-wing liberal media: *The New York Times*, *Washington Post*, *The New Yorker*. They all routinely published anti-Israel articles, and still do. Ever hear of Peter Beinart?"

"No."

"Good. Anyway, Joe and I got into arguments. He looked down on me because I was just in high school, and he's a Harvard graduate. Really, he was condescending. He more or less shut me up, and I left feeling not great. For the next year or so we discussed none of this, just family stuff. Then, about three years ago, as I began to study the Israeli-Palestinian conflict in some depth, and came across books and articles supporting my views. I started up with him again."

"How so?"

"One small piece left," he said, pointing to a sliver of pie on the plate. "Want it?

"No, I've had enough."

David ate the piece, took a sip of coffee, and continued. "I sent him Amazon links to books I thought he should read, starting with Alan Dershowitz's *The Case for Israel*."

"Dershowitz the lawyer? The speaker mentioned him."

"Yeah, he's written great stuff, several pro-Israel books, and argues strongly against all the propaganda published by those Jewish authors that Geddy mentioned."

"What happened?"

"Joe attacked me!"

"Attacked you?"

"Yeah, in an email, he wrote 'Don't quote me Dershowitz!!' Double exclamation points. He was furious at Dershowitz for supporting Trump in the first impeachment, and other cases."

"So, he didn't read the book?"

"Hell, no. He told me I was an extremist for reading or quoting Dershowitz."

"Then what?"

"I lay low for a while. Then I came upon websites like Camera.org, Algemeiner, and Jewish News Syndicate, which point out the hypocrisy in many of the media my brother loves to read. I sent him several articles from these websites. Rather, links to them."

"Then?"

"He replied, 'all media is biased,' which in his mind negated the validity of anything I sent him. He didn't comment on the articles, never read them. His mind was closed."

"Did you quit?"

"For a while. But then I started up again. This guy Beinart I mentioned, he's a Jewish journalist, very much against the very existence of Israel, and writes frequent essays in *The New York Times*. I took one of these essays and notated all its misinformation, omissions, and double standards. To me, just a bunch of propaganda, aimed at ignorant *Times* readers."

"Such as?"

David thought for a moment, then said, "I really don't want to bore you."

"I'm not bored. Just give me one example."

"Okay, give me a minute." David pulled out his phone, did a quick search. "I have all the emails I've sent Joe, in a separate folder. There are dozens. Here it is, an essay by Beinart in the *New York Times*. Beinart wrote that the political system in Israel is not a genuine liberal democracy for Palestinians, that it's a movement to save liberal democracy only for Jews."

"What's wrong with that?"

"Fair question. I notated right after that paragraph, in yellow highlight, that Beinart's comment was highly misleading, since all Arab citizens of Israel, which is about 20% of the population, have full voting rights. Several Arabs serve in the Knesset. For Israeli citizens, there is *no* distinction between rights of Jews and rights of Arabs. The 'Palestinians' referred to by Beinart are not Israeli citizens, I explained. All the Arabs living in Gaza and the West Bank are *not* citizens of Israel."

Rebecca nodded. "Okay, I get that."

"I went full throttle and in my email and explained how Hamas and the PLO are *not* democracies, and make no pretense of offering any semblance of 'democracy' such as voting rights, freedom of speech or press, to the Palestinians. I pointed out that Hamas is recognized as a terrorist organization worldwide, and offers *no* equality to women, LGBTQ, or to any person who is not an Arab. Beinart mentioned none of this. Beinart wrote his essay for ignorant readers. Like my brother."

"Sounds like you were lecturing your brother. How did he respond?"

"With more condescension. He criticized me for criticizing *The New York Times*. He repeated again that all media has bias, and that Beinart's essay was labeled as opinion, and should be read as such. In other words, he never addressed my comments, but just attacked the messenger. And it's been that way ever since."

"That's so sad. Is that the Harvard way?"

"I don't know. All I know, for all his smarts and education, he lives in a bubble, and can't or won't read anything that doesn't agree with what's printed in the anti-Israel media."

"So, is he really anti-Israel?"

"No, he professes not to be. It's just that he is willfully ignorant. Here's one good example, Are you ready for this?"

"Ready."

"Well into these email exchanges, he called me one day, on my birthday. After birthday greetings, he wanted to make sure I knew he is pro-Israel but that there were two sides, and that I didn't appreciate his wisdom and understanding of the Israeli-Palestinian conflict. I agreed there were two sides, and then, rather slyly, mentioned how complicated the whole conflict is, with all the nuances. Then I asked, 'Joe, what do you think about the BDS movement,' not mentioning anything about it. From the way I asked the question, the movement could be pro- or anti-Israel."

"And he answered?"

"Quote: 'What is the BDS movement?'"

"Really?"

"Really. From a guy who kept telling me how all-knowing and understanding he is. I replied, sort of off the cuff, that it's just a movement to boycott Israel products. Then he said, 'no, never heard of it.'"

"I did not tell him that it's a total contradiction to claim awareness of the conflict and not know about BDS. It convinced me, more than anything else, how truly ignorant he is. He is the perfect audience for Beinart propaganda. Willfully ignorant. Well, I think I've beaten this subject to death. Thanks for listening."

"Yeah, it *is* interesting. I do need to get back and finish writing a paper for tomorrow's Econ class. Thanks for the pie and coffee."

"Back to your dorm?"

"Yes. Back to my dorm. I need some alone time."

ELEVEN

# The March

The October weather turned cooler during the week. After Friday's Shabbat dinner, the Hillel meeting focused on the planned BDS march for Saturday, an event now known around campus, especially among Jewish students. However, most students viewed it as just another march or street demonstration, and no big deal. Since the school year began, there had already been several: for transgenders to compete in all non-contact sports; for unionization of graduate student teaching assistants; and against a planned skyscraper tower in the downtown area.

Adele Birnbaum addressed the assembled students in the meeting room. "I don't recommend any type of counter-demonstration at tomorrow's march," she said. "In other cities that type of response has often led to altercations, and just more publicity for the BDS movement. If you want to go individually and view from a distance, take video or whatever, that's up to you. But Hillel is not sponsoring any type of organized response."

Some discussion followed. David was present but did not speak. He also decided not to show up for the march. No point, he thought; can't change minds by counter-demonstrating.

* * *

Saturday afternoon brought clear skies, a high of 55 degrees. The Great Lakes BDS students planning to march assembled outside the student union at 12:30. Several carried signs that read "Justice for the Palestinians" and "End apartheid in Israel." Rebecca and Michael began walking with the group toward the downtown plaza.

"Ever been on one of these marches before?" Michael asked her.

"No, never. Kind of exciting."

"There's supposed to be students from other colleges meeting us at the plaza," said Michael. "I think Gordon said three or four other colleges. We have about thirty kids from Great Lakes. There could be well over a hundred altogether."

"I wonder what the local merchants think of these marches. I guess as long as they're peaceful, they don't mind."

"No. In fact, I was thinking afterwards we could have some coffee at Mona's Coffee Shop. Ever been there?"

"Once." *So similar. Same lines, same questions.* "Where do we end up after the march? I don't even know."

"It's a loop around downtown. Doesn't end up at campus. Ends back at the plaza. That's where the busses will be for the out-of-town students."

"Okay. Yeah, Mona's will be fine if it's not overcrowded. Then we can walk back to the campus."

As the group approached the plaza, they saw three buses parked on a side street. Students exiting those buses also carried signs, many larger than the ones carried by Great Lakes BDS. By one p.m. at least 100 students had assembled on the plaza, milling about. Nearby were two police cars and several policemen, as was always the case with downtown demonstrations. Adjacent to one police car was a van from the local television station.

Gordon Geddy stood on a bench in the plaza, bullhorn in hand. "Welcome, BDS participants. I want to thank all the out-of-town students for joining us. The march will be short, total of one mile around the town. We'll stay on the sidewalks, obey all traffic lights. In a couple of places, the Township's officers will hold traffic until we cross the street.

"We'll start down Jefferson Street, turn right at Adams, and enter the pocket park at the corner. From there we'll come back via Harriet Tubman Way, and end up back here at the plaza. I'll start the march." With that, he jumped down from the bench and proceeded to lead the way.

"I notice he's not walking with his girlfriend," said Rebecca.

"What's that supposed to mean? Did they break up?"

"No, they just never seem to appear together," she replied. "I heard they are very close, though."

"Heard? From whom?"

"Just a rumor." *Dumb, dumb. I should keep my mouth shut. Obviously, it was from David.*

Some of the signs were new to Rebecca, and created a feeling of unease. "From the River to the Sea, Palestinians will be free." Does that include Israel also? she wondered. Aren't the Arabs free in Israel?

Another: "End the Jewish Occupation. No more Jews. None. Zero." *None? Zero? Referring to the whole area?*

She also saw two women wearing Palestinian *kuffiyeh* scarves and draped in Palestinian flags. *Are they college students?* She did not raise these concerns with Michael, just kept them to herself.

The television van preceded the front group, stopping periodically to film the march. Local news always carried some part of these street demonstrations, to meet the interest of curious Township citizens.

"I don't want to be in any of these videos," she said to Michael, "let's stay back a bit." She met another girl from the group, and began talking to her, while Michael started to chat with another guy. She and Michael became separated, several yards apart, as the crowd continued to move forward.

Fifteen minutes into the march, a teenager behind Rebecca took off a long sleeve shirt, under which he wore a brown sweatshirt. He started moving up, perhaps to get into the view of the TV cameras. He brushed past Rebecca, hitting her arm, turned and said "sorry."

She saw the front of his sweatshirt. It read, "Camp Auschwitz," and under the title was a human skull.

"What is on your sweatshirt?" she yelled, above the noise of the crowd.

"Yeah," the teen said. "You like it?"

"What? Are you crazy. Camp Auschwitz? Do you know what you're wearing? He turned around to show her writing on the back, in large letters: "*Arbeit macht frei*. Work sets you free."

"Do you know anything about Auschwitz?"

A few people had stopped to hear this conversation. Michael was still several feet back, unaware.

The sweatshirt guy came up close to Rebecca, inches from her face and said, "Are you *Jewish*?"

She pushed him back. "Out of my face!" she yelled.

This caught Michael's attention and he proceeded toward Rebecca. Before he could reach her, the teen pushed on Rebecca's right shoulder, sending her back a few feet.

Michael approached the boy, saw the sweatshirt. "Who the hell are you?"

"Oh, look. Another damn Jew!"

Michael grabbed the kid's right arm, pushed hard, then used his left leg to swipe under the offender's groin. Within seconds the sweatshirt wearer was on the ground, Michael on top, twisting the teen's arm into a painful flexion. "Do I kill you now or later, you fucking Nazi?"

Other students came up, pulled Michael off. Sweatshirt got

up, made no attempt to attack Michael, yelled "Goddamn kikes," and stormed away.

"Michael, let's get out of here," implored Rebecca.

"Yeah, this piece of shit doesn't deserve to live. Let someone else do the dirty work. Let's go." He grabbed her hand and they crossed the street, moving in the opposite direction of the march.

Neither one said anything until they reached the campus. Then Michael asked, "What the hell happened?"

She explained the quick encounter, and what she read on the sweatshirt. "How did that get into the BDS march?"

"I don't know. What school was he from? Not Great Lakes."

"I don't know."

"Did Geddy see any of this? I don't think so, it happened so fast."

They came upon a bench in the quadrangle. "I've got to sit for a minute," she said.

They sat close and he held her hand. "Are you all right?"

"No, I'm not. I feel short of breath." She began crying. He put an arm over her shoulder.

Her tears subsided. "Michael, I'll be okay. Really. Thanks for rescuing me. I don't know what would have happened if you hadn't been there."

"Glad I was. If they hadn't pulled me away, I might have hurt him bad. That was not a Bahá'í move. It's a primitive reaction, and I can't help it sometimes. But everything turned out okay. We certainly won't go to Mona's. If you want, we can go to the student union, have coffee there."

"Michael, I'm really exhausted. I think I need to get back to the dorm, maybe try to get some sleep. You've been wonderful, you really have. Please, just walk me back to the dorm."

"Sure. No problem."

They stood from the bench and began walking toward her dorm.

TWELVE

# Rebecca's Decision

Rebecca entered the dorm and returned to her room. It was now just after 3 p.m. Her roommate was out, fortunately. Even though she had her own small bedroom, she didn't want to encounter anyone just now. She could not hide her tear-stained face and didn't want to answer any questions. After a quick stop to the bathroom, she plopped on the bed, fully clothed.

She thought back, not to Michael's rescue, but to an earlier conversation with David. She recalled his words: *Honestly, Rebecca, as much as I like you…I don't think you fully understand this group. I don't want you to get hurt.*

How did he know? Have I been so wrong for so long? He's been trying to tell me, hasn't he?

She opened her laptop, downloaded the websites David had sent her. She scanned several in a row, searching for "BDS" in each.

www.jewishvirtuallibrary.org
www.camera.org
www.algemeiner.com

www.memri.org

On the website Jewish Virtual Library, she read the quoted words of BDS founder Omar Barghouti.

"Definitely, most definitely, we opposed a Jewish state in any part of Palestine. No Palestinian, rational Palestinian, not a sellout Palestinian, would ever accept a Jewish state in Palestine."

"If the refugees were to return, you would not have a two-state solution, you'd have a Palestine next to Palestine."

She found quotes from other BDS advocates, leaders of the movement.

"Ending the occupation doesn't mean anything if it doesn't mean upending the Jewish state itself...BDS does mean the end of the Jewish state."

"BDS represents three words that will help bring about the defeat of Zionist Israel and victory for Palestine."

"The real aim of BDS is to bring down the state of Israel...That should be stated as an unambiguous goal."

So explicit! Just as painful, was the analysis by pro-Israel websites of BDS's influence on colleges. College kids who adhered to BDS in the name of justice and peace were merely pawns, fodder for the movement to destroy Israel. Dupes. Ignorant of what they were marching for. *I do feel duped. Did Geddy know Nazis would be joining the march? Did he invite them?*

Then she remembered hearing about the Hamas Covenant, perhaps from David or her mother, she wasn't sure. The Covenant, she was told, called for the destruction of Israel, which made all talk about peace with the group meaningless. She had never looked it up, didn't even think about it during the JVP talk by that woman from Berkeley.

She googled "Hamas Covenant," and found it discussed in multiple web sites, including Jewish Virtual Library and The Avalon Project from Yale Law School. The Hamas goal was not hidden at all.

"The Islamic Resistance Movement is a distinguished Palestinian movement, whose allegiance is to Allah, and whose way of life is Islam. It strives to raise the banner of Allah over every inch of Palestine."

"Israel will exist and will continue to exist until Islam will obliterate it, just as it obliterated others before it."

Was the JVP speaker, a seemingly smart, Jewish woman, also duped? She said JVP has been around for two decades. Surely, she must know about the stated goals of BDS, and the Hamas Covenant. How, then, could she advocate for terrorists who wanted her dead? *This makes no sense!*

Her mind reeled. She closed the laptop, picked up her phone, then put it back down. She lay down on her bed, in the fetal position, began crying again, cried until there were no more tears. She fell asleep.

She awoke an hour later, feeling no better. Worse – despondent, lonely.

She kept a handwritten diary, with sporadic entries. Recent notes included her first meeting with David and Michael, the Boycott movie, and the Hillel presentation. Mostly facts and dates, just a few sentences about feelings. Now she felt the need to write more, much more.

She unlocked a desk drawer, retrieved the leather-bound book, turned to the first blank page and began writing. A summary of the march, the encounter, the rescue by Michael, the internet search. A full page of just events. Then she opened up.

*I'm giving in, I can feel it. I need someone to love me. I'm a fool, playing hard to get. All that with Judson last spring, now I'm like a nun.*

*I could make love with either Michael or David. Where would it lead? Start of a relationship? Both love me, or at least my body. What's the difference? Michael respects me more, I think, at least for now. David's more mature, more aware - he sent me the info. He knows I can grow.*

*Marriage? Have to think of the long term. I owe Michael so much, but don't see a future with him. He's got a streak, not a healthy one altogether. He's struggling to find peace, distance from his rough childhood. Does he feel duped by BDS like me? Is Bahá'í the answer for him? Is he Jewish or Bahá'í? Can Bahá'í raise Jewish kids?*

*I sound like my econ professor, weighing the over-under odds, or something like that he discussed. I feel stupid. Truth is, I need to be held, to be loved. Now, today. I feel so depressed!*

She closed her diary, locked it in the drawer, picked up her cell phone and stared at it for several minutes. Then, with a deep sigh she punched in a number. David answered.

"Rebecca? Is that you? What happened at the march? Are you okay?"

"I'm fine," she said, her voice a little shaky. "David… where are you now?"

"In my apartment, microwaving some dinner. Why?"

"Are you alone?"

"Yes. My roommate's not here. Why?"

"Can I come over? Spend the night?"

## THIRTEEN

# Michael's Plan

After bringing Rebecca to Newell Hall, Michael had returned to his own dorm, where he lived as a junior. His mind turned to the afternoon's march, first to Rebecca. *I think she likes me, but I sense she has something going with that guy David.*

Then to BDS. Did he really understand the organization, its goals? Was the sweatshirt Nazi just a party crasher? Or a welcomed guest? *Do I even give a shit about BDS? I thought it has something in common with Bahá'í, but maybe not. Bahá'í Gardens and Shrine are in Haifa. What if...?*

He crafted a plan, one that required his special computer skills – and some new equipment. He left the dorm and drove to a computer emporium a few miles north of Great Lakes Township. There he purchased a burner phone and a cheap laptop, good enough for internet surfing.

Back in his room he signed on to Google from the new laptop with an alias, and registered a new email address. For two-step identification he used the burner phone and an area code of 212: New York City. Then, using his alias and paying with untraceable crypto, he signed on with Nord VPN, a virtual private network that meant his computer could not be traced to its location when he surfed the internet.

To this point, he had not revealed his real name, location, any credit card information, or his regular cell phone number, the one registered with the school. Now he was Myron Khalid, email mkh22@gmail.com.

The burner phone still had to use local cell towers, so the CIA or FBI could trace him, but not likely ordinary users of the internet, so he didn't worry about this one aspect. Furthermore, his use of the phone would be brief, a few minutes at most; then it would be turned off, sending no signal.

At six o'clock he checked the local news channel's website to see its coverage of the afternoon march. To his relief, nothing about Rebecca's brief encounter; the TV van wasn't close at that point. The video also did not show the offensive sweatshirt. It did show the front row of marchers carrying signs that read "From the River to the Sea, Palestinians Will be Free."

He took screenshots of the video, then created a webpage that would only be traceable to mkh22@gmail.com, someplace in New York.

*Geddy's probably drinking with the Nazis. I'll wait until tomorrow to contact him.*

## FOURTEEN

# The Morning After

Rebecca arrived at David's apartment shortly after her phone call, with a knapsack containing fresh clothes and toiletries. On entering they hugged, their first physical contact beyond a handshake.

Are you okay" he asked. She said yes, just a bit hungry. Over dinner – prepared food from Trader Joes, heated in the microwave – she provided a brief history of the day's events. David asked no questions. He understood her emotional need to talk, to have someone listen who cared about her. She would spend the night, but he did not assume she wanted to share his bed.

"Rebecca, if you want, I can sleep on the couch tonight and you can have my bed."

She gave a slight, provocative smile. "David, I didn't come over here to sleep alone."

\* \* \*

The next morning they awoke within minutes of each other. He moved over to hold her.

"I'm so glad you have a queen-sized bed," she said. "When I made up my mind to call you yesterday, I was a little worried it might be one of those narrow twins."

"That's all you were worried about? Not about my manhood, whether I had condoms, whether my roommate would be an asshole? Whether you would enjoy losing your virginity? None of that?"

"No. About your manhood, no doubt. And I assumed the school gives out condoms to every guy on arrival."

"Do they give out birth control pills to the girls?"

"No, all the girls got them in high school. Except me. But I do have a morning-after pill, in case you weren't prepared."

"Really? So, you knew all along—"

"No, no. Just in case I ran into a serial rapist. Girls have to be prepared. As for losing my virginity, it was the right time. I am thankful you were ready, willing, and able."

"You're such a tease. Flattery will get you anything you desire, including many repeat performances. As far as my room-mate, I was up in the middle of the night, told him you're here, in case he found the bathroom occupied not by me. He's okay with it."

"Does he have a girlfriend?"

"Yes, sort of, but not one who's slept over, to my knowledge. And he just has a twin bed. But when I rented the place, I knew I needed a bigger one."

"For all your girlfriends? Don't answer. I don't want to know."

"For just one girl. My future wife."

"Come again?"

"Do you want to get married today, or wait until your parents can attend the ceremony?"

"I'm only eighteen. Ask me in a few years."

"Only eighteen? You make love like... Oh, never mind. How about this plan? I get my own apartment, and you move in."

"And then when you go off to medical school. I follow you, change schools, and do your laundry, cook your meals, and have your children?"

"That's the nineteenth-century model. Think twenty-first century. You finish college while I'm in med school, then enter law school while I'm in residency. After your graduation we have the kids, and function as a high-powered, pro-Israel, professional couple."

"Are you writing a play or something? Where's the drama, the disappointments? I've read some Shakespeare, you know. At my age, Romeo and Juliet were dead."

"Rebecca, I knew when I first laid eyes on you that you are one smart girl. How you ever fell for that BDS crap was a puzzle."

"I think we're still far apart on what ails society. Let's not discuss. I have to go to the bathroom."

# FIFTEEN

# Michael's Zoom Call

To: Mr. Gordon Geddy
    ggdd2010@gmail.com
    Subject: BDS on campus

Mr. Geddy,

I am organizing a BDS movement in upstate New York university. I saw on the internet, the march yesterday from Great Lakes University, and found your name associated. Good job!

We've so far recruited two dozen students, including a couple of Jews. Though I fully support the movement, I am not an expert, and questions have been raised. Since you are most active in college BDS, I thought of asking you. Is this something you could help with?

Myron Khalid

\* \* \*

To: mkh22@gmail.com.

Subject: BDS on campus

Will be pleased to help. If I don't know the answers, I know who to contact.

Gordon Geddy

* * *

To: ggdd2010@gmail.com

Subject: BDS on campus

Thank you. One student is concerned about the signs carried in the march, "From the River to the Sea, Palestinians Will be Free." Does that mean one state for all people, or the land just for Palestinians?

Myron

* * *

To: mkh22@gmail.com.

Subject: BDS on campus

You will find many interpretations. BDS wants all people in the region, West Bank, Gaza, and what is now claimed to be the state of Israel, to be equal, have voting rights. That is the goal.

Gordon

* * *

To: ggdd2010@gmail.com

Subject: BDS on campus

Thanks for your response. Wouldn't that goal erase Israel as an independent country, if all the Palestinians could vote? This question keeps coming up by one Jew. I don't want to lose him; he brings needed diversity. I need to try to keep the Jews on board.

Myron

\* \* \*

To: mkh22@gmail.com.

Subject: BDS on campus

Sometimes you have to give up on the Jews. BDS wants equality, Jews don't. But I am a student just like you. I suggest a contact with someone who has been with the movement almost from the beginning. Perhaps a three-way phone call.

Gordon

\* \* \*

To: ggdd2010@gmail.com

Subject: BDS on campus

That would be appreciated. I have a cold, and my voice is a little raspy, but if you could arrange it, thanks.

Myron

\* \* \*

Later that day:

To: mkh22@gmail.com.

Subject: BDS on campus

I contacted Mr. Abu Moussa, a professor of Religious Studies in California. He would like to set up a Zoom call. He can do it tomorrow afternoon at 5 pm our time, if that's acceptable. I gave him your email and he'll send the link. Let me know.

Gordon

\* \* \*

To: ggdd2010@gmail.com

Subject: BDS on campus

5 pm tomorrow Central Time is good. Thanks.

Myron

Michael/Myron had a day to prepare. Halloween was coming soon, and he'd have no trouble finding what he needed for the Zoom call: Hoodie, mustache, goatee, glasses. He had spoken at a couple of BDS meetings, but never up close with Geddy, so with a disguise he didn't think he'd be recognized on a Zoom call. He would also keep the computer camera several feet from his face.

* * *

On Monday, Michael/Myron clicked on the Zoom link a few minutes before 5 pm, his laptop set up so the background revealed nothing to suggest his dorm room. In another minute his face appeared, followed by Geddy's, then the professor's – a man in his forties, of Middle Eastern origin.

"Myron, you're muted," said Geddy.

Michael/Myron unmuted his video. "Sorry about that," he replied in a coarse voice, one that he had practiced.

"As I explained," said Geddy," Myron is a student at New York University. He is organizing a BDS movement there and has some questions."

"Actually, in upstate New York, not the university in Manhattan," explained Michael/Myron. "A Jew has joined our group, and he raises questions about the ultimate BDS goal."

"Be careful he's not a plant," said Moussa. "We've had that situation, where the Jew joins, then spreads lies about our movement."

"He's not the brightest kid," said Michael/Myron. "I doubt that."

"Well, then, you want to keep him. Emphasize the positives. Are you of Arab descent?"

"My grandparents were Christians, from Lebanon. So no,

not really Arabic. Can't wait to go to Palestine, and hopefully make it up to Lebanon."

"Mr. Geddy told me you wondered about the slogan, 'From the river to the sea'."

"Yes, to explain to the Jew what BDS means by the slogan."

"Tell him it means equality for all," said Moussa.

"Then the Jews will finally lose Israel?" asked Michael/Myron.

"There is nothing to lose. It was not their country to begin with. It's stolen. But don't tell that to your Jewish student. Always, you must emphasize equality, that all the Palestinians want is peace."

"What about other religions? Druze? Baháʼí? Christians?"

"However long it takes, we will have an Arab nation in all of Palestine. That's the great thing about BDS. It gets young people to understand the Zionist oppression, brings them to our side, so when the time does come, there will be widespread support. As to your question, there are many Arabs in Palestine who follow Christianity, not Islam."

"How many Christian Arabs?" asked Geddy.

"About 50,000 in the West Bank," said Moussa. "Mostly in Bethlehem and East Jerusalem. As for Druze, if they can live under our laws, they will be welcomed. If not, there are other countries for them. Same for the Jews."

"And Baháʼí?" asked Michael/Myron, expecting an answer to confirm his suspicion.

"There are no Baháʼí in Israel," said Moussa, "except for volunteers who support the Baháʼí tourist sites. They are all citizens elsewhere. No more than a few hundred at any one time, and they rotate."

*Is that true? Why didn't I know that?*

"Oh?" replied Michael/Myron. "I read about those beautiful gardens in Haifa, assumed there was a native Baháʼí population."

Unseen on the Zoom video, Michael did a quick internet search and found the answer in Wikipedia.

In fact, although there are adherents in close to 170 countries, there is no resident Bahá'í population in Israel. The 700 Bahá'í s who can be found there at any given time are all volunteers who have come from multiple countries to do service for varying periods of time.

"No, not native," said Moussa. "A common misconception, because so many tourists go to Haifa to see the beautiful gardens."

"Will the gardens stay under Bahá'í when Palestinians take over?" asked Michael/Myron.

"Interesting question. You seem to have an acute interest in Bahá'í."

"Actually, no," said Michael/Myron. *Be careful!* "I have an interest in Haifa. Before my grandparents passed away, they said the one city I should visit in Palestine is Haifa. So, I read about it, and how the Jews expelled all the Arabs during the Nakba in 1948. That's how I first learned about those gardens. I've seen pictures."

"Well, here's a bit of history you and Mr. Geddy may not know," replied Professor Moussa. "Bahá'í originated in Iran in the 1840s, as an outgrowth of The Shi'ite branch of Islam. The faith was proclaimed by two young Iranians, one known as the Báb, and his follower, Bahá'u'lláh. They and their followers were persecuted by the Muslim hierarchy. Bahá'u'lláh was eventually executed because his teachings contradicted a point of Islamic faith – that Muhammad was the final prophet. Still, the religion grew and spread worldwide, and now there are followers in dozens of countries. Bahá'í is considered a separate religion from Islam, Judaism, and Christianity."

"Interesting," said Geddy. "I didn't know that. We actually have a Bahá'í student in our BDS for Justice club."

Michael/Myron did not blink at Geddy's comment, and

without missing a beat, asked, "Are Bahá'i followers still perse-cuted by Muslims in Iran?"

"Unfortunately, yes. There is persecution ongoing. It's a complicated situation, given that the religion originated in the country."

*I better get off this subject.* "I will try to keep the Jew as a member," replied Michael/Myron, "emphasizing your points. He does understand how Israel oppresses the Palestinians, and wants to change that, and have Israel get rid of all the settle-ments in the occupied West Bank. But I don't think they he wants the destruction of Israel. So, I will work on steering him away from that possibility."

"Know this," said Geddy. "It *will* come. You and I and the professor know it. BDS is but one pillar in the foundation. But it is inevitable. God Willing."

They said goodbyes and ended the Zoom call.

\* \* \*

Within a minute a text message popped up on Geddy's phone, from Professor Abu Moussa. "Call me."

Geddy made the call. "What's up?"

"Do you know this student?"

"No, he contacted me via email, about our BDS march here at Great Lakes University. Why?"

"Something fishy. His questions. A true BDS leader would not be so ignorant. And his appearance; never really got a good look at his face. What university is he with, somewhere in New York?"

"He said it was in upstate New York."

"But he didn't give you the actual school?"

"Apparently not."

"I may be overly concerned, but this could be a sting. You are confident you have not been hacked?"

"All contact for our project has been via the dark web. Nothing searchable on my computer without two-factor authentication. If Myron got into my computer, I don't think he'd find anything."

"Good. Let me suggest you have no further contact with him. If he emails you again, ignore it. Just to be safe."

"Okay. Glad you texted me right away. I *was* thinking of following up with him, to ask about his Lebanese heritage. My girlfriend's parents are from Lebanon."

"Don't do it. Let it go."

"I understand."

* * *

Sitting in his dorm room, Michael removed the fake facial hair, took off his hoodie.

*That did not go well. The professor is quite smart, and I came across like a dolt. But I do have a better grasp of BDS. Its goal is the destruction of Israel. And Geddy – he's a scumbag. Probably invited the Nazi to the march.*

# SIXTEEN

# Taste of India

With November, cool weather set in, accentuated by wind off the nearby lake. David texted or called Rebecca daily. They planned to have dinner together Friday and she would come to his apartment afterwards, but not spend the night.

On Wednesday she stopped at Walgreens and picked up a prescription for birth control pills, prescribed by a nurse practitioner at the college infirmary. The package insert stated the pills would not become fully effective for at least a week.

On Friday they walked over to Taste of India, on Jefferson Street. David loved the restaurant's lamb korma and naan bread. Rebecca ordered an eggplant dish.

The bread arrived in a few minutes. David tore off a piece. After a few quick munches: "Umm, their naan is excellent. You can almost make a meal just out of the bread."

Rebecca ate a piece. "Not bad. It's amazing how many restaurants are downtown, especially Asian. Maybe try Chinese next time? That's my favorite."

"Good idea. I do like it when you say, 'next time'. Gives me confidence. I think about you every day. Did you get the pills?

"Yes, but they take at least a week to kick in. So, stay safe."

"Of course. Like a boy scout. I'm prepared. Things are quiet this week, since the march. Have you heard anything?"

"No, thank goodness. Most students couldn't care less, if they even knew about the march. I saw one little article in the school paper. Nothing about me or the Nazi. Thankfully."

"Yeah, things are quiet here. I started up with my brother again."

"You did? Why?"

"Couldn't help it. He sent me a link to an article in *The New York Times* critical of Israel's right-wing shift, which has led to some demonstrations in Tel Aviv and Jerusalem."

"What's wrong with that? It is a problem. Concerns me, too."

"Nothing, except all the years we've been sparring he's never expressed concern about Hamas, Hezbollah, Islamic Jihad, or Iran – the real, existential threats to Israel. Or BDS, for that matter. Or the Haredim, with their insistence on not serving in the military and only studying the Talmud. Those are all threats to Israel, but nada from him. Then there is yet another in a long line of right-wing shifts in Israel politics and all of a sudden, he's very concerned. It's democracy in action, these political shifts, and now that concerns him. Not the missiles, tunnels, terrorists, suicide bombers, Haredim. Never comments on those."

"Aren't you being a little too critical? I'm sure those threats bother him also, if as you say, he is pro-Israel."

"Rebecca, he has no idea what the hell is going on. He's never been there. And he's never once expressed any concern about the terrorists or the real threats to Israel's existence. But the government shifts rightward, gets criticized in *The New York Times*, and now he's worried about the country. You can cut the hypocrisy with a knife. I let him have it. Want me to read what I wrote?"

"Not really. Honestly, David, you should let it go. You're not going to change him, from what you've told me. You just get yourself worked up. Why do you persist?"

The lamb korma and eggplant arrived and they began eating. "Umm, this is delicious," he crowed. "How's your eggplant?"

"Pretty good."

"Here, taste some lamb."

She took a bite. "A little too spicey for me"

"You can add some yogurt to make it less spicy."

"No thanks."

"Rebecca, I'm not ignoring your question. You're right about Joe. I'll cut back, stop egging him on. What galls me is his all-knowing attitude. To him, I'm still his ignorant little brother. It's beneath him to respond with any information, any cogent argument, any fact-filled discussion. It's always, I'm 'extreme' or some other put-down if I criticize him or *The New York Times*. You never had disagreements or arguments with your sister?"

"Not arguments, but I do have issues with her. Being older, she never much cared for my views, but we didn't argue politics and certainly nothing about Israel. That's not an interest of hers, as far as I know. When she got married and became pregnant, her focus turned inward. Now, when we do talk, guess what? It's all about her. She rarely asks more than one question about how I'm doing. And if I didn't ask her about her life, her family, her career, there would be no conversation. Just silence. But I don't email her, at least never anything with criticism."

"Have you told her about us? Or your parents?"

"No, not yet. Too soon."

"Why, are you expecting it won't last?"

"No. No. I mean we've had just a couple of dates. What am I going to say, I met this guy, shacked up with him, lost my virginity on our first date?"

"No, just that you met the most wonderful man in college, who's in love and wants to marry you. Ask if it's okay if they come here for the wedding, or do we have to get married in Palo Alto."

"Your humor hasn't improved, David. I'll tell them in due time."

He ate some more lamb korma. "Are you going home for Thanksgiving?"

"That's the plan. Why?"

"If you could change the plan, I'd like you to come to Cleveland, meet my family. We'll stay in separate bedrooms. That won't be an issue."

"Thanks for the invite, but my parents are really expecting me home. And to be honest, I'm a bit homesick. But I'll only be gone four or five days."

"I'll miss you."

# SEVENTEEN

# Report to the President

Ten days after the BDS march in Great Lakes Township, Attorney Zimmerman entered the school president's office. Hightower started off with a question. "So, what have you learned?"

"Not a whole lot. I had two law students attend the BDS parade last week, and one of them saw the attack on that female student. He got a snapshot before her rescuer came and floored the guy. Her name is Rebecca Goldman. The attacker was some Nazi-wannabe kid who's not even in college. He's a high school senior in Oslandia. That's twenty miles away, so he was likely bussed here with students from Oslandia Junior College. He had on an Auschwitz-themed sweatshirt which initiated the confrontation.

"So this was just a random act of Nazi aggression?"

"Yeah, by a radicalized kid. Doubt he's involved in anything intelligent."

"Okay, what else?"

"The BDS leader, one Gordon Geddy, has a girlfriend of Lebanese descent. She and he have been very vocal about Israel.

Vocal that is, in refuting the Israel narrative, as you would expect."

"No threats made?"

"No, not according to my sources."

"Your two student spies – where'd you recruit them?"

"Not hard. Two Great Lakes law school students who work in the legal office. Paid them for extracurricular work, which is a common expense."

"Lester, please tell me all this snooping is legal."

"When you're investigating a case, what's legal and what's not is subject to judicial review. Tracking somebody without trespassing is, in my opinion, legal. I don't think the FBI stopped by just to be nice. They want any information we can give them."

"Okay, I won't ask again. So, what's the relevance here?"

"Nothing obvious, I admit. And really, I doubt anything learned so far is new to the FBI. At least, not if they are doing a competent investigation. They won't tell us what they have, so we really don't know how or why they're concerned about our campus."

"That's true, but you're homing in on BDS. What about Students for a Socialist America?"

"Checked them out. They don't agitate, they don't march. Their thing is writing letters to Congress and posting on websites. I just don't see anything alarming with that group."

"So, if there's anything at all on campus, you think it's BDS? I hope this isn't becoming personal in any way."

"What do you mean?"

"You're Jewish, the FBI says there's a threat, you focus on BDS. And before you jump down my throat, remember Ruth is Jewish, What I don't hear about anti-Semitism on campus, she fills me in at home."

"It's not personal. I like to think I'd be just as vigilant if I saw a potential threat against Asians or Blacks or Gays. And I have not excluded other potentials. It's just that the FBI visit and the

BDS march seem too close to ignore. If you hear anything from our Asian American Club or any other ethnic group, let me know. Now, where was I?"

"You were telling me about BDS."

"Oh, yeah. So given what happened on the downtown demonstration, I had one of my law students contact the young woman who was attacked. In that way we were able to get the names of several other Jewish BDS members. To keep this from mushrooming, the only other one they interviewed is a student named Michael Solomon, Rebecca's erstwhile rescuer. Now, both know to call my office if they hear anything about another 'Nazi demonstration.' Of course, that's not the concern, about some high school punk wearing a sweatshirt. The concern is the one the FBI alerted us to, which was not mentioned – a possible terrorist attack. Still, I think if they hear something fishy, we'll find out."

"Pretty thorough job, I must say. I'm impressed. Anything else?"

"Oh, yeah. One other interesting tidbit."

"I'm listening."

"Geddy and his girlfriend live in the same house. Other students also live in the house. It's one of those large Victorians near campus. Whether they share the same bedroom is unknown, but not especially relevant. What is relevant, or may be, is that Geddy sometimes visits another large house a few blocks away, the home of the Muslim-cultural Students Association."

"Wait a minute, your lawyer sleuths are following Geddy around town?"

"No. One of my student investigators slapped a GPS device on the inside of Geddy's rear bumper. Then he tracked the signal. Geddy's made two visits there the past week. Each one lasted about an hour. The law student will keep checking."

"Is *that* legal? Never mind, don't tell me. In any case, what's the big deal about him going to MCSA. It's been around longer than I have. Entirely legitimate group."

"I know. And I just assume he may go there to recruit new students to his BDS club. It's just a feeling that there are dots, and I don't know how to connect them. If the FBI hadn't stopped by with their veiled threats, nothing we've found would raise the slightest concern. Frankly, I think they are worried about another synagogue mass shooting like the one in Pittsburgh a few years ago."

"As I recall, that shooter was a white male. Nothing Islamic about him."

"Right, but now the FBI is telling us about these money transfers between the Middle East and our zip code. Do you think Al Qaeda is recruiting a white male to do its dirty work? I don't think so."

"Lester, my head is reeling. Keep up your investigation, and please just let the FBI know when you have something, anything, that can help them. Right now, everything we are seeing regarding out own students seems to be on the up and up."

"Fair enough."

## EIGHTEEN

# BDS Meets Again

The next BDS meeting was full of congratulations over the successful march downtown. Michael Solomon was not sure if he would say anything. And if he did, would Geddy make any connection between him and the guy Myron on the Zoom call?

Fifteen minutes into the discussion Geddy asked if there were any suggestions for improving the next BDS demonstration, which was planned for late spring. Instinctively, Michael stood and said, "Yes, I have one?"

"Okay, let's hear it."

"Don't invite the Nazis next time!"

"Excuse me?" Geddy stared.

*Does he make any connection to the Zoom guy?*

"Mr. Geddy, are you not aware that one of the marchers is a self-identified Nazi? He's the one who wore that disgusting sweat-shirt, advertising Auschwitz concentration camp."

Before Geddy could respond Michael asked the group, "How many saw this pimp with the sweatshirt?" Several hands went up.

"Sorry, I didn't see that," said Geddy.

"Well, he attacked one of our members, who has since left the club. How did he get invited?"

Geddy raised his voice. "For the record, we don't invite Nazis to our march. For the record, we don't invite Nazis to anything. If some punk wore an offensive sweatshirt, that was something we can't control. If you have any information that we in any way have anything to do with Nazis, please share it now, or shut up!"

Michael did not shut up. "He may not be card carrying members of the Nazi party. But many BDS members have the same values—get rid of all the Jews, from the river to the sea. Do you deny that?"

Several people cried out, "Sit down. Cool it, Mr. Bahá'í," remembering his previously announced affiliation.

"I will cool it. Let me just state for the record, the goal of BDS is not to improve relations with Israelis. It is to destroy Israel, get rid of all the Jews. Look it up, google BDS and its founder, a guy named Omar Barghouti. Read what he and other leaders state is their real goal. That Nazi kid marched with us because he knew his values and BDS values were aligned. That's the type we're attracting. No, not we. You. I'm done with your racist club."

Michael walked out. Several people remarked as he left, "Good riddance."

* * *

Back at the dorm, Michael called Rebecca. She answered right away.

"Just want to let you know I quit BDS a few minutes ago. After calling Geddy a fucking racist and Nazi lover."

"That must have gone over well," she said. "Why did you bother?"

"Couldn't help it. We both have some feelings that things need to change in Israel, in its relationship with the Palestinians, but BDS is not the way to do it. I've done a lot of reading since the march. Do you know about the Soda Stream factory in the West Bank?"

"No, what's that?"

"Oh, years ago BDS encouraged people to boycott this West Bank factory that makes seltzer devices for home use. Turns out almost all the employees were Palestinians. The boycott was effective, and the factory closed. All the Palestinians lost their jobs. Then the factory moved to the Negev, and now employs mostly Israelis. So, Palestinians were the losers. That's the BDS way. BDS is poison. They don't give a shit about Palestinians, just want to hurt Jews." *I'm getting too excited. Need to dial it back.*

"Well," she said, "I'm out. Are any Jews left in the club?"

"I don't know, maybe one or two. After my harangue, maybe none." *I've got to ask.* "Rebecca, are you still with David Applebaum?"

"Yes, Michael, I am. But I do want to stay friends with you. And I very much appreciate what you did on the march. Please, feel free to call if there's anything I can help you with."

A few more pleasantries and the call ended.

* * *

Bordering part of the campus, where it meets the lake, are huge boulders placed to block waves from washing ashore. Their surfaces are ripe for graffiti, and students paint on them love messages, "class of" notes, obscure quotes, and other trivia. Occasionally hate messages appear, and when this happens the administration has a strict policy: erasure.

The day after Michael's outburst at BDS for Justice, one of the boulders spouted the following message in bright-orange letters a foot tall.

## Bye Bye Bahai

## Good Riddance
## Jew-boy

Some anonymous source sent a picture of the boulder to Michael, via email. The dark sky backdrop and artificial illumination showed it was taken during nighttime. Michael saw it mid-morning. His attempt to reply to the email elicited "address not found." The boulder was just a ten-minute walk from his dorm. If the thing was real, and not some photoshopped image, he would buy two cans of spray paint at the Student Union – always in stock for graffiti writing –paint over it and write "Fuck You BDS."

When he arrived at the boulder, the very one in the picture, two maintenance crew were just completing a coating of purple paint; only the word "boy" remained uncovered. He questioned them, but all they knew was "orders to paint over it," and showed him a picture, this one taken during the early morning, presumably by a student passing by.

# NINETEEN

## The Breakup

The Saturday before Thanksgiving Rebecca and David went out for dinner to Luigi's, an Italian restaurant just a few doors from Mona's coffee shop. After dinner, she planned to return to his apartment, for one last time in bed before flying to California on Tuesday.

Luigi's serves great deep-dish pizza and they split a large pie: Mushrooms, pepperoni, and cheese.

"I feel like I'm on a world tour, with all these restaurants," she said.

"Yeah, college students are an eclectic bunch, so they try to cater to us."

"I see some non-college students here also, at least judging by age."

"Probably a smattering of faculty, parents of college kids visiting, some locals not connected with the university."

"Guess who called me a few days ago."

"Let me guess. Judson, your flame from high school. He's learned you're no longer a virgin and wants you back."

"Wash your mouth out with soap."

"Your sister?"

"No."

"Gordon Geddy?"

"Yeah, right. No, Michael Solomon, my rescuer."

"Oh. And?"

"He told me he reamed out Geddy at the last BDS meeting, for letting that Nazi into the march. Geddy denied having anything to do with it, of course, and they got into a sparring match. Michael walked out, quit the club, won't go back."

"Good for him. In less than a month two Jews have quit, you and Michael. Now if more could follow."

"We still have strong feelings about the situation in Israel. But also see that BDS is not the solution. It sounded good when we first went. It's easy to corral in naïve college students like us, I guess."

"Bravo! You're learning fast."

"Now we need to find another channel to promote our goals for peace."

*Maybe not learning so fast. She still has these Kumbaya fantasies. Need to tread carefully.* "I wish there was a path, Rebecca. But everything I've learned is that the Palestinians, or at least their leaders, don't really want peace. They want to perpetuate the conflict, to keep the money flowing, and themselves in power."

"But how do the settlements help? What happens when new Palestinian leaders do come along, and there's no land left to make a Palestinian state?"

"Honestly, I don't see them ever wanting a state side by side Israel. They've had multiple opportunities, turned them all down. The only thing they want, the only thing they will ever accept, is Israel gone. Aaron Peretz called it in his book. No possibility for a resolution any time soon."

The pizza came and they each took a piece.

"Pretty good," he said.

She nodded agreement, her mouth full of cheese and crust.

"I plan to go to Israel for the summer before medical school, and want you to come with me. We'll tour all the sites, meet some interesting people. Did I ever tell you about the student who is making Aliyah to Israel?"

"You mean, he's moving to Israel?"

"Yeah, name's Steve Mandelbaum. Don't know if you know him. After graduation he's moving there, joining the IDF."

"IDF?"

"Yeah, the Israel Defense Force. Their military. Includes army, navy, air force – the whole shebang. He says it's the only way to fight the threats to Israel, and that all our efforts here in the U.S. are a waste."

"Well, I'm not moving to Israel."

"Don't blame you. Women have to serve in the IDF as well as men, right after high school."

"I've heard that. It's barbaric."

"Not really. It's a service to the country and a way to keep up the military strength. One thing you'll see when you go there are young girls, your age, carrying machine guns as they walk on patrols It's sobering – and reassuring."

"Yeah, and if they get killed in combat, that's one way to cut down on the Jewish population. Sounds like a dumb idea."

"I think combat for women is optional. You have a point, but the female soldiers I've met are proud to serve in the IDF. When your country's very existence is threatened daily, it's a small price to pay."

"Israel is so strong now, I don't see its existence threatened daily."

"But it is. If they let their guard down, Hamas and Hezbollah and the PLO would swoop in, take over in a flash. Then they would fight among themselves, another Arab civil war."

"Don't you think the larger risk is oppressing millions of Palestinians so they will eternally hate the Israelis? I mean, I know about the terrorist groups, I get it. But if the ordinary, everyday Palestinian feels he or she is being screwed over by the Israelis, that creates a huge negative. It's like a volcano that could explode anytime. And that concerns me."

"It concerns me, too, but the cause isn't Israel, it's the way the Palestinian leaders treat their own people. They want them subjugated, with few of the rights we take for granted. Here, have another piece of pizza."

"Let me digest what I just ate. It is good."

"What exactly do you want Israel to do?" David asked.

She took a sip of water. "I guess, for starters, cut back on the settlements, rather than keep expanding them."

"Well, that's a long-standing argument. Some Israelis would certainly agree with you. For my money, I don't think there's anything the Israelis could do that would matter. Don't forget, between the 1948 War of Independence and the 1967 Six Day War, there were zero Jewish settlements in the West Bank. The land was controlled by Jordan, and there was no move whatsoever to form a Palestinian nation. They didn't do it then, and they won't do it now. They don't want a nation coexisting with Israel. The Palestinians want all the land. And they won't quit until they get it. Which means a conflict in perpetuity."

"You keep saying that," her voice rising. "You're like a machine. Have you talked to any Palestinians? Been in peace talks with them? Seen how they live? Walked in their shoes?"

*I'm really making a mess here. Need to pull back.*

"No none of that, I agree. But I've studied the history, I've read the websites. Are you familiar with MEMRI.org? I think I sent you that link. MEMRI monitors all Arabic media. What the imams and Arab politicians say in Arabic is different from what they speak in English. Sometimes, the exact opposite. In Arabic, it's 'remove all the Jews, kill all the Jews, reclaim all the land if it takes 100 years. We will prevail, God is on our side.' You should check it out. See what they really believe, what they really want."

Rebecca stared at David and did not respond right away.

"What's the matter?"

"Honestly, you treat me like you treat your brother Joe, like I'm some willfully ignorant no- nothing and you're the hotshot know-it-all. My views don't count because you don't agree with them."

*She's got it backwards. That's how Joe treats* me.

"Rebecca, that's not—"

"Shut up! Please, just listen. I know the history, not as much as you, and I've not been over there. But I know the harm people can inflict when one side controls the lives of others. Don't discount my views because I don't read English translations of Arab speeches. My God, there's a real crisis in Israel, it may be unsolvable, but I can't believe it's all one-sided like you do. So, stop putting me down because I'm so ignorant."

"Rebecca you really misunderstand what—"

"No, I don't misunderstand! I get it. Right now. I'm just upset over your preaching."

*What have I done?* "Sorry, I didn't think I was preaching. Want some more pizza?"

"No thanks. Right now, I want to go back to the dorm. I fly home Tuesday. I'm just not in the mood for anything else right now. Let's put some space between us for a few days. That will be good."

"I'm sorry, Rebecca, I really am. You know how I feel about you. I'm sorry for being so strong in my views. I am not in any way putting you down. Just expressing how I feel, that's all."

"I see that, I do. It just blunts any desire for intimacy. I'm sorry. Just being honest."

"Okay, I appreciate that. Can I call when you get back? I think we can work this out, I really do. Please?"

"Okay, but it won't be for another week. I return on Sunday."

"Good. I won't stop thinking of you."

# TWENTY

# What About Michael

Rebecca returned to her room, depressed, mad at herself. What am I trying to do? I was looking forward to being in bed with him, but he made me angry. Now, I'm alone. I hate this!

She opened her diary, began writing. About the dinner. The conversation. David's preaching. Her reaction. Then, suddenly, Michael popped into her head. She stopped writing.

Michael! I owe him. Such a nice guy. He likes me, maybe as much as David. I know it's sex, that's what they want, but with the right guy there's also love and affection. How can I thank him with something more than words? I know he would sleep with me, but can I have two lovers – am I a whore like Cynthia, that high school bitch?

I owe nothing to David. I owe a profound thank you to Michael. I could make him happy like I used to do with Judson. Not intercourse, but he would love it. Yes, I'll do it! I'll explain that David and I have broken up temporarily, that I cannot go all the way with him right now, but that I can get very intimate in other ways. What guy would turn that down? I'm wicked! Eighteen and immature, anyone would say. But if I work this right, I can pay my debt to Michael, and return to David as well. There is a future with David, much more so than with Michael.

Then she thought: what if I do it and he takes advantage, forces himself inside me? He's so physical. My plan would backfire. I am Cynthia!

She went back and forth, trying to decide.

*I need someone.*

She picked up her cell phone and called Michael.

"Hello. Rebecca, is this you?"

"Yes, hi Michael. Can we talk for a minute?"

"Uh, sure. What's up?" Then, in a voice partially removed from the phone but still audible to Rebecca, he spoke to someone in his room. "This is the girl I told you about. The one on the march."

"Oh," said Rebecca, "I'm sorry, are you with someone?"

"Uh, yes, but that's okay. Her name's Amanda Stanwyck. She knows about the march, and all that shit with BDS. So, what's up? Are you okay?"

"Yeah, I'm fine. Is Amanda like, your girlfriend? I don't want to intrude."

"Hey, Rebecca, no problem. You can call anytime. Amanda and I are dating. Yeah, well, she's in my room, so it's kind of heavy at times. But don't tell my parents." He laughs.

"Well, I'm so happy for you, Michael. I just wanted to call and again thank you for what you did for me on that march. I'm going home to California for Thanksgiving, but maybe we can all get together when I return."

"You're still dating David, right?"

"Right, yes. Well, I'll let you go."

"Okay, Rebecca. Thanks for calling."

She ended the call, crawled into bed and cried, a cry of sorrow and of relief. Sorrow for her emotional mess. Relief that Michael was with another girl, and didn't need her.

*Oral sex with Michael would have solved nothing. I can return to David clean. I need to grow up.*

# TWENTY-ONE

# The Professor

The day before leaving to spend Thanksgiving in Cleveland, David walked over to an office in Fanuel, Hall, home of the history department. The sign on the third-floor office door read "Prof. Mordecai Shapiro, Mid-East Studies."

David knocked and was met with "come in."

He did not know for sure why the professor wanted to see him but thought it might have something to do with recent discussions at Hillel. He had never met Prof. Shapiro or seen him at Hillel.

David entered, introduced himself. "You wanted to see me, Professor?"

"Yes, yes, thanks for coming. Steve Mandelbaum told me about you, and I wanted to just chat for a moment. Take a seat. Sorry for the all the mess."

By mess, he meant books, strewn everywhere; desk, floor, one overcrowded bookcase. David had looked up basic facts about Shapiro: age sixty-seven, at Great Lakes for decades, tenured professor. On a student-run site he found a popularity ranking of 4.4 out of 5. Not bad. All the internet pics showed a clean-shaven man, younger and slimmer than the man at the desk: now with full beard, overweight by fifty pounds, tired eyes beset by wrinkles.

"No problem. What's this about, Professor?"

"How did you ever avoid taking my class?"

"On Middle East history?"

"Yes, that one. Steve told me of your knowledge of the history as regards Israel, at least."

"Thank you. I'm pre-med. I've taken several humanities courses, but yours wasn't one of them. I'm sorry."

"No need to be sorry! There are many other courses our graduates miss. Art, music, literature. But we have to have careers, and Middle Eastern history would not be that helpful to yours. Are you accepted to medical school?"

"Not yet. The applications are in."

"Where do you want to go?"

"I will stay in the area if I get into Great Lakes. But I'm also applying to two schools in Cleveland, my hometown, and a couple in New York."

"Well, I'm sure you'll get in. But I have no pull."

*What does he want of me?* "What did Steve tell you that prompted this invitation?"

"I'm coming to that. Do you know anything about me?"

"No, sir. I mean, I've heard your name, but you're not one for the college newspaper. Only what's in the school catalogs. No controversy, I assume."

"Good, that's what I prefer. At least to this point. Steve took my course last year, as a junior. In the course, I give a couple of lectures on the history of the Israeli-Palestine Conflict, and assign some reading that is strictly historical, not slanted one way or the other. From Steve, I know you are familiar with this history."

"Thank you. I've done a fair amount of reading, and we've had speakers from time to time at Hillel, on the subject."

"Yes, I know you had Aaron Peretz recently. Did you know he stayed at my house for that visit?"

"Really? No, I didn't know."

"Yes, Aaron and I are friends. In some respects, I have been a silent mentor for his work."

"Why silent?"

"My choice, to this point. "Anyway, back to the course I teach, the one Steve took last year. After the lectures and reading assignments, I ask students to write a review of the history, adding in their point of view, their assessment of the conflict. I make it abundantly clear that I am not advocating any particular viewpoint, but that history is often presented with one, and they should now offer their own. You've heard the expression, 'the victors write the history books?'"

"Yes, something to that effect."

"Well, in the I-P conflict, there are no victors, per se, so I make it clear I am open to all viewpoints The only thing required in this assignment is that they get the facts right. After that, their grade is based on the writing and how well they integrate their viewpoint with the known facts."

"Do they have to agree with the facts?"

"Excellent question, David! See, I really wish you had taken my course. The answer is yes, they have to agree with the facts, but they are few. For example, it's a fact that around 750 thousand Palestinians left their towns and villages during the War of Independence, and became refugees. What's disputed is why they left, so that's open to interpretation, and believe me, there are many viewpoints.

"It's a fact that armies of five countries invaded Israel the day after independence was declared in May 1948. It's disputed what their goals were.

"It's a fact that Israel fired the first shots in the 1967 Six-Day war, when the Israeli Air Force bombed Egyptian airfields. It's disputed whether this was justified at the time.

"It's a fact that the holocaust took place during World War II, killing six million Jews. If they make up new facts, including holocaust denial, they will flunk. I make it very clear that they have wide latitude for expressing their viewpoint, just don't mess with the facts."

"So, I imagine you got different viewpoints."

"Yes, over the years. Can you guess the results?"

"Well, the way you're presenting it, I think most of the students will find fault with Israel, and come out on the side of the Palestinians."

"Good Guess. And you're correct. Out of 100 plus essays I've received on this theme, over eighty per cent take the view that Israel has been at fault, or the cause for the conflict, both its initiation and continuance. The other twenty percent have been more or less pro-Israel, from mildly so, to what one might call radical. Or rather, one was radical."

"Steve?"

"Yes."

"What did he write?"

"Let's just say he caught my attention. He did not know at the time that I'd been writing a book about how college professors are at fault, how they foster anti-Israel bias and anti-Semitism on campus. His viewpoint was straight out of my book, and blew me away."

Since Mr. Peretz stayed with you, I assume you know about Steve's outburst during his talk, calling the local BDS club leader a liar and stating his goal was to kill all the Jews?"

"Yes, that didn't surprise me. Steve likes to speak the truth, not mince any words. I'll tell you a little secret. Aaron was delighted by the outburst. First, he pretty much agreed with Steve's comments. And second, it woke up his audience, who he said was tending to drift away. So he wasn't upset at all."

"Good. I thought Mr. Peretz handled it very well. Back to your class, what did Steve write in his essay?"

"He understood that the problem isn't just an inherent bias against Israel by many faculty. The problem is that the whole educational structure is set up to brainwash students not to think, not to use reason or even common sense when confronted with anti-Israel propaganda. In effect, to support any latent anti-Semitism the students may have brought with them when they entered college. In other words, the problem is a flawed education. I'll give you one example. You read *Industry of Lies*, by Ben-Dror Yemini?"

"Yes, I have."

"In his Introduction, Yemini talks about confronting two young women protesting Israel's genocide of Palestinians. They literally had no knowledge of a single fact to back up the claim, but spouted some off-the-wall academic garbage generated by warp-minded professors. Well, I've encountered that here and in other colleges as well. Students claiming Israel is 'apartheid,' 'practices genocide,' or 'is like the Nazis in World War II.'"

"Yes, Mr. Peretz talked about those crazy claims at Hillel."

"So, assuming they are believed, what kind of intellect are we fostering in our colleges? A book published several years ago, called Anti-Zionism on Campus pointed all this out in detail. Multiple examples. It shows how the BDS movement is eroding our colleges, including free speech, respectful discourse, even research. I venture to say the situation's even worse now. If Israel ever got into a full scale war with Hamas, it I think the campus antisemitism would explode."

"What do you mean?"

"So many students have been radicalized, that if Israel was in a war, where there were any significant number of Palestinian casualties, these students would rise up *against Israel*. Out of total ignorance, with no understanding of the history, or the true meaning of words like 'occupation,' 'apartheid,' or 'genocide,' they will march against Israel, waving the Palestinian flag. It doesn't matter if Hezbollah or Hamas initiates the war by firing a missile at Tel Aviv or Jerusalem that results in killing hundreds – I believe a large number of college students will march against Israel, as soon as Israel retaliates. Including – and this is really insane – groups supporting gay rights or women's rights or freedom of speech. In Gaza these groups would be silenced or killed the moment they spoke up. But you will see them marching *for* Palestine."

"And you blame the professors?"

"Yes, to a large degree. Along with labeling Israel as "apartheid" or "genocidal," consider that now we have craziness like 'women can become men,' 'men can become pregnant,' and so forth. No sane person believes this gender shit, of course, but rational belief is not the goal of our teachers. The goal is to condition students not to challenge such obvious irrationality, which can then extend to more important topics." The professor paused for a moment.

"Like Israel?" asked David.

"Yes, like Israel, and its conflict with the Arabs. If students do question propaganda, they risk being degraded – literally. So, students keep their mouths shut, or worse, believe that maybe it all does make sense – 'men can become pregnant' or 'Israel practices genocide.' All this indoctrination takes place *sub rosa*, as it were, without formally espousing anti-Semitism in the class room. And, if they were closet anti-Semites to begin with, they now see academic support for believing lies about Israel. Ugh! I sound like I'm lecturing to you. Sorry about that."

"No, no, it's fine. Professor, I get your point. The students are being taught not to challenge dogma, even when it's obvious bullshit."

"Certainly not challenge openly, David. Students will succeed as long as they keep quiet, or if they speak out, they must never challenge the immorality and duplicity of their professors. Steve saw this right away as a root cause of the problem, and I was impressed. I invited him to discuss the issue privately, and learned much about this remarkable young man. Once I had his confidence, I asked him if he would read portions of the book I was writing. He was the first person on campus for whom I made that request."

"And did he?"

"Yes, he was happy to do so. He made some suggestions, and he's been reviewing changes made since then. He and Aaron Peretz are my main beta readers, you might say."

"And you're telling me this, why?"

"The draft is done. Steve suggested you would be a good choice as another student, to review it."

"Well, thank you. I assume it gets into BDS?"

"Of course. But unlike your Hillel discussions, and your own efforts to counter BDS propaganda – which are admirable, don't get me wrong – my book is an indictment of the whole rotten core of academia. The intellectual dishonesty that pervades academia, to the point of accepting propaganda as truth, purposely mis-educating our youth. It's not college education, it's college indoctrination."

"I see why you and Steve were attracted to each other."

"Let's just say we have a similar perspective."

"What's the title of your book?"

"*Useful Idiots: How Academia Fosters Anti-Semitism.*"

"That's some title. The useful idiots are…?"

"The students. It's an old term, meaning people who adhere to propaganda spouted by leaders of a cause, without any under-standing of the goals of that cause, or where that propaganda will lead. One good example is the followers of Lenin during the Russian Revolution, which of course led to the deaths of millions."

"But why all the secrecy? I'm sure plenty of people would agree with what seems to be your premise."

"Not plenty of people in academia. I have tenure, so don't really risk job security when the book is published. But I do risk faculty calumny, student boycotts, eggs thrown on my house. So I've decided to wait until retirement to publish it. I'll be sixty-eight next fall, and will announce my retirement then. If all goes well, the book should come out a short while later."

"Do you have a publisher?"

"Yes. A small one, pending completion of the book. They agreed based on a few chapters, but have not yet seen the whole book. So, no contract yet signed. But I have confidence."

"There must be other books out there documenting campus anti-Semitism. How are they received?"

"Actually, only a few. And they are not specifically geared to students, or about the teacher-student relationship. The best one came out several years ago. It's on my shelf somewhere." The professor got up, walked over to a shelf and pulled out two books. David noticed he walked slowly, and his breathing appeared a bit labored.

"Ever heard of it?"

"No, I must admit."

"Yes. Being multi-authored, it's more wide-ranging than my book. It goes into all aspects, including faculty censorship by administrators and smear campaigns by faculty colleagues, all rooted in academic anti-Semitism. It even includes essays by students who have experienced anti-Semitism at Oberlin, Brown, University of Michigan, and other top schools. My book is much more narrowly focused, on the teacher-student dynamic. And my goal is to have the thing read – by students."

David closed the book, put it on the desk. "What's the other book you pulled out?"

"On a somewhat different subject, but one you should be aware of." He handed it to David, who read out the title.

*"Betrayal: The Failure of American Jewish Leadership."*

"I assume you've not read this one either?"

"No, sir."

"You will, in due time. This one documents how Jewish organizations, supposedly set up to fight anti-Semitism, are in fact enabling it."

"Enabling it? How so?"

"By refusing to condemn or call out overt anti-Semitism by progressive elements. They pretty much only acknowledge anti-Semitism if it comes from right-wing whites, and ignore the anti-Semitism from the left wing, from progressives, from Blacks, and Muslims. Thus, for example, anti-Semitism on campus gets a pass if it comes from minority groups."

"You say 'Jewish organizations.' Which ones?

"Several, one of the worst being the Anti-Defamation League, or ADL. Another is the American Jewish Committee."

"Professor, I see I have a lot to learn, and you're opening my eyes. I'll get to these books at some point, but right now let me concentrate on your book."

"Yes, or course, I don't' mean to overload you. Just want to point out that there are books out there documenting the disaster of how poorly we're dealing with the rise of anti-Semitism, on and off the campus. My book is narrowly focused on colleges, and what should be their main purpose – to educate students."

"What kind of feedback are you looking for from me? I'm not an English major, my spelling is atrocious."

"When you do a beta-read, anything is fair game. My main concern is clarity of thought. Is there anything that doesn't make sense? Obviously, people are going to disagree with what I've written. That's expected. But I want to make sure, to the college students who might read the thing, that my points are clearly made. Of course, if you find typos, let me know."

"Well, I'm flattered, Professor."

"So, you'll agree?"

"How much time would I have?"

"If you could read it over the next month, that would be fine. Oh, one other thing. You can't tell anyone about it. Girlfriend, family, other students. Will you agree to that?"

*I'm sure it's something Rebecca wouldn't want to read.* "Yes, yes, of course."

"Okay." Professor Shapiro opened a drawer, pulled out a thick manuscript and handed it to David. "Here it is. Send me a note when you're done. My contact information is in the front of the book."

## TWENTY-TWO

# Palo Alto

Thanksgiving dinner in the Goldman home was a small family affair: Rebecca's parents, her sister Julie, brother-in-law Henry, their two-year old son Jeremy. Henry was a vegetarian, so Rebecca's mother cooked tofurkey for him, regular turkey for everyone else.

Rebecca had arrived late Tuesday, and most of Wednesday she spent visiting a couple of high school friends. She also helped her mom make the turkey, plus potatoes, gravy and salad.

"Mom, did we have tofurkey last year? I don't remember."

"No. Henry went full veggie this year. I think Julie is going to follow soon, though she said she wanted to have real turkey today. Your dad thinks the tofurkey is vile."

"Whatever. A lot of the kids at school are veggies, or vegans. I'm not even sure of the difference."

"Vegetarians will eat eggs and cheese. Vegans won't eat anything processed from a live animal. Only plant-based foods."

"Ugh! How do they survive?"

"Quite well, I'm told. I have a couple of patients, kids who are being raised as vegans. They are not suffering in any way that I can tell."

* * *

Julie and her family arrived mid-afternoon on Thanksgiving. There were hugs, but no real conversation, as Julie had to put Jeremy down for his afternoon nap. To have an uninterrupted meal, dinner was served at four. Rebecca and her mother placed all the food on the table. Mr. Goldman sat at the head of a rectangular dining table, Rebecca to his left and her mom, Julie, and Henry, on the other side.

"It's so great to have us all together again," said Mrs. Goldman. "I've hardly had a chance to talk to Rebecca since she came home Tuesday."

"Yeah, you're too busy cooking," said her father. "I talked to her. She's tearing up Great Lakes University."

"Why did you choose to go there?" asked Henry, "instead of Stanford?"

"Oh, just a chance to get away. It's cold, but otherwise a good place to be."

"Are you dating anyone?" asked Julie.

"Asked and unanswered," replied Rebecca's mom.

"Let's not be too nosy," said her father.

"What ever happened to that guy Hudson you were so close with in high school?" asked Julie.

"Judson, not Hudson."

"Whatever."

"We broke up, you know that."

"Well, what are the boys like at Great Lakes?"

"Men, Julie. Men. We don't call college students boys anymore. For the record, I've had a few dates with one guy. We're kind of broken off for a while, but may get back together."

"Why'd you break off?" asked Julie. "Let me guess. Politics."

"No. Israel."

"Israel?" asked her mother. "I've never heard that reason before."

"Yeah, we have different views, and got into a heated argument. He's very pro-Israel."

"Well, aren't you?"

"This is Thanksgiving," chimed in Mr. Goldman. "We should be thankful. No need to rehash old arguments."

"What old arguments, Dad?"

"Your mother and I have had some differences abut Israel. Buried our hatchets years ago."

With this comment Rebecca's mother turned to look at her husband. "You buried yours, dear. Mine is out and poised to strike."

"What the hell are you two talking about?" asked Rebecca.

"I better go check on Jeremy," said Julie, "still part-way through her meal. "Be back in a moment."

As she left, Henry shrugged his shoulders, raised his eyebrows – giving a look of puzzlement. "She may need help. Be back in a minute." He excused himself and went to join his wife.

"Nice family get together," said Rebecca.

"Juile's a little overwhelmed with Jeremy," replied her mother. "She's working full time. They have a nanny, but she's still stressed out a bit. Henry doesn't help that much with the kid."

"How's his job?"

"His job's great. He's one of Apple's top engineers. Working on a new type of virtual reality, which he's explained and neither your father nor I understand."

"Makes a good salary?"

"More than me or your father."

"I think you and dad are doing okay. I certainly appreciate not having to take out loans."

"What's your on-again-off-again boyfriend's major?"

"He's premed."

Rebecca's mom dropped her fork.

"Don't fret, Mom. There's nothing that serious with us."

"Just don't tell me he plans to be a surgeon. They're the worst."

"I don't think so. He once mentioned cardiology."

"And you are still committed to pre-law?" asked her father.

"Yes. That's my goal. Want to hear something interesting?"

Mom and Dad nodded.

"His father's a doctor, his mother a lawyer. The reverse of you two."

"So, what is the argument about?"

"It's not an argument, just a different outlook about what Israel should or should not do regarding the Palestinians."

Her mother looked at Mr. Goldman, suggesting 'here we go again.'

Julie and Henry returned to the dining table and took their seats.

"Everything okay with Jeremy?"

"Yes, Mom, he's fine."

"Henry, Mom tells me you're designing a new invention at Apple."

Henry laughed. "No, just some improvements in our virtual reality devices."

"Major improvements," said Julie. "May equal the iPhone in importance."

"Oh? That's exciting. Some college students are using those devices. You see them walking around the dorm with these giant goggles. Really weird looking."

"With Henry's device, you won't know it's even being worn. Looks like regular sunglasses."

"It's at least two years away," offered Henry, "if it comes to market at all."

"While you were out," interjected Mrs. Goldman, "Rebecca

was just going to tell us about this boy she met, who is very pro-Israel."

"Sounds like your kind of son-in-law," said Julie. "What's his name?"

"David Applebaum."

"Yeah, and he's pre-med," added Mr. Goldman.

"Match made in heaven. Jewish girl meets pro-Israel pre-med," snickered Julie.

"What are you guys talking about? I've only had a few dates."

"Have you, you know, have you two…?"

"Julie, none of your business," snapped Mrs. Goldman.

Rebecca stared at her sister. "I'm on the pill." *That should shut them up.*

"Are you running into any anti-Semitism at Great Lakes?" asked her father. "We're having some issues on the Stanford campus. I imagine it's a problem everywhere."

*How much do I tell them? Anything I say will just lead to more questions.* "There's a BDS group on campus. I went to a couple of meetings. But I don't think their boycott idea is the way to peace, so I quit."

"Good for you," replied Mrs. Goldman "They actually advocate for the destruction of Israel."

"It's more nuanced," replied Mr. Goldman. "Some do want to just pressure Israel to relax restrictions on Palestinians. The more radical elements want Israel out of the picture altogether, I agree."

"This is not a legal brief, dear. You know damn well BDS is anti-Semitic at its core."

"Then why do Jewish students join it?" asked Rebecca.

"For an answer to that, you need a Ph.D. in psychology. Why did you join?"

"To advocate for justice for the Palestinians."

"But BDS doesn't care about the Palestinians. They are only interested in getting rid of Israel. Their advocacy more often ends up hurting the Palestinians who work for Israeli companies."

*I know, Soda Stream. Please, not again.*

"Can I change the subject?" interjected Mr. Goldman. "Stanford. plays UCLA this weekend. Who do you think will win?"

## TWENTY-THREE

# Night
—————

Before going to bed that night Rebecca opened her diary to start a new entry. There was a knock on the door.

"Who is it?"

"Mom. Can I come in?"

"Sure, Mom." She put away the diary and her mother entered, dressed in a nightgown.

"What's up, Mom?"

"I just wanted to discuss something with you. Lay on the bed, I'll sit on the edge."

"Are you going to tuck me in like when I was four or five?"

"No tucking in. Just wanted to talk for a minute. Things can get difficult with you and Julie, and that's not the best environment to have a discussion."

"As you said, she's pre-occupied."

"Yes, Jeremy is a handful. Anyway, more to the point of why I came. It's about you. I only have the barest glimpse of your new relationship, but it does raise a concern."

"About what?"

"What to expect in any relationship. Your father and I have

had our differences in several areas, politics a little bit, Stanford, Israel. We've never let these disagreements get between us in any serious way."

"Stanford? What's wrong with Stanford?"

"Oh, Becky, don't get me going. The home of not-so-free-speech and cancel culture. He sees things a bit differently in the law school than I do from reading the newspapers and conservative websites. But that's not the point. Just some differences, trivial in the scheme of things. If David's a nice Jewish boy, and you genuinely like him, don't put up a wall over Israel. And pre-med is not an issue for me. He can be a doctor or a truck driver. So, my question is, how serious is your relationship and your disagreement? Are you having sex with him?"

Rebecca didn't answer right away.

"I'm your mother. No need to be coy."

"Okay. To the second question, yes. He ended my virginity last month. Fully consensual. To the first question, I don't know. He's so pro-Israel that it's hard to discuss anything with him unless I agree. Now he wants to take me to Israel next summer, to see things firsthand, as he puts it."

"That's wonderful!" Her mom stood. "Rebecca, do that! Please go. We'll cover the trip. Dad and I'd love to join you."

"Mom!"

"Just kidding, just kidding. Has he already been accepted to medical school?"

"He's waiting to hear, but I have no doubt. He plans to start when he returns from Israel."

"I love the idea. Your father and I should go again. We haven't been since you were eight years old. Remember? Dad was invited to lecture at Tel Aviv University, and we didn't want to take you and Julie out of school for a whole week. You stayed with Aunt Marjorie."

"Yeah, I remember. Hell week."

"Naughty girl. She was very nice to you two. Well, I'm going to sleep. Think about all this. Your whole life's ahead of you. If he's not the right guy, there will be many others knocking down your door."

*Yeah, Michael for one. He would love to be let in.*

"How long have you and Dad been married?"

"Anniversary next month. Twenty-five wonderful years."

Rebecca jumped out of bed, hugged her mom. "Mom, I love you."

"And we love you, Rebecca. See you in the morning. Have a good night's sleep."

Her mother gone, Rebecca returned to her diary.

*Mom just here. Always reassuring. Like when I was a child. Now I'm a woman, or have body of a woman, fully grown, able to have children. But the mind of a child, no, an almost-child the way I am treated sometimes. Do this, don't do this, you're ignorant, you've got a lot to learn, your life's ahead of you. No! My life is now, not ahead of me.*

*I pity women years ago, no career outside the home. I will have my own career, don't need a man for that. I will help bring justice to the world, or my small part of it.*

*Israel, I don't know. So <u>confusing.</u> Why is 'kill all the Jews, kill all the Jews.' all I seem to hear these days when people like David talk about the Palestinians.*

*That was Hitler's goal. Why does it always come up now, about Israel?*

*Strange, I don't ever remember grandma or*

*grandpa using that expression, and they came this close...*

*I never asked them. And they never told me. Why not?*

\* \* \*

The next morning Rebecca met her mother in the kitchen. Her father was off to the law school, her sister and family back in their own home.

"Mom, thanks for the pep talk last night."

"Did you get a good night's sleep?"

"Yeah, finally. Went to sleep around eleven. Can I ask you something? About your parents?"

"Of course."

"They never talked much about what happened in Auschwitz. I mean, the basics, they lost their parents, aunts, uncles, I get that. But they never talked about what it was like, day to day. Just that they lost family and they survived, met later, reconnected, married, came here, had you. I know those basics. But nothing more."

"Did you ever ask?"

"No, but I was only twelve when they both died. I was a kid. What was I going to ask?"

"But you studied the holocaust in high school."

"Yeah, again the basic outline. The statistics, the cattle cars, the ovens, the liberation. And I saw *Schindler's List*. But Grandma and Grandpa never talked about it. So, my question is, did they talk about it when you were growing up? To you and Aunt Marjorie?"

"No. And I'll tell you why. They didn't want to talk about it, and we didn't want to ask. Like you, we knew the basic history.

But as far as a first-hand account, it is not something to 'tell' your kids."

"Why not?"

"That's a great question, Becky. Two reasons, if I think about it. The more obvious one is that it's just too painful to bring back those memories. The other reason is that kids should learn on their own. Not be "told." When you tell people something, it tends to be not fully believed, or not even heard. In one ear and out the other. When people learn on their own, it sticks, stays with them. You have to learn on your own. I sound like a school teacher, but that's my assessment."

"So, since they're gone, I have to do my own reading. Stop being 'told' by people like my friend at school?"

"Well, that's one good way to look at it. Since you're now asking these questions, I'll recommend a book, just one to start. From there, branch out, do more reading on your own, books or websites you come across."

"It wouldn't happen to be a book by Alan Dershowitz, would it? I hear he's very pro-Israel, writes about it a lot. Always seems to be mentioned."

"Your father met Dershowitz once at a convention and came away impressed with the man's intellect. Yes, he's very pro-Israel, but no, not one of his books. A different kind of book. I have a copy. I'll get it for you. Be back in a minute."

She retrieved the book from her office and handed it to Rebecca.

"Read it, then branch out, see where it takes you. I'm so proud of you!"

Rebecca glanced at the title. *Night*, by Elie Wiesel.

# TWENTY-FOUR

# Calls Made

David read the professor's book while in Cleveland for the holiday. *Professor Shapiro's nailed the problem. Joe is a classic example. So common. Colleges are supposed to be for education, not anti-education, as he points out time and again.*

He drove back to school Sunday evening, and the next morning sent an email to Professor Shapiro.

Professor Shapiro:

Thank you for allowing me to read your manuscript *Useful Idiots – How Academia Fosters Anti-Semitism.*

I had some misgivings by the title "Useful Idiots," referring to college students, but now see it is apt, and should draw readers' attention. Your detailed exposition of mis-education by the nation's faculty – something ongoing for a long time – explains a lot. While the book's focus is on anti-Semitism, you do expand toward the end to include other areas. If college students are rarely taught to think, to challenge, to investigate, they do end up as useful idiots for all the anti-Semitic propaganda.

The book resonates with me on several levels. For one, I have a brother who went to an Ivy League school, supposedly had a "great education," yet is unable to recognize propaganda when he reads it. He simply cannot appreciate when he's being lied to, or given mis-information, even when I point it out in detail. Without doing any research whatsoever, he usually replies "all media has bias," or some other BS. Some might write this off as "sibling rivalry," but I don't think so; he's eight years older, so there never was any rivalry as such. I was seven when he entered Harvard as one of those lickety-smart high school graduates. He ended up in New York, became one of elite progressives who love *The New York Times*. Somehow, he never learned to appreciate propaganda if it's printed in The NYT or other media that he likes; they could tell him 2+2=5 and he would find a way to agree. He learned nothing at Harvard.

On another level, I now appreciate what Steve was telling me a while back, that I may be wasting my time trying to "educate" the pro-BDS Jewish students here on campus. What he meant, I think, is that I am trying to use facts, recorded history, documented information, to show these students how misguided they are. The problem, as you so ably point out, is that these students are taught to disregard "facts, recorded history, documented information," if they don't agree with their pre-set world view.

Thus, time and again I have run into Jews who support BDS – willfully ignorant of BDS's goal, which, ultimately is the destruction of Israel as a Jewish nation – for whom facts are irrelevant. Their progressive viewpoint trumps all facts on the ground. Now I see that this is how they are taught. Not logic, not common sense, not research, but go with how you feel. So, in that sense, I see Steve's point. The root problem is one of horrible mis-education, led by a faculty that wishes to turn students into "useful idiots."

One concern about the book is your citing some Great Lakes faculty by name. For example, you write on page 45:

"One Econ 101 student was severely criticized when she quoted Ayn Rand in a term paper. She wasn't advocating Rand's position, just quoting her for an alternative point of view about laissez faire capitalism. Her economics professor, Stuart Affalbarb, wrote in big letters on her paper, 'Don't ever quote Ayn Rand in this class!' No explanation was given. Since the whole tenor of the course was anti-capitalism, the student was literally afraid to ask for any explanation. She was intimidated, silenced, as it were. And, of course, she never quoted Rand again."

I suggest you leave off actual faculty names, since adding them will have no meaning to people outside the campus. I know you plan to retire, but not naming actual people will lessen the chance of literary retribution. There are other examples. Just a recommendation.

Also, I found a few typos, which I've marked. I can return the manuscript at your convenience. Please let me know a good time.

Thanks again,

David Applebaum

* * *

During the day David checked his email, hoping to see a reply, but found none. Also, nothing from Rebecca. *Is she back on campus? I need to call her. First, call Professor Shapiro.*

He wondered if the email to the professor simply did not go through, though he had received no error message. In the late afternoon he called the cell phone number listed in the book's front matter. No response, only a "Please Leave Your Message," which he did.

Then he called Rebecca's cell phone.

"Hi, David," she said, sounding happy for the call.

"Are you back on campus?"

"Yes, arrived late last night. Exhausted. Flying from California is the pits."

"Yeah, I can imagine. I drove home. Six hours, not bad. Is everything okay at home?"

"Oh, yeah, hunky dory. Parents are doing great, my sister's a piece of work. How about with your brother. Did he come for Thanksgiving?"

"Yes. With his wife and kid. Cordial the whole time. No politics."

"Did you mention me?" she asked. "Tell him about another no-nothing student in your specialty area?"

"Rebecca, I'm really sorry about all that last week. I hope you forgive me."

"Forgiven. I know I can be a bitch sometimes."

"Well, I have the perfect plan. Are you ready?"

"Not. Getting. Married."

"No, no, no. Nothing so dramatic. This coming weekend, if you agree, and I hope you will, we are going on a field trip."

"Oh? To where?"

"Taliesin, in southern Wisconsin. The home of Frank Lloyd Wright."

"Oh? Is that a day trip?"

"Un, no, we will have to spend the night in Madison, just an hour away from Taliesin."

"So, you're asking me two things. Go with you to Taliesin. And spend the night with you."

"Uh, yeah. We've had some good times together. In fact, my plan is for you to spend the night with me Friday night, and then we leave for Wisconsin Saturday morning around eight am. It's a three-hour trip. Then after the tour, which starts at one, we drive to Madison and visit another Wright building downtown, then check into the hotel. I have it all planned."

"So now we're up to three things. Friday night. Saturday trip to Taliesin. Then Saturday night."

"Sounds like fun, doesn't it?"

"Are we a couple again, David?"

"I sure hope so. No more spats."

"Can I have some time to check my workload for the week, and let you know?"

"So, that's a maybe?"

"Yes, a maybe. Give me a day."

"Okay, wait to hear from you. I love you."

TWENTY-FIVE

# Mrs. Shapiro

David awoke the next morning, checked his email. Still nothing from Professor Shapiro. He called the number again and got the same request to leave a message. He decided to go to class, and later that afternoon walk over to the professor's office with the manuscript.

At that moment his cell phone rang; it was Steve Mandelbaum.

"Hi, Steve, what's up?"

"Did you meet with Professor Shapiro, about his book?"

"Yes, I did last week. And I've read it. A great book. I emailed him yesterday, and haven't heard from him."

"There's a reason, David. He's had a heart attack. He's in the hospital, in the ICU."

"What!?"

"Yesterday morning, in his office, he developed chest pains, apparently knew it was his heart, and called 911. When they found him, he had very low blood pressure and was about to go out. Medics revived him, saved his life."

"How'd you find all this out?"

"One of his history students was in the building when the medics came. He called me later and this morning I was able to reach Professor Shapiro's wife, who I've met once. She said he's stable in the ICU, and they're running tests, but the doctor told her it was a serious attack. He may need heart surgery. Apparently, he's very weak."

"Wow. He seemed kind of run down when I saw him. Overweight, tired."

"His wife asked if I would visit him, maybe cheer him up. I would like you to come also."

"Me? Why?"

"You're premed, aren't you?"

"Yeah, with emphasis on the 'pre'."

"Will you come if I go? The visiting hours are only an hour a day, from two to three. She suggested I come tomorrow. Can you make it?"

"I suppose so. The way this presents, I feel a little obligated."

"It's more than that. I think we have to establish some relationship with her if we end up having to secure publication of his book."

"We?"

"We. You and me. Not many people even know about it."

"What about Aaron Peretz?"

"That's three."

* * *

The next day David met Steve in the hospital lobby and they took the elevator to the fourth floor ICU. There they met Shapiro's ICU nurse, who ushered them into the cubicle. Mrs. Shapiro had not yet arrived.

"Hello professor Shapiro, how are you feeling?" Steve asked. "I brought David Applebaum with me."

"Hello professor," said David. "I read your book, liked it very much. Sent you an email."

"Oh, yes, yes," came a weak voice. He had a nasal cannula feeding oxygen to his nose at three liters/minute, two IV lines running, and a foley catheter inserted into his bladder. He appeared pale, wan. David noticed the monitoring equipment, the continuous EKG, the pulse oximetry reading of 95%. *This is going to be my workplace in a few short years. Take notice.*

"So, you liked the book?"

"Yes, you hit the proverbial nail on the head, sir. Can we help in any way, while you are still in the hospital, with the book?"

The professor closed his eyes.

"I think he fell asleep," said Steve.

"Yes," said the patient, eyes suddenly open. "If something should happen to me—Sylvia, we have visitors."

Mrs. Shapiro had just entered the cubicle. A short, thin woman, she appeared about the same age as her husband.

"Sorry I'm late. Uber took a wrong turn, hit a construction zone. Hello Steve, thanks for coming. Who is this?"

"Mrs. Shapiro, this is David Applebaum. He has also read Professor Shapiro's book."

"Oh, good. And please call me Sylvia. No time for formalities."

David reached out his hand. "Nice to meet you, Sylvia. I was just talking to the professor about his book."

"Oh, yes, his magnum opus. So, he gave you a copy?"

"Yes, and I read it."

"Well, I did also, about two years ago. He keeps dragging his feet, to get it published."

"Syl'viya, nikakikh semeynykh sekretov," said Mordecai, with a weak smile. [Sylvia, no family secrets.]

"Eto vash stimul zakonchit' delo, bystro popravit'sya." [That's your incentive to finish the thing, to get better fast.]

David glanced at Steve, puzzled.

"Russian. They're both from Russia."

"Mordecai, speak English," she asked.

"Is Rachel coming?"

"She can't today. Has to pick up Jacob at school. She'll come tomorrow."

David aimed another puzzled glance at Steve.

"Rachel's their daughter, Jacob's her child."

"I'm so full of tubes," said Mordecai. "Feel like I'm floating."

"Did you see doctor today?" she asked. "The nurse wouldn't tell me anything."

"Yes, they have a very limited vocabulary, these doctors and nurses. 'Tests', 'pending', and 'tomorrow.' That's it. Three words. Say, David, you are premed as I recall?"

"Yes, sir."

"Learn more words in medical school."

"Will do, sir."

Mr. Shapiro's nurse entered the room. "His heart rate has increased in the last few minutes. I think it best if we let him rest, maybe get some sleep. If you want, we have a small room where you can sit, come back in half an hour if he's awake. Hope that's not a problem.

"Oh, you see," said Mordecai, "that's another word. 'Rest'."

"Good idea," said Sylvia. "That will give me a chance to get acquainted with these mensch."

They walked to a small waiting room down the hall, took seats and closed the door.

"I do appreciate you coming to see Mordecai," she said. "I am very worried. The doctors think he's going to need heart surgery. Survival I'm told is not assured."

"Now I notice your accent, Sylvia," said David. "But the professor has none. You're both from Russia?"

"Yes, he came over as child, learned both languages growing up. I came over after high school. Learned English, but accent remains, yes."

154

"Where did you meet?"

"At university in Cleveland, where we both settled."

"Cleveland? I'm from Cleveland. Case Western Reserve?"

"Yes, Case. He was history graduate student. I studied accounting. Our backgrounds brought us together. And where did you live in Cleveland?"

"I grew up in Shaker Heights. And you?"

"First, in university housing. Our last year there, after marriage, apartment in Cleveland Heights."

"I do remember there was a large immigrant Russian population in Cleveland. They had lots of support from the Jewish community."

"Yes, they paved way for my immigration. Forever grateful."

"Small world," said Steve. "Sylvia, did the doctors mention the possibility of a heart transplant?"

"Not mentioned. It's more like major repair is needed, rather than whole new heart. But what do I know? I was only an accountant."

"Are you involved in helping him publish the book?" asked Steve.

"No, it's his project. He's held it as you say, close to his chest. I don't think anyone else on campus has seen it, but you two. I read early draft, not the latest. Oh, and Mr. Peretz, who stayed with us when he came to speak. He read it."

"Why the secrecy?" asked David.

She did not answer right away, then, "Well, I'll tell you. Family secret," she replied, followed by a short laugh. "You'll keep this to yourselves?"

"Yes, of course," they both agreed.

"About five years ago he entered friendly debate with another history professor, about the Middle East. You know, origin of the conflict between Jews and Arabs. As I said, it was friendly, only for the students majoring in history, in the department. I attended. They both made reasonable arguments. This other professor, a specialist in Egyptian history, blamed the situation on European colony-ism."

"Colonialism?" offered Steve.

"Yes, colony-alism. Mordecai concentrated on the root cause being the intolerance of Islam for any other religion, especially Judaism, and how that's an ancient problem. Anyway, no win-lose in the debate, but during the discussion phase there were some student questions bordering on the anti-Semitic: about why Jews stole land from the Arabs, why do Jews want to expel all the Arabs, typical lies of the Jew-haters. The Egyptologist – his name was Abu Moussa – didn't do anything to counter the lies. He sat quiet, but more, he smirked as his students put these questions to Mordecai. Anyway, Mordecai countered the lies with his version of the truth, and that was it."

"Abu Moussa?" asked David. "Is he still on campus?"

"No. I'm coming to that. The next day, Mordecai's office door was plastered with swastikas, and hateful, anti-Semitic graf-fiti. Steve discovered it on arrival around about eight that morn-ing. The staff had it all cleaned up in half an hour, but not before pictures were taken.

"Mordecai complained to history department administration. The next day Abu and Mordecai were called into chairman's office. Moussa denied any involvement, of course, but the suspi-cion was there. His smirking during the debate, and the fact that the anti-Semitic students were in his class at the time. Raised suspicion of at least tacit support, if not outright complicity."

"Had this Mr. Moussa been known to be outwardly anti-Semitic before the debate?"

"If so, Steve never mentioned it. Of course, we both knew anti-Semitism can run deep in society without thugs painting swastikas on your door. We left Russia for that reason."

David and Steve nodded in agreement.

"Worse," she continued, "it soured any relationship between

Abu and Mordecai. To that point, at least, they were friendly colleagues. And it cast a pall in the history department. They both had tenure, but within a year Abu had decamped to California. Good riddance."

"I took Professor Shapiro's class two years ago. Never heard any of this."

"No, he never spoke about it, except to me. But since that episode, he decided not to publicize his book while still teaching. He doesn't want to create any controversy within department while he's around. If he's gone, won't have an office door to paint swastikas. So his plan is to publish after he retires. Later this year."

"So, he has a publisher?"

"Sort of. Yes. No. They've agreed, pending review of the finished product."

"So, you'll send it to them?" asked David.

"Me? I don't have a copy," she replied. "If you have a copy, that's it."

"Can we search his computer for a digital file?"

"You'll have to ask Mordecai. I don't know his passwords."

The nurse entered. "Mr. Shapiro is sleeping, so I think it best we let him be for now. His heart rate is back to where it was."

"Yes, good," said Mrs. Shapiro. "I will return tomorrow with my daughter."

\* \* \*

For David, the week started on a downer, but then he heard from Rebecca, via email. She agreed to half the plan.

Can you pick me up Saturday am for planned trip?
    That will work best for me.
    R

He was not going to question her reason for avoiding Friday night. Maybe she had a lot of homework to do. No matter. He went online and secured the tour tickets, and a reservation at the Hampton Inn in downtown Madison.

# TWENTY-SIX

# Michael's Gambit

Geddy opened his computer to check emails, saw one from Professor Abu Moussa.

> Gordon,
>
> Attached is a list of midwestern college BDS clubs, with their approximate membership, current leaders, and contact information. I am also compiling a list for the Eastern and Western states. My goal is to create a comprehensive website so students and BDS leaders can interact without difficulty.
>
> Please check to make sure I have the information accurately stated for Great Lakes University.
>
> Abu

A quick glance at the email showed it was indeed from the professor, so he clicked on the attachment. It loaded quickly, and he scanned the Word file. Fifteen colleges listed. Reading through the information, he noticed something a bit odd. A few typos, and a couple of places with obviously incorrect listings. For one, his first name was spelled "Gorden," not Gordon. Then he noticed that "University of Indiana" was used instead of the correct designation "Indiana University." And, the listing had it located in Indianapolis, not Bloomington. The University of Chicago was listed as being located in "Hyde Park, IL," when Hyde Park is only a Chicago neighborhood, not a town in Illinois. A few other gaffes raised his suspicion about the list.

Then it hit him. *Oh, no!* He turned off the computer, grabbed his cell phone and punched in Abu Moussa's number.

"Yes, Gordon?"

"Professor Moussa, did you just send me an email, with an attachment about BDS clubs in the Midwest?"

"No."

"No?"

"No, I have no such list, why would I send something like that?"

"I've been hacked."

"Calm down, my friend, tell me exactly what happened."

Geddy recounted the last several minutes.

"Did you shut down your computer?"

"Yes, then I called you right away."

"Do you have anti-virus software installed?"

"Yes, Webroot."

"That may help, depending on the hacker's sophistication. Don't restart your computer. You have to assume it's now infected with a virus. You are no longer connected to the internet?"

"No, the computer is shut down."

"Not good enough. Unplug your modem. Now."

Geddy did as told. "Okay, that's done. But I need to use Wi-Fi at some point."

"Yes, but not with this computer anywhere near it. Put it in your car, far from the modem. Then, I'm afraid you'll have to get another laptop, to be safe. I assume you have backup files?"

"Yes, on an external hard drive. But Abu, it was your email. I checked. How was someone able to send me a message from your email?"

"If you're computer savvy, these things are possible. What we don't know is what information was sent before you shut down the computer and disconnected the modem. How many minutes altogether, from when you first downloaded the file?"

"Oh, maybe ten minutes at most."

"Lot of info can be transferred in ten minutes. Were any passwords in there, especially the ones to access the dark web?"

"No, they are all on paper, in my locked file cabinet."

"Good. Secure yourself another laptop, and check all the passwords you have using the new computer, from the most benign, to the ones for the dark web. Keep a handwritten diary of what you find. Can you get another computer today?"

"I have an old backup but haven't used it in a while. And my girlfriend has one."

"Don't. Neither option. Go buy yourself a new one. Doesn't have to be fancy. Sorry this happened, but we've got to be careful. Call me with your results."

"So, who do you think?"

"We know, don't we? Likely your 'friend' in New York. If that's where he is."

"I don't think he is. I think he's right here, on campus."

TWENTY-SEVEN

# To Wisconsin

David pulled up to Rebecca's dorm, parked the car and entered the building's foyer. She was there by the door, holding a stuffed backpack as if about to go on a long day hike; it included all she needed for the overnight trip. She told her roommate not to expect a return until Sunday afternoon.

David wanted to kiss her, but held back. Once in the car, he leaned over and kissed her on the cheek.

"I've been lonely," he said. "Welcome back."

"Per your plan, we'll have time for that later."

"You are wicked!"

"And you are horny."

"And you?"

"David, are we going? What time is the tour?"

"One o'clock." He started the car and drove toward the expressway. On the way he told her about Professor Shapiro and his book.

"Sounds like a mystery novel. He's still in the hospital?"

"Oh, yeah. They plan to do open heart surgery Monday."

"So, what are you going to do with the book?"

"Get it published, at some point." He went over the meeting with Mrs. Shapiro in the hospital. "Hey, let's change the subject. I've been rehearsing a new subject for you."

"Not comedy, I hope."

"No, tragedy."

"Shakespeare?"

"Rebecca, not even Shakespeare could think up what I'm going to tell you about Taliesin."

"About the murders?"

"You know about that?"

"I did a quick read about Taliesin on Wikipedia. But frankly, it made no sense. So if you want to tell me your version, I'll be happy to listen."

"It's not my version but what really happened. In August 1914 Frank Lloyd Wright was living with his mistress and her two kids by a previous marriage in Taliesin. Her name was Mamah Cheney. She had moved there in 1911."

"You pronounce it May-mah?"

"Yeah, that's the correct pronunciation. It's discussed in his biographies. Anyway, back to 1914. Since the house was always a work in progress, Wright had a lot of workmen employed there at the time."

"But he wasn't home, as I recall."

"Correct. On August 15, 1914, Wright was working in Chicago, on Midway Gardens, a huge outdoor entertainment area he designed. On that morning he got a phone call, with the message 'Taliesin on fire.' He had no idea what to make of it, but knew he had to return home. His son was with him, also working on the Gardens."

"He was still married at the time?"

"Yes, but his wife, who was living in Oak Park, wouldn't give him a divorce. So Mamah Cheney was considered his mistress, and there had been lots of tabloid publicity about their relationship. In fact, the whole affair was a scandal, since they had both abandoned their spouses five years earlier, to run off to Europe. He left behind his wife and six children, and she left behind her husband and two kids. Imagine that."

"I can't."

"Well, it happened. Anyway, in 1914 Wright and Mamah were considered by society to be living in sin. But they were happy and really didn't care what the world thought."

He paused the story to pass a couple of cars in his lane.

"Go on. I'm listening."

"So, he gets this call, and arranges to take the train back to Spring Green that afternoon. That's where Taliesin is located, an hour west of Madison, where we're headed. Well, he gets on the train and guess who else is on board?"

"I don't recall reading that."

"His mistress's ex, Mr. Cheney, the father of her two children. He had also received notice of the fire."

"Oy, vey"

"No, by all reports they were cordial to one another. However. this was a local, and the train stopped numerous times on the way to Spring Green. And at each stop there were newspapers for sale, with updated headlines about the Taliesin fire. And that's how they both soon learned of the murders. Several, by a truly deranged servant, who had only recently been hired by Wright. A Negro from Alabama by way of Barbados."

"That's what I don't understand. Why?"

"No one knows, but some think he went crazy over racial slurs by other workers. But what he did is way beyond Shakespearean tragedy. During lunch, when Mamah Cheney and her two kids were eating, along with six workers in an adjacent room, he locked all the doors but one and set the entire wing on fire using gasoline. As everyone tried to escape through the only open door, he hacked them with an ax. Seven died, either from the fire or his ax. Four workers, plus Mamah Cheney and her two kids, a young boy and a girl."

"How awful!"

"Yes, one of the worst mass murders in the U.S. up to that time. Well, by the time the train reached Spring Green, the deaths were known to Wright and Cheney. Tragedy beyond belief."

"And the murderer killed himself?"

"Well, he swallowed poison that day, which eventually did him in, but he didn't die until seven weeks later, in prison. No motive was ever discerned. Anyway, Wright buried his mistress, in a family sanctuary down the hill from Taliesin. And Mr. Cheney buried his two children. Wright went on with his life, which evolved into more trouble with women. That's a tale for another time."

"David, how do you find time to learn all this stuff? Israel history. Frank Lloyd Wright? And still study for Premed?"

"Well, Israel, you know how I got involved in that history. As for Wright, I took an Art History course as a sophomore. For the term paper you could choose any subject. I'd always had an interest in his work, so I went deep. Read several biographies, including his autobiography, which he published in 1932. There's a joke about his autobiography."

"At this point I could use a little humor. What is it?"

"Librarians don't know whether to file his autobiography under fiction or nonfiction."

"Fiction?"

"Yeah, he was a notorious liar. He lied about his birthdate, claiming he was born 1869 when it was 1867; wanted to make himself seem more precocious than he was. He lied about his education at the University of Wisconsin. Said he came within three months of graduating when he took only two courses there before leaving for Chicago. Lots of other fibs. Scholars have had a field day parsing his writing."

"I'm getting an impression. A genius with flaws. Leaves his wife, shacks up with a mistress, lies."

"Yeah, you got it. Genius is often associated with major personality issues. Picasso, Van Gogh, Einstein, Rand."

"Rand?"

"Ayn Rand. Married, entered into an affair with an acolyte twenty-five years her junior."

"Is she another of your in-depth subjects?"

"No, no. When I delved into Frank Lloyd wright, I learned he was an inspiration for Howard Roark, in *The Fountainhead*. You read that novel?"

"Ashamed to say, no. Didn't read *Atlas Shrugged*, either, though I know about them. My mother is a big Ayn Rand fan. They're all about individualism."

"Yeah, Rand developed her own philosophy called Objectivism, and attracted a lot of followers. Anyway, when she began writing *The Fountainhead* in the 1930s, she contacted Wright to get his input. He wasn't very nice to her, and didn't help much. But his life was definitely an inspiration for her character of Howard Roark, so I learned something about her writing in my research on Wright."

"It's nice how you get so involved in things that interest you."

"We all do, to some extent. I bet you have subjects you're fairly expert about."

She did not respond right away.

"Well?"

"In high school I wrote a term paper on Harriet Tubman, which got me the top grade, so I guess I know about her and the Underground Railroad. Did a lot of research on slavery in the Civil War. Speaking of autobiographies, do you know how many Frederick Douglass wrote?"

"Autobiographies? About his own life?"

"That's the definition."

"Okay, you got me. I'll guess one, but the way you asked, it's probably more."

"Three."

"Three?"

"Yeah, three different ones, the first in 1845, the second 1855, and the third, 1881. His first is by far the most popular, the most widely read. Now I sound a little like you, Miss Pedantic."

"No, that's great. Not pedantic at all. See, that's what I mean. Once you get hooked on a subject, it's easy to learn. I hope one day you'll hook on to Israel's history."

"Maybe I already have."

"Really?"

"Did you ever read Elie Weisel's memoir, *Night*?"

"In high school. What brings that up?"

"Oh, nothing. Sort of relates to what my grandparents went through."

"You want to discuss it? I'm all ears."

"Not really. Maybe another time."

"No problem. We'll be there in an hour.

# TWENTY-EIGHT

# Taliesin and Madison

They parked in the Taliesin visitor's center, from where buses carried ticket holders to the home, two miles distant. Tours ran every day in the summer, weekends other months. David had signed up for the two-hour tour of just the main house, not the surrounding structures also built by Wright.

Their group of fifteen boarded the bus, and the guide, a middle-aged man, introduced the tour. "Just a little background," he said. "Taliesin was the summer home of Frank Lloyd Wright. It was originally built in 1911, and has since been remodeled and parts rebuilt since then. No one lives there now, and it's run by the non-profit Taliesin Preservation. When we get there, guides will take you through sections of the house, and feel free to take pictures. We only ask that you not touch any of the furniture, as some of it is quite old and fragile."

"Will he mention the murders?" she asked David.

"Nah. Nothing much about Wright's personal life at all, from what I recall on my last visit. They really concentrate on his work, not his scandals."

Ten minutes later they were in the Taliesin parking lot. Exiting the bus, David said, "you won't appreciate what he designed until you get into the living room and look out over the hill."

At the entrance the group was turned over to another guide, who took them inside. This guide commented on the low ceilings, a feature of Wright's entrances, and pointed out which furniture was original, and which rebuilt during one of the house's many restorations. Then they came to the living room. And the view.

"Pretty amazing," said Rebecca.

The guide pointed out a small structure down the hill, about a mile away. That's the chapel where family members are buried. After the tour, on your own you can stop there if you wish. Now we'll go into the bedrooms.

In Wright's bedroom Rebecca commented, in an aside to David, about the small size of the bed, and the general modesty of the room.

"King size beds weren't common back then, as far as I know."

One tourist asked the guide just how many women slept in the bedroom with Wright. He replied there were "three we know of," which elicited some giggles. "His mistress Ms. Cheney, and his last two wives, Miriam and Olgivanna. Of course, after he built a new Taliesin in Arizona, in the thirties, Wright came here only in the summers. But until his death in 1959, the house was always occupied by workers and various servants when Wright was out west."

Rebecca looked to David, who nodded in agreement with the guide's information.

* * *

They decided to drive from Spring Green to Madison, and not visit the chapel. The trip took just one hour. David found a parking spot near Monona Terrace Plaza. "This is our next stop. After this, we'll check into the hotel, just a few blocks away."

They walked toward a modern civic structure. "No tour here, except by me. Wright designed this civic center in 1938, but had trouble securing public funding for the project. He died before money could be found to build it. Wisconsin finally approved funds for what's now called the Terrace Community and Convention Center, in 1992, 33 years after Wright's death. It wasn't built until 1997."

"The original design?"

"Oh, I'm sure there were some modifications sixty years after he drafted the plans. But as you can see, it's unequivocally Frank Lloyd Wright."

The building was open, and they toured the main public areas. David took several photos with his phone, including a selfie with Rebecca. "Well, it's almost five o'clock. Let's check in, then go to dinner."

"Sounds good."

They parked in the hotel lot, checked into the front desk – David Applebaum and partner – using his credit card, then found their room on the third floor.

"I need to use the bathroom," she said.

"Me too. I'll do a little unpacking, plug in my computer, and go in after you."

After both had used the bathroom they stood before the bed, poised to go out...or not. He pulled her gently toward him. "Why are we playing games? Can't dinner wait?"

She did not respond, but her gentle pressure against his groin showed full agreement.

"Let's lay down for a minute," he said. They plopped onto the king-sized bed. He kissed her on the lips, unbuttoned her bra, then the button of her slacks. In another minute they were undressed.

"It seems so long," he said. "I really missed you."

"Shhh," she said, and moved one hand down to change his words into a soft moan.

# TWENTY-NINE

# Michael's Trove

Technically, Michael's hack of Geddy's laptop was a success. He got in, and before Geddy had shut down Wi-Fi was able to download dozens of files. But, a mess. Jumbled text and computer code from Word, Excel, Downloads, PowerPoint, Instagram, the old Twitter, and other apps.

Michael had inserted a sophisticated virus in the attachment sent to Geddy. The problem was that Geddy also had virus protection software, so it was a battle between protection and invasion. Sometimes hackers win, sometimes it's a draw.

Michael ran a check on all the files secured from Geddy's computer: 10.2 gigabytes of data. He decided to approach the information slowly, to see if anything popped up of interest. Out of curiosity he took one corrupted Word file, sent it to his favorite AI program with the command, "Please format into standard English to reflect the original message."

A few seconds later came the disappointing, "Sorry, message not formattable as written."

The most corrupted downloads were just a series of computer code. He sent one segment of code to the AI program and got back only "retrograde association, please resubmit," which made no sense. So much for AI, he mused. This task will require *human* intelligence.

He decided to load everything into a single file, then search that file for key words or phrases. Since contact by the school's legal department, regarding the march, he had kept his eye out for any new information about the Nazi kid. He would begin his search with related key words.

\* \* \*

It took Michael hours, spread over several days, to load all the disparate files into one super file. He then uploaded the super file into the AI program, with instructions to "search for Nazi."

Voila! The term came up twice, though only in snippets.

"The Nazi jerk from Oslandia" in an email from Geddy to… Abu Moussa.

In another email: "I let them have it, made clear don't ever send Auschwitz Nazi again…Might raise…Pittsburgh. No local publicity, fortunately."

"Pittsburgh?" Michael saw the connection. The 2017 massacre of Jews at the Pittsburgh synagogue. Why is Geddy writing about that?

He printed out the relevant email, called his contact at the school's legal office. He was told not to send anything via email or text, that the law student who had interviewed him would come by in person and pick up a copy of the information.

\* \* \*

Michael's snippets quickly found their way to Attorney Zimmerman, who met with President Richard Hightower to explain the latest development. He showed Hightower a copy of what Michael had uncovered.

"One of our students hacked Geddy's computer?"

"Yeah, the kid's a computer genius, for sure. I checked his profile. He's here on scholarship. Won a big award in high school for his work on artificial intelligence."

"Glad we got him. We always look for the best and the brightest. They don't all go to Harvard and Yale. Is he Jewish?"

"With the last name Solomon, I assume so. In addition to this information, he gave us a flash drive with all the files retrieved before Geddy shut down his computer. It's mostly virus-modified gibberish, but he thought maybe the FBI could find a way to unlock what's there. So now the FBI has everything we have."

"Kid's a mensch, for sure."

"Frankly, Richard, from what I've learned, I don't think the FBI can do any better. In fact, when he graduates, I'm going to recommend him to the FBI for his computer skills."

"Who'd you talk to at the Bureau? One of the guys who was here?"

"Yeah, Thomas McDowell. After I reached him on my cell phone, he said to hang up and call another number. The new number is a line that records automatically, and at the same time can detect any attempt at tapping the conversation. All very high tech."

"Okay, but spare me the techie stuff. What'd McDowell say?"

"They think we might be on the trail of another mass shooting. They already have the local synagogues and Hillel with metal detectors at the entrances."

"Before this Hillel didn't have metal detectors?"

"No. Nor do our libraries, the student union, or any of the classroom buildings. If a shooter is determined to get in, there's very little to stop him. We're just not there yet."

"No, I understand, but a Jewish institution, I would have thought—"

"Only recently. It's getting worse. So yeah, now it's synagogues and Hillel. Hope it doesn't get to the point where every building on campus has to function like a TSA checkpoint."

"What about bringing in Mr. Geddy for questioning?"

"My impression is, they don't see any reason to. He's broken no laws, and there's no guarantee that an interview with him would stop any planned attack. Instead, they've put him under limited surveillance."

"What the hell does that mean?"

"It means they don't follow him, but they've installed cameras to monitor the entrance to the group home he lives in, to see when he leaves, and with whom."

"Installed where?"

"On a telephone pole across the street."

"Okay, back to the metal detectors at synagogues and Hillel? What's to keep an active shooter from firing from the sidewalk?"

"I asked that also. Cops outside, in unmarked cars, during services."

"Not 24-7?"

"No. the profile of mass shooters is that they go for the maximum kill, not just one or two individuals. They won't crash a synagogue to kill the janitor, or even a lone rabbi. Not enough publicity. Has to be many killed to make it worthwhile. Sick, I know."

"Lester, I'm still unclear on this one point. Is Geddy involved in a plot or not?

"We don't know. Everything about him seems to fit his role as nothing more than just the student head of our university-sanctioned BDS club."

"How long can this go on?"

"We don't know."

* * *

Michael continued to plow thru his trove of downloads. He had the latest software. ChatGPT-5, BingAI+, and Google AI-Plus. These programs were always evolving, improving. With the latest versions, he was able to store all the data in 'standby' mode, and then receive an alert if any new interpretation surfaced.

# THIRTY

# Geddy Goes Fishing

The day after he met with the law student to turn over his information, Michael found an unexpected email in his inbox. From Geddy, subject "Reconciliation?"

> Michael,
>
> I'm sorry you felt the need to walk out of last month's BDS meeting. It upsets me when any of our members feel mistreated, and I want to apologize, and invite you back. I understand your concerns about Israel, and the Bahá'í, Temple and Gardens. Please consider, and let me know.
>
> Gordon.

So, he suspects me, thought Michael. In the BDS meeting, before I walked out, I never mentioned the Bahá'í, Temple and Gardens. That only came up on the Zoom call with him and Professor Moussa. Either he thinks I'm an idiot and don't remember that, or he's just letting me know of his suspicion. Then when I reply, he'll check the IP address of my computer to confirm his suspicion. Since I used a different computer for the email I originally sent him 'from New York,' that's not an issue. The question, is how to respond.

He thought for several minutes, then typed a reply.

* * *

Gordon,

Thank you for your invitation, though your comment is a little puzzling. I don't recall ever mentioning any concern over the Bahá'í Temple and Gardens in Israel. I've never been there, and as part of the faith there are other countries higher on my bucket list to visit. Bahá'í is a worldwide religion, with followers in over 70 countries. Right now, I'm planning a summer tour of India, where there are many Bahá'í followers. The Bahá'í Temple in Delhi is particularly striking (google it to see).

Perhaps you've been in contact with other Bahá'í here in Great Lakes? If so, please let me know.

I do remain concerned about possible racist attitudes in BDS, which of course are anathema to all of Bahá'í faith. So, I respectfully decline your offer. However, thanks for asking.

Michael

* * *

Michael did not expect to hear back from Gordon. And he didn't.

# THIRTY-ONE

# The Shiva

Professor Shapiro did make it through the surgery, but died that night in the recovery unit. Whether he died from an embolus, sepsis, or another heart attack was never ascertained. Mrs. Shapiro declined an autopsy, and he was buried the next day.

David and Steve visited Mrs. Shapiro the second night of Shiva. There they met his daughter, who thanked them for their efforts on behalf of the book. "Mom wants Dad's book published, and I understand you can help with that."

David felt awkward discussing the book during a week of mourning, but Steve saw an opportunity, since Rachel brought it up. "Thank you. We have some ideas, but this may not be the best time to discuss it."

While Mrs. Shapiro was accepting condolences from other guests, Rachel pulled the two college students aside. "My Dad's death has not yet hit her. I am very worried she's going to go into a deep depression, and may not even be able to live alone. I'm spending the night, as I did last night. Tomorrow, if she seems okay, I'll return to my husband and son tomorrow. As awkward as it may seem, now is the best time to iron this out. Could both of you possibly stay until the end, so we can have a private meeting? Trust me, this is the best time."

"Un, sure, I'm okay with that," replied Steve.

"Yeah, sure," said David, looking at his watch. *At least another hour.*

* * *

The last condolence departed, Rachel spoke to her mother, pointing to David and Steve. "Mom, I asked them to stay, to discuss Dad's book. This will only take a few minutes."

"Okay, dear, came the reply," with a tone of resignation.

"They want your approval to proceed with getting it published. They said they will work with Mr. Peretz, who is a known author, and they'll start with the company Dad had contact with. They just need your approval to proceed, so there's no misunderstanding."

"They have the book?"

"I have a print copy," replied David. "Here's the thing. We really need a digital copy, and assume it's in Professor's computer, though probably behind a password. If we could get access to it, we still might be able to get it." Turning his head toward Steve, he said, "I know of someone who could get it if anyone can."

"Oh, dear. His office is a mess. The school brought everything over this weekend, put it in the basement."

"Is the computer plugged in?"

"I don't think so."

"Mom, can I take them down to the basement, see what's there?"

"Sure, dear."

Rachel led them to the basement. In one corner they found all personal belongings from his university office: boxes of books, a few pictures, and on top of one box, a large desktop computer. On top of another box a briefcase, and inside...a laptop computer. No desk or chair, as those were the property of the school.

"David pulled out the laptop and searched in the briefcase for a flash drive, but found none. He checked the back of the desktop for any attachments, but again, no flash drive.

"I can only assume he has a digital file in each computer. Or, he may have sent the file to himself as an email attachment. Can I plug these in, just to see what loads?"

"Sure," said Rachel.

David plugged both computers into a nearby socket. As expected, each came to life and asked for a pin number.

"I know someone who might be able to get into these without a PIN or password. Obviously, we don't want to invade his privacy. What do you suggest?"

"I don't think you'll find any porn in my father's computers," replied Rachel. "Or love letters to another woman. When can you bring this person over? It sounds like a good idea. Before you suggested it, I was thinking of taking them to Best Buy and have Geek Squad download all the data. I understand they can do that."

"Probably. But this guy I know out-geeks the Geek Squad, and he should be able to do it here, in the basement. I'll contact him tomorrow and let you know."

* * *

Michael was flattered to be asked. "Yeah, it's like duck soup. Only thing I need to know, are they Mac's or windows-based PC's?"

"PC's," said David. "And I assume the latest Windows software."

"I'm done with classes at two," said Michael. "How about three?

"That should work." He called Mrs. Shapiro to confirm.

\* \* \*

Michael brought along two reset disks, and in only a few minutes had both computers unlocked. "I see there are a lot of files, and there may be others with financial information I don't want to touch."

"That won't be a problem," replied Mrs. Shapiro." We only have two accounts, with the local bank and Fidelity, so I have full access. Just see if you can search for the book."

David typed "Useful Idiots" in the search bar, and up popped several files – dated copies of the book. "I assume the latest date is the one you want."

"Actually, said David, if you could put them all on a flash drive, I can discern what changes he made over time. But I assume the latest date is the one I have in paper."

"Will do."

\* \* \*

Outside, David thanked Michael for his work. "I'll put you in the acknowledgment section."

"Thanks. Can I ask you a personal question, while we're here?"

"Sure." *I think I know what.*

"Are you still dating Rebecca? She called me last month, and something seemed to be on her mind."

"She did? Can you remember just what date she called?"

"Yeah, let me think. Oh, it was before she left for Thanksgiving, so, that weekend, either Saturday or Sunday."

"What did she want?"

"She said it was just to thank me for helping out during the march, and that when she returned maybe the four of us would get together. But I never heard from her again."

"Four of us?"

"Yeah, I was with my girlfriend at the time."

"At the time? She is still your girlfriend?"

"Yeah, but nothing serious. Or rather, nothing that will lead to permanency."

"Michael, I really appreciate your work. To answer your question, Rebecca and I are still together. One day, I plan to marry her."

"I get it, David. That's what I wanted to know. You've answered my question."

THIRTY-TWO

# Writing the Forward

With the digital file in hand, David contacted Peretz to explain all that had happened. Peretz agreed to contact the publisher about the professor's demise, and how he and a couple of students were now involved in getting the book published.

As expected, the publisher's editor said any contract would have to be with Professor Shapiro's widow. So, step one, send us the manuscript. Give us a few weeks to look it over. Step two, a published contract with Mrs. Shapiro. Before one was sent out, they would need a copy of the death certificate. Step three, publication in about three months after the contract was signed.

Over the next two weeks Aaron and David edited the manuscript, then Peretz sent it to the publisher. He called a week later with good news.

"Well, they've accepted it! Congratulations, David."

"Same to you"

"However, there is one caveat."

"Oh?"

"They require a Forward written by a college student. They

think the title "Useful Idiots" will both attract and repel students, and a Forward by a student will help tip the balance. So realistically, that means you David."

"Me? I'm a good reader, not a great writer. And besides, I'm going to medical school. I don't want to do anything that might create controversy. You never know where anti-Semites lie. What about Steve? He's read the book and he's moving to Israel. He'll be the perfect author. Certainly, I'll help write it."

"That will be okay," said Peretz. "As long as we have one student author. Is he a good writer?"

"I don't know. But we'll write the Forward together, and then you can edit it."

"I figured you'd suggest that. Keep in mind, the voice has to be the student's, not some pro-Israeli businessman."

"How much time do we have?"

"Send it by tomorrow, that will be fine."

"What?"

"Just kidding. Take your time, but the quicker you get it done, the quicker we can get the ball rolling."

David called Steve with the news. "Me? Sure, I'll sign it after you write it. My way of giving the finger to all these anti-Semitic professors."

They're not all anti-Semitic, thought David. But no point in arguing with him. Need his byline.

David then called Rebecca with the news. He did not mention Michael's question about their status. "They want a Forward by students. That's me and Steve. But only Steve will sign it. I don't want to be distracted in medical school. Being pro-Israel in a published book can be very distracting."

"Well, I understand that. You've both read the book, so should be easy to write the Forward. Heard from medical schools?"

"Not yet. This week, I think. After Steve and I write the

Forward, would you review it? It's really got to be from a student's perspective, per the publisher."

"How long is it?"

"We're limited to 1000 words, so not long. About two-three pages."

"Okay, let me know."

David began working on the piece, and in the space of two hours had his thoughts down. He emailed the draft to Steve. "Please read this now, and edit as you see fit. I think if we go back and forth, with iterations, we can get this done right."

A half hour later Steve called. "David, looks good. I changed one or two words, just to make it legitimate to put my name on the bottom. But it captures the essence of the book. So, I really don't have much more to contribute. It's attached."

"I'll look it over again before sending it to Peretz. Something tells me this is too easy. Hope he accepts it."

David reviewed the file Steve sent him, reading the "one or two words" contained nothing offensive. *Okay, now to Rebecca.* He sent her the file by email, and waited.

She replied that she was studying for an exam, would read it tomorrow and get back to him later that day.

"Great. Thanks."

* * *

David felt a little anxiety that night, over how she would respond. She might not agree with all of their points, but his concern was the writing, not the book's arguments.

She replied the next morning.

David, I read through the Forward and made some comments. I don't want to be too critical, and I know how passionate you and Steve are about the work, but there are issues. If this is to be read by students, it (in my opinion) needs some reworking.

My comments are attached, in bold-faced type inside brackets. If you want me to continue to work on this, I would like to see the full book. Thanks,

    R

David opened the attachment and read through the first two paragraphs of his Forward, with Rebecca's bolded comments.

Professor Shapiro was a professor of Middle East Studies at Great Lakes University, before his untimely demise just before the book was published. [**was…was; passive voice weakens the first sentence; suggest rewrite**.] I was privileged to read his manuscript while a senior at Great Lakes University, and found it wonderful. [**"wonderful" sounds like a movie review; need to be specific; perhaps 'enlightening'?**] He nicely [**"nicely" is an unneeded adverb; would delete**] lays out many arguments showing that college professors across the nation have failed to teach students how to think, question and analyze information, at least in regards to issues that impact or influence issues relating to anti-Semitism. [**wordy phrasing; suggest "…to issues relating to anti-Semitism"**].

His main theme has been [**should use active verb "is"**] anti-Israel propaganda prevalent on campuses, accepted by students [**obviously not all students, so need qualifier here, e.g., "many" or perhaps "most"**] as "the truth" because their professors never taught them to challenge this information in a logical way. [**"information" seems antithetical to "propaganda," so would use a different descriptor, e.g., "anti-Israel writings,"**] He later expands on this to cover other areas including economics, politics, popular culture, and language. [**I read this**

**sentence twice, trying to get my head around "this,";
it's just too vague in context, so would be more
specific, e.g., "...he expands the critique of how
students are taught to other areas, including..."]**
Don't be put off by the title "Useful Idiots." College students
are inherently smart in terms of IQ. But in the way professors
treat them, they are merely receptacles for indoctrination of
the worst kind: how not to think, question, investigate. **[I like
this last sentence, but would add the word "often"
before "merely."]**

David stopped reading after these two paragraphs, saw much
bold-faced type in the remaining paragraphs and decided it was
too painful to continue.

*Who the hell does she think she is? Probably just the smartest girl I've
ever met. She's been hiding this talent. I can't write worth a shit; neither can
Steve.*

He thought about her request to see the whole book. *Can I
send it? The Professor said no, when he was alive. Now, it should be okay.
She'll keep it close.*

He wrote back:

Rebecca,

Well, I am impressed with your changes. Did not know you
were a young Hemingway. Attached is the whole book as you
requested. Please don't share it with anyone. Re-do the
Forward with your changes and get it back to me. I don't want
my name on it for reasons explained, but considering your
effort, you should be the first author.

David

She replied:

David,

I should have told you I am taking a creative writing course, so I've learned to be picky when asked to review or edit something. What you wrote is not that bad, just needs some tuning up. I'm going to skim thru the professor's book – probably won't read it cover to cover – and then will re-do the Forward.

However, I share your mis-giving about publicity. I have 3+ more years to go before entering law school. While I don't mind participating in controversial activity on campus, I am not looking for notoriety that could come from the book's publication. Can we sign the Forward "anonymous students"?

R

Rebecca placed a funny-face emoji after her initial.

* * *

Two days later David received Rebecca's revision, with "please call after you read it."

After a quick read, David called. "This is great, Rebecca. Much clearer than what I wrote."

"I tried to adhere to what you and Steve wanted to say, though in all honesty that's not my impression."

"What do you mean?"

"I spent time going through the book. Read or skimmed every page. I can understand why you and Steve like it so much. But if I was reviewing this book from a distance, say for a newspaper or magazine, I would find issues."

"I'm all ears."

"Well, Professor Shapiro criticizes the way many professors teach, or rather don't teach. He blames the anti-Israel sentiment in our colleges in large part on students' inability to recognize propaganda, or lies if you will. Which, he blames on the professors – who have done nothing to teach how to question, investigate or even recognize propaganda. And he gives many examples."

"So?"

"David, it's wholly one-sided. He gives anecdotes, dozens, but those are ones he's selected, sent to him from email lists cultivated over the years, and from news items he gets from those websites you like."

"That I sent you weeks ago."

"Yes. Camera.org, Jewish News Syndicate, Algemeiner, MEMRI. Those websites. So there's no lack of examples showing blatant propaganda, censorship, cancel culture, group think, Orwellian terminology – I think that's the right term, yeah, Orwell. Altogether it's a horror show, I admit. But he never makes the connection between these anecdotes and his main theme – that professors in general aren't teaching students how to think, evaluate information, recognize propaganda relating to Israel mainly, and then to other subjects. So, he automatically blames the professors for the students' prejudices, biases, irrational anti-Semitism."

"I see your point. But the whole idea of college is to get an education, to learn how to think, read, investigate, challenge, that sort of thing. It's a total failure if a student writes that Israel is apartheid, and the professor doesn't challenge that statement, doesn't demand a logical explanation. Instead, too many faculty get away with teaching anti-Semitism, though it is in the guise of some progressive ideology, such as teaching about personal trauma and the atrocities of men."

David, talk English. What 'personal trauma,' what 'atrocities.'

"Another anecdote, Is that okay?"

"I'm listening."

"Princeton pushes a rabidly anti-Semitic book *The Right to Maim*, which teaches a wholly made up, blood-libel charge that

Israel harvests the organs of Palestinians. Absolute lies, but no one challenges. Professor Shapiro calls them out. What's wrong with that?"

"I agree, but these are still anecdotes, and don't support widespread professorial anti-Semitism or incompetence. In my case I came here feeling strongly that Israel shared blame for the plight of the Palestinians. You can't blame my teachers for that. If anything, I've moved away from that belief, thanks to you and Michael and others."

"But Rebecca, if you had not met us, and had that horrible incident on the march, where in Great Lakes University are you going to learn that claims of apartheid are a lie, that much of what you hear in BDS is propaganda. Not from your professors."

"So, you're saying that college is supposed to set us straight, in our beliefs?"

'No. But look at Geddy's girlfriend. Smart, I assume, because she's a student here. But dumb, dumb, dumb, because no one has taught her to evaluate information. So, she quotes Human Rights Watch and Amnesty International, wholly ignorant that they are nothing but propaganda agencies aimed to destroy Israel."

"David, you make no sense. Geddy's girlfriend is anti-Semitic, granted. The professors are supposed to fix that? What do you want, re-education camps like I read they have in North Korea?"

"Okay, I see we have two different views. Professor Shapiro has a point, and maybe he's expecting too much of college teaching these days."

"Way too much. From my perspective, his book is not much more than a collection of anecdotes all in favor of his argument. I counted all the colleges named. Thirty-one, including four Ivies, plus my father's college, Stanford. That's like one percent of all the U.S. colleges."

"Yeah, regarding Stanford, I'm curious what you thought

about that administrator who tried to justify squelching a conservative speaker."

She did not respond right away.

"Rebecca, are you there?"

"Yes, just looking something up...Okay, found it. That administrator was fired, deservedly so. But a one-off like that doesn't prove students are mis-taught across the board. Here's the basic argument. Professor Shapiro, like you, is upset that students too readily accept propaganda, like Israel is apartheid or Israel harvests Palestinians' organs. He therefore goes fishing for anecdotes to prove his theory that it's their teachers' fault, because they are never taught to recognize propaganda, to question and investigate statements for which no evidence is provided, or for which the evidence that is provided is obviously false – if they did any digging whatsoever. Those are pretty much his words."

"But Rebecca, the anecdotes aren't invented. Don't you think they're more like the tip of the iceberg?"

"Perhaps, but nothing in this book proves it. His multiple tales from some thirty colleges fit what we call confirmation bias. A jury would move to acquit."

"Rebecca, you'll make one hell of a lawyer."

"One other issue, David. The book may turn off many students, who won't like to be called 'Useful Idiots.' Any chance of changing the title?"

"No, our agreement with Mrs. Shapiro is the title stays as the Professor wrote it. Look, the book may bomb, but it's going to be published. I think it's great that you could edit our Forward in light of your negative opinion."

"Well, it was fun, actually. I don't want my name on the Forward. Promise?"

"Your name will not appear. Unless you want to change it to Rebecca Applebaum, then no one will know."

"Silly you are. I'm still only eighteen!"

"Oh, by the way, I just got accepted into two medical schools."

"You did? Congratulations. Where?"

"Great Lakes and Case Western Reserve in Cleveland."

"And?"

"I'm staying in town. Great Lakes University School of Medicine!"

## THIRTY-THREE

# The Unexpected and Unexplained

The next morning, shortly before 8 am, David's phone beeped with a text message. At first he thought it was some sort of joke, but then realized it was not.

> Great Lakes University Student shot
> dead! Gordon Arthur Geddy murdered
> walking to school this morning. Drive -by
> shooting. Developing story.

His first instinct was to call Steve. As soon as David punched in the number. Steve answered with, "I just saw it. It's real. I have no idea."

"What the hell is going on? Who could have done this? Or ordered it?"

"Well, for people in the anti-Israel mob, we'll be blamed."

"Me? You?"

"Jews."

"Yeah, maybe so. What about Mossad? Gordon was just the head of a local BDS club, no real power. Why would Israel do him in?"

"Actually, I don't think it was Israel. And I can't imagine any of our students getting into something like this."

"So, who does that leave?"

"Local enemies. He must have somehow been involved in something nefarious, that pissed somebody off."

"Great specificity, Steve. That's really helpful."

"Think, David. What does this remind you of?"

"I'm clueless."

"Gang warfare."

"Gangs?"

"Yeah, gangs kill each other's leaders all the time. Gordon must have been part of some gang or organization, and another gang didn't like what he was doing. Sort of like Shi'a and Sunni in the Middle East. They both want Israel gone, but in the meantime they kill each other in multiple wars. So maybe there are competing BDS factions. I don't know, but that's my guess. But no matter, Jews will be blamed."

"By whom?"

"By assumption. It may be unstated, but it'll be lurking in the minds of the masses. Students. Faculty. Town folk. I can't wait until I get out of here, home to Israel. Where I'll feel safe."

* * *

Rebecca picked up right away.

"I just heard," she said. "It's on the news."

David had not thought to turn on the TV. "Wait a minute, let me turn it on."

The banner at the bottom repeated the text message. "Local student shot dead on way to school."

"Let me listen to this. I'll call you back later, okay?"

The local news did not give much more information. A local reporter stood outside the group home where Gordon lived.

Police cars were on the street, and yellow tape cordoned off the front lawn.

"He apparently left the home around seven this morning, and as he crossed the street," said the reporter, pointing to his left, "people in the house heard shots ring out. From what the police have learned so far, at least two shots. Students in the house ran out and saw his body on the street. They called 911 but when the medics arrived, he was dead. A student walking to school from half a block away reports seeing only a 'black sedan,' but no license plate information."

The TV anchor asked her reporter, "Do the police think this was gang-related?"

"They don't know, but over the few minutes I've been out here, I've learned that Mr. Geddy was head of the local BDS movement on campus. That's an organization that seeks to boycott Israel, to influence the country's treatment of Palestinians. It raises the possibility of a hate crime, and it's my understanding the local police are going to ask the FBI for help."

That's good, thought David. They're already involved. I bet they have some ideas.

# THIRTY-FOUR

# The Campus Reacts

Geddy's murder gave excuse to unleash anti-Semitic bias among various clubs, groups, and heretofore silent students. Always there, under the surface, but now it was on full display. Within two days of the murder the campus was plastered with two-by-three-foot poster pictures of Gordon Geddy, with the headline: "BDS Martyr. Contribute to the Cause." Below each picture was a website for donations to support BDS, and below that, a list of sponsoring student organizations, including BDS for Justice, Students for a Socialist America, LGBTQ on Campus, and the European Studies Club.

Pro-Palestinian vigils were held every afternoon outside the administration building, with the usual, by now familiar slogans: "Palestine will be free, from the river to the sea," and "Free Palestine." The demonstrations were peaceful, and fell within the speech guidelines of the university.

The pro-Israel crowd, fewer in number, was not so visible. Neither Hillel nor any other campus club organized a demonstrations, and the students who showed up connected via social media. Thus small groups of students, carrying the Israeli flag, also demonstrated outside administration. The nightly news showed both groups, one manifestly larger. To any viewer, it was apparent where the main sentiment lay: anti-Israel.

The *Great Lakes Campus Daily* covered Geddy's murder with national news sources, and reporting on local police efforts. Two days after the shooting it published several letters directly or indirectly blaming the Jews/and or Israel for the murder. One student wrote:

> Gordon Geddy's murder is not difficult to understand if you know anything about Israel and how Mossad operates against its enemies. And make no mistake: Mr. Geddy was an enemy of Israel, given his position here at the University and with BDS.
>
> I refer students to a book on the subject, *Rise and Kill First*, that came out a few years ago. In this book the author meticulously documents how Mossad and other secret Israeli agencies kill anyone perceived as a threat to Israel. The book even documents how Mossad killed someone by mistake. No matter, to the Israelis. If Mossad has you in their sights, you are toast. No trial, no evidence needed. They're called "extra-judicial" killings.
>
> So, yes, the FBI is working on the case, I know. But I don't think they extend to checking out Israel. They should.
>
> Bernie Singleton
>
> Junior, Arts and Sciences

* * *

After reading this and other letters, David called Steve. "Steve, I think we should write a rebuttal to this guy Singleton. He makes it seem like Israel is just a bunch of killers. Doesn't mention how the Mossad targets are all terrorists who have killed Israelis. Like the Munich gang in the 1972 Summer Olympics."

"Be my guest," replied Steve, with a touch of sarcasm. "You'll be wasting your time. Worse, you'll be inflaming the loonies. Have you seen the posters? I'm sure you have. Notice the sponsoring organizations?"

"Yeah, you can't miss them. They're everywhere."

"And one of the sponsoring groups is LGBTQ on Campus. Can you believe that? Their members wouldn't last a day in Gaza or under the PLO. And they're advocating for Palestinians? Do these people have any idea what it's like for their kind in Arab countries?"

"Evidently not."

"Given this lunacy, you think your well-reasoned letter is going to change their thinking? Not happening. They'll just double down. David, I've said this time and again. Your efforts are admirable, but you're up against insanity. Israel is the only country in the Middle East where queers and transgenders can live in the open. And here on campus they're pro-BDS, pro-Palestinian? They advocate for governments that would not tolerate them, indeed outlaws their kind? You can't reason with these ignorant anti-Semites. Make Aliya, join the IDF. That's your only hope."

"Well, thanks for the advice. I'll think about writing the letter."

"Good luck. Leave me out of it."

After disconnecting, David thought about the brief conversation. *Of course, he's right. But making Aliya is not the solution.*

# THIRTY-FIVE

# The First FBI Interviews

David didn't have to wait long. At noon he received a phone call from attorney Zimmerman.

"David, I don't have to tell you how serious this is. We are cooperating fully with the FBI. You are one of a number of students who've had interactions with Mr. Geddy. The FBI needs to interview all of you, and has asked me to set it up. Let me add that there is absolutely no suspicion you or other students are involved in Geddy's murder. The interviews are just to get information, possible leads. However, the interviews are not optional, I'm afraid. I will be your attorney of record, but if you choose to have your own personal attorney present, that's your choice. Again, it's simply to get a handle on the situation."

"Thanks, Mr. Zimmerman. I don't need a personal attorney. I hope the interview times are flexible."

"I have three options, starting tomorrow, December tenth. The interviews will take place here in the administration building, and will be recorded." He gave the choices and David opted for the next day at three pm, after his last class.

"Can I ask who else is being interviewed?"

"I can't give out names, but I'm sure you can figure out most of them."

By the end of the day, he knew. Steve, Michael, Rebecca, were also contacted. And likely Geddy's girlfriend, and others in their group home.

Steve told David he had objected to the interview, which David thought was dumb, since it could cast suspicion. Steve said he relented only when Zimmerman told him he could be expelled. If the school could expel him because he wouldn't talk to the FBI, they could also revoke his passport, nixing his move to Israel. On the phone he repeated his earlier statement: "Can't wait to get the hell out of here, return home."

David's interview was just as Attorney Zimmerman had stated, for information only. Two FBI agents, plus David and the attorney, sitting around a long table. The most uncomfortable part concerned Professor Shapiro's book.

"You state the first time you heard of Professor Moussa was in a discussion with Professor Shapiro?"

"Yes, sir. He told me about the incident I just recounted. I came to Great Lakes the following year."

"And you're read Professor's book?"

"Yes, sir."

"Is Professor Moussa mentioned by name or identified on any way?"

"No, he is not. In fact, Professor Shapiro recounts numerous situations to support his thesis about campus anti-Semitism, but that incident is not one of them."

Turning to Lester Zimmerman, the FBI inquisitor stated, "We will need to see this book. Before it's published."

"That is possible, and I can have my student client submit it, but you know first we'll need a statement of exclusivity. For FBI eyes only." Turning to David, Zimmerman asked, "do you have a Word file of the book?"

"Yes, I'm still working on helping to get it published. There's nothing in there that will help this investigation."

"Young man," said the FBI agent, who himself could not have been more than thirty, "that's for us to decide. Lester, have Mr. Applebaum send you the file, then you can forward it to us on the encrypted email server. It will not go anywhere outside our purview."

"Will do. Send me the exclusivity paperwork, and we'll get it to you right away. Let's not get into a squabble that leads to a subpoena. It's just a routine information transfer."

The FBI agent looked to his partner, who simply nodded. "Okay, will do."

The rest of the interview was stress-free, and it ended after forty-five minutes. As David left the room, he found Rebecca in the waiting area. She was next. He was careful not to mention any details about his interview. *If she's asked about the book, she won't have anything to add beyond what I told them.*

"I'll wait for you," he said. "Outside the building."

Half an hour later she came out.

"Well, that was fast. How'd it go?"

"Okay. They asked more stuff about the Nazi, and about why I quit BDS. How about with you?"

"Similar. About my interactions with Gordon over the past two years. I said it was just two students with different views about Israel. Steve and Michael are not until tomorrow. I think they'll have more to say. Did they ask you anything about a guy named Abu Moussa?"

"Yeah, they did. Never heard of him. Was I supposed to know something about him? They said he was on the faculty here several years ago."

"He was a colleague of Professor Shapiro's. Not worth going

into now. Good you never heard of him. Did they ask about the Professor's book?"

"Yeah, that too. I gave my opinion."

"Did they want to read it?"

"No. No one asked. Didn't seem too interested."

"That's interesting. Hey, how about an early dinner?"

"Sure. Chinese, though."

# THIRTY-SIX

## Additional Interviews

"Please state your name, age, and address."

"Michael Solomon, age nineteen, and I live here on campus. Bradley Hall."

"Mr. Solomon –"

"You can call me Michael."

The young FBI inquisitor smiled, said, "Okay. Michael, tell us how you knew Mr. Geddy."

"I didn't really know him, except that he ran the BDS for Justice Club here on campus, and I was a member for a while."

"Why did you leave the club?"

"I learned that the ultimate BDS goal is to eliminate Israel, not change its behavior toward the Palestinians. And that bothered me."

"Can you explain how you came to this conclusion, and just when you quit the club?"

Michael went over the events leading up to his walking out of the meeting, but made no mention of hacking Geddy's laptop.

"Now you turned over some files to the FBI, from Mr. Geddy's computer. How did you get those?"

"Excuse me," interrupted Zimmerman. "Let me talk with Michael just for a second." He pulled Michael aside, out of hearing range of the two FBI agents.

"Michael, this is just an interview. However, don't misstate anything. You're not going to get into trouble for hacking Geddy's computer. You could if you don't answer everything truthfully. Just want to give you a heads up."

"Okay, thanks, I understand." They returned to the table, and Michael went over details of his hack.

"What happened after that?"

He explained the email from Mr. Geddy, and his reply.

"Did you have any further contact with him after that?"

"No, none. He didn't reply to my last email. I did assume he suspected me of being the guy from New York on the Zoom call."

"What about Professor Moussa. Did you hear from him?"

"No, nothing. My only contact with him was on that Zoom call."

"After that last email from Mr. Geddy, with whom did you discuss all that had transpired.?"

"What do you mean?"

"Who did you tell about the hack, and the email from Mr. Geddy?"

"No one, that I recall."

"You are of the Bahá'í faith?"

"Yes, I converted. From Judaism."

"Did Mr. Geddy ever criticize you for that reason? Or make light of your conversion?"

"No. On the contrary, in one meeting he pointed me out as an example of the great diversity of BDS, as inclusive of all religions."

"Do you have any speculation as to who might have wanted Mr. Geddy killed?"

"I've thought about that a lot. In all honesty, I think a lot of students, well not a lot, but some, would wish he was gone, given his perceived anti-Semitism. But it's inconceivable any student could be part of a plot. He may have alienated people he was working with, however. Maybe some of that is in those files I downloaded. I just don't think the crime was connected with any students."

"Tell us about your work in AI."

Michael related his interest starting in high school, his science fair award, and his use of AI to decipher the downloads from Mr. Geddy's computer. He followed that with, "Let me ask a question, if I may. What has the FBI done with that file?"

"We're not privileged to discuss that. I'm sorry."

*Translation. Nothing.*

"You are majoring in computer science?"

"Yes."

"Okay, I think that's all the questions we have. If you learn of anything that you think might help in this investigation, you'll notify Mr. Zimmerman?"

Michael nodded.

"I'm afraid you have to answer verbally."

"Yes, of course, I will"

## * * *

"Please state your name, age, and address."

"Steve Mandelbaum. I'm twenty. I live off campus."

"Your address, please?"

Steve answered.

"Mr. Mandelbaum, what was your relationship to Mr. Geddy?"

"None. Zero. Which makes me ask, why am I even being interviewed?"

"Fair question, Mr. Mandelbaum. Your name has come up several times in previous discussions, as someone who is close to

Mr. David Applebaum, and who has very strong views on Israel. Since Mr. Geddy was a proponent of boycotting Israel, we felt you might be able to shed some light on recent events."

"Well, I know you want to be thorough, but I'm afraid I will be of no help."

"What are your plans after graduation?"

"You probably know. But for the record, I am moving to Israel, and plan to join the IDF."

"Which is?"

"The Israel Defense Force. The army that prevents the world from exterminating Israel."

"And when will you move there?"

"Sometime on June, after graduation."

"You have been accepted into the IDF?"

"Yes, pending my arrival, and some basic fitness tests. Which shouldn't be a problem."

"You have relatives there?"

"No. none."

"What were your views of BDS and Mr. Geddy, if you could summarize?"

"Are you joking?"

Zimmerman chimed in. "Steve, they just have to get your responses down for the record. They may know your views already, but it's got to be recorded. So, please, just cooperate."

"Okay. BDS is devoted to the total destruction of Israel. No question about it. Geddy was a phony, a hypocrite, a rabid anti-Semite in sheep's clothing. He professed to just wanting to change the way Israel treated Palestinians. That was total BS. Anyone with a brain knows what they are after. I was and remain pretty disgusted how our students fell for this BS. Especially Jewish students. Is that sufficient?"

"Thank you," said one of the agents. "We get it. So, in your own thinking, who would want Mr. Geddy killed?"

"Any sane person."

"Steve," intoned Zimmerman. "They're not looking for a diatribe. We all know how you feel."

"Okay, a lot of us would, in all honesty. But I also have no idea who might have done it. If I had to guess, I would say he pissed off some fellow travelers, and they did him in. I strongly, strongly doubt Israel had anything to do with it. That's my strong opinion."

"Okay, thank you. I think we're done."

* * *

"Please state your name, age, and address."

"Lena Nadir. I'm nineteen, and live off campus, at 2121 Tokken Street."

"Is that the same group home where Mr. Geddy lived?"

"Yes, eight of us live in the house. It's quite large." Without being asked, she offered, "we all have our own bedrooms."

"How long have you known Mr. Geddy?"

"Two years, about. We met here in Great Lakes."

"Did you see him the morning before he left for school, when he was shot?"

"No, he left early, for an early class. I only heard when the others did. Someone came running into the house, yelling "Gordon's hurt," or something like that. It was chaos after that, with the police, the ambulance."

"Please understand we are trying only to get information to find who committed this crime. Do you have any idea why someone would do this, or why someone would arrange to have him killed?

"I have idea, but no proof."

"What is your idea?"

"My boyfriend was very much pro-Palestinian, as I am. Who would want him killed? Jews, I assume."

"By Jews, any group in particular?"

"The Jews have connections to Israel. Israel has Mossad, which targets people in other countries. That is well documented. You can even read a book about it, called *Rise and Kill First*. So that would be my first guess."

"And apart from Mossad?"

"I don't know. Local Jewish killers for hire?" she asked.

"Who would hire them?"

"Look, you know my feeling. I think the Jews were somehow involved. That's just an opinion. I have no evidence. So, I'm just offering an opinion. But some Jewish students recently quit the club, over disagreements with Gordon. I don't say they did anything, but maybe they were involved somehow."

"Apart from other Jewish students, did Gordon have any enemies that you know of?"

"No."

"Do you know of a Professor Abu Moussa?"

"I've heard of him. Gordon mentioned him, said he used to be a professor here."

"In what context did Mr. Geddy mention him?"

There was a slight pause, then she said, "Something about the BDS club, some advice or something. Apparently, he is an expert on the Middle East situation, and Gordon may have consulted him on some topic. I assume he had learned about him after enrolling here. I really don't know anything more. I personally never met the man."

"Do you know where this Professor Moussa lives, where he teaches now?"

"I believe somewhere in California, that's all I know."

"Thank you, Ms. Nadir. I think we're done.

# THIRTY-SEVEN

# Zimmerman's Recap

The day after the last FBI-student interviews, Attorney Zimmerman met with President Hightower to go over the findings.

"Lester, before I ask you about the interviews, did you hear anything from Geddy's family? As far as I know, they made no attempt to contact my office or any administrator.

"I learned his parents are divorced, and his mother did come to claim the body after the autopsy. His father is apparently in Europe somewhere. And yes, as far as I know there's been no family contact with the university. Of course, we may hear something in the future. I did look up his file. He was from St. Louis, went to a prestigious private school there. Nothing in his application to suggest radicalization in high school."

"That's like saying none of our applicants are serial killers. These kids are seventeen, eighteen. Wouldn't expect a rap sheet on any of them."

"Well, there are some applicants who do have a history. DUI, petty theft, other things. But nothing on him."

"So, back to the interviews, how many were there?" asked Hightower.

"Fourteen altogether, including the eight students who live in Geddy's house, plus two other Jewish students who have remained in the local BDS club."

"You sat through all of them?"

"Yes, as the student's attorney of record. I also had a senior law student with me as backup."

"The same student the whole time?"

"Three different ones."

"And your overall take?"

"I couldn't help thinking of Agatha Christie. You know, *Murder on the Orient Express*, where everyone had a motive and participated somehow in the murder. Could be the Jewish students, Mossad, local BDS agents who found some major disagreement with him, or an agent of this Professor Moussa. Or – you ready for this? Even his girlfriend."

"His girlfriend? A student?"

"Yes, name's Lena Nadir. She is of Lebanese descent and has been as vocal as Geddy over the Israeli-Palestinian conflict. Well, one resident in their group home said there were rumors of Geddy having an affair with another girl he meets at the Muslim-cultural Students Association, and that's why he often went over there. But when Lena was asked about this she poo-pooed it, said she and Geddy had a great relationship. Still, it raises the possibility of jealousy, and perhaps Lena was involved in the plot somehow, as revenge. So, when you think of all the possibilities, his murder is not implausible as it seemed at first."

"And your opinion?"

"Only one, that I would bet the house on. No Jewish students were involved, directly or indirectly."

"Why the modifier 'Jewish'?"

"Because I think someone in the group home may have

made a call or sent a text message at the moment Geddy was leaving to walk to school. Just my hunch."

"Can't they search all the phones of the students?"

"Any message would be erased. I also think, if the plot was as sophisticated as I think it was, that any phone used would not belong to any student, probably a burner phone long buried somewhere."

"What did they find when they searched Geddy's room?"

"From what I learned, not much. He was too smart to leave anything lying around that could be found. As to his laptop, I don't know. I assume they have it. Don't know if it's the same one Michael Solomon hacked."

"He's our famous computer nerd?"

"Yeah. He seems above board, not really anyone who would be involved in a murder plot. I did learn a few things from the agents, however."

"Such as?"

"Do you remember I told you they set up a surveillance camera across from the group home?"

"Yes."

"It got a video of the car passing by Geddy, and then Geddy is on the ground. So, the shooting was opposite the camera's position. They identified the car as a black Honda SUV. Unfortunately, no license plate recognition. And the widows were tinted. And the sun was barely up, so altogether no one in the car identified."

"So the Honda is now the automobile of interest?"

"They assume, if these guys are professionals, that the car's now in another state, and will never appear within a thousand miles of Great Lakes University. But it's still a tiny lead."

"And what else?"

"This professor Moussa. FBI agents in California went to interview him at his home in Santa Cruz, as he's definitely a person of interest. He was a professor at the University there."

"Was?"

"He's gone. Left for Egypt the day before the murder."

"Wow! He's their man. What did the school give as his reason for leaving?"

"He apparently told them it was a family emergency, would let them know of his return as soon as he took care of personal affairs. Right now, he's beyond any chance of being interviewed."

"Can't the FBI file for extradition?"

"No. They have no evidence of his committing a crime, so unless he returns –which seems unlikely – he's gone."

"So, we're back to murder by Honda?"

"Afraid so."

"What about the Muslim-cultural Students Association? The place where Geddy often visited, and may have met a secret girl-friend. I think that would be a place ripe for investigation."

"Definitely, but the staff there are privately employed, not by the University. They have many student members, and if any of them were to be interviewed, I would not be the attorney of record. I was informed they would arrange for their own attorney to sit in on any student interviews. So, I'm not privy to what went down with that group."

"Lester, this is not good for our school. It's been a nightmare for the Administration. Just about every newspaper and TV channel has come through. I've had Public Relations handle things as well as possible. On your advice, I've given no interviews."

"Good. At least we can say, 'the FBI is handling the investiga-tion.' Fortunately, the Christmas holiday begins this week, so most of the students will be gone and we'll have some reprieve."

# THIRTY-EIGHT

# Return from Christmas Break

The campus went dormant during a two-week Christmas break. Hillel shut down, as did all school activities. Rebecca's parents booked a week-long family cruise from San Francisco to Mexico, to include both sisters, and Rachel's husband and son. Despite entreaties from David for Rebecca to come to Cleveland for at least a few days, she opted to stay with her family and take the cruise. "Mom and Dad are paying for everything. They want us all together. I'm going."

David spent some of his vacation in Cleveland, during which he worked on editing the professor's book. Steve would be doing the same, and they planned to get together on return to campus, iron out a single final edit, and then send it to Peretz for his review.

The second week of Christmas break David joined his parents on a trip to New York City. They stayed in a hotel, and when not hanging out with their Joe and his family, went to Broadway shows, Lincoln Center, the Bronx Zoo, and other attractions. They had a two-room suite at the Hyatt, so David had his privacy. As for their get-togethers with Joe, no politics was discussed. Joe did congratulate David on his getting into medical school.

The day after returning to campus, David got together with Steve to go over the manuscript of Professor Shapiro's book. They each had made minor changes, and page by page they agreed on the editing.

David had not yet called Rebecca since his return to campus, but planned to do so when done with Steve. She called before they finished.

"Hi," he answered. "I was just about to call you. I'm here with Steve, going over the professor's book."

"Good. Did you have a nice vacation?"

"Great, yeah. Got to go to New York with my parents. How about you?"

"I did that cruise with my parents. Had a nice time. I just got a call from Michael Solomon."

"Oh?"

"He wants the four of us to get together for dinner this Saturday."

"You, me, him and who else?"

"His girlfriend, Amanda. I don't remember her last name, but I think I mentioned her to you."

"Oh, yeah, you did."

"Can I confirm it, then?"

David looked over toward Steve. *He should be included.*

"Wait a minute, Rebecca. Maybe we can add two more."

"Who?"

"Just a minute."

His hand over the phone, David asked, "Steve, are you dating anyone?"

"No. Why?"

"Dinner this Saturday. Me, Rebecca, and Michael and his girlfriend. Want to join us?" *It's only right that I ask.*

"I'll be like a fifth wheel."

"Nonsense. Maybe you can recruit Michael for the IDF."

"Well, if you're sure it's okay with everyone."

"I'll make it okay."

David resumed his phone conversation with Rebecca. "Please tell Michael that Steve Mandelbaum is going to join us. Right now, Steve doesn't have a date, so it'll just be him. I'm sure Michael won't mind."

She agreed to convey the request, then he asked: "One more thing. When can we get together? How about this Friday?"

"Not Hillel. I need some quiet."

"No, I'll skip that Shabbat dinner. Just the two of us."

"Call me later?"

"Okay."

David turned off his phone, turned to speak to Steve. "Michael will pick the restaurant. It'll be a fun evening."

\* \* \*

David waited an hour after Steve left, then called Rebcca. "You said to call you later. Steve is gone."

"I checked with Michael," she replied, without being asked, "and it's fine with him if Steve joins us Saturday."

"Good, but that's not why I called back. I really want to get together again with you."

"We are together," she replied. He knew full well she knew what he meant.

"You are such a tease, Rebecca. Didn't you miss me on the cruise?"

"The cruise was great. Warm, sunny."

"But you slept alone."

"Hardly. The first cruise night with one of the stewards, Jose Ortega," she said. "The next night with a ship's cook, Miguel Hernandez. The third night with one of the late-night performers, Pedro Gonzalez. He was great on the stage and in bed. Mexicans are great lovers, don't you know?"

"Okay, okay, I deserved that. My bad."

"I'm having my period. Friday should be okay. Dinner only."

"No problem. I'm just glad to have you back."

"Anything new on the investigation?" she asked.

"Not that I know of. I've had email contact with Attorney Zimmerman. He's either being tight-lipped, or they're no closer to finding the murderer."

"David, did you read the article in *The New York Times*?"

"Yeah, I did. Just a general rundown. Nothing new, except that Professor Moussa skipped town. Sort of implicates him in some way, but the FBI made it clear there was nothing they could do. They have no grounds for even pursuing an extradition, which I don't think we have with Egypt anyway. Do you remember reading about that notorious Arab anti-Semite Amin al-Husseini, who conspired with Hitler?"

"Yeah, I've come across his name."

"After World War II he escaped to Egypt, where he lived several years safely as a wanted war criminal. Egypt simply ignored all requests to deport him. And Moussa is only wanted for questioning, with no pending charges."

"All very puzzling, David. Is there some plot? Or not?"

"Rebecca, you know as much as I do. On to something more mundane. Where is Michael making the reservation for Saturday night?"

"Luigi's."

"Good. How about us going to Bistro Bills on Friday. Haven't been there in a while."

"Just dinner?"

"Just dinner. Maybe after Saturday night we can have dessert in my place."

"All five of us?"

"Rebecca, you are too cruel."

## THIRTY-NINE

# Dinner at Luigi's

Saturday night's dinner at Luigi's was planned for six pm. Michael made a reservation for one of the round tables that could seat five or six.

David and Rebecca entered the restaurant and found Michael and Amanda waiting in the foyer. Steve had not yet arrived. Michael introduced Amanda. She was not what David expected. The girlfriend of short, rather shlumpy Michael Solomon stood about an inch taller, and had blond hair and blue eyes. Very attractive and obviously not Jewish. *Shiksa pretty. What does she see in him? Wonder if she's Baháí?*

The four were seated in the restaurant, with an empty chair waiting for Steve. "Is he bringing someone," asked Michael?

"No, no girlfriend," replied David. "Told me he doesn't want to get romantically involved before he goes to Israel."

Just then Steve bounded into Luigi's, walked over to stand behind the empty chair. "Sorry I'm late. Let's see, I know Rebecca and David. You must be Michael, and this is your beautiful girlfriend." He shook hands and sat, commenting "I've not been here before. I suppose all of you have?"

"We have," said David, nodding toward Rebecca.

"Yeah, Amanda and I have eaten lunch here," said Michael. "Good pasta."

The round table facilitated easy conversation. And, as a bonus, the restaurant was quiet, an ambience somewhat uncommon in Township eateries. Menus were delivered and for drinks, everyone just requested water.

After a few minutes the waitress returned. David and Rebecca ordered a large pizza to share, Steve ordered a small pizza, and Michael and Amanda ordered chicken parmesan.

"Amanda, what year are you?" asked David.

"Junior year."

"Studying?"

"Architecture. I'm in the school of Architecture. It's a five-year program."

"Really? That's great."

"David, ask her about you know who," said Rebecca.

"Who?" queried Amanda.

"Amanda, David is pre-med. But he's a nerd on Frank Lloyd Wright. Give him a minute and he'll unwind for about, oh, an hour or so."

"Well," replied Amanda, "Wright certainly had an interesting career. And he's historically very important, but no longer really an influence in modern design."

"Amanda is crazy about architectural history," said Michael. "Whenever we walk about the campus, she's always pointing out different styles. My mind reels. Georgian, Victorian, mid-century modern."

"I assume you've been to Taliesin," said Rebecca.

"Oh yes, just the one in Wisconsin. Haven't been to Arizona."

Touching David's arm, Rebecca whispered, "I think you've met your match."

"Amanda, I really don't know much about architecture

design," offered David. "I just got interested in Wright during a humanities course, and wrote a term paper about his early life. Got to know all the sordid stuff as well."

"Yeah, pretty bad. He left his wife and kids to run away with another man's wife."

"Sounds interesting," said Steve, who to this point had not spoken after ordering pizza. Since then, David noted Steve had looked only at Amanda.

"Steve is getting a degree in engineering," said David. "Steve, what do you think about modern design?"

"Uh, oh, civil engineering is my gig. Bridges, tunnels, not houses. Wright doesn't enter the picture. Amanda, where are you from?"

"Philadelphia. How about you?"

"Well, we have something in common. Same state. I grew up in Pittsburgh."

"That's interesting," replied Rebecca. Only one of us is from the Midwest, attending a midwestern university."

"I don't think of Cleveland as Midwest," replied David. "In fact it was once part of the Western Reserve of Connecticut."

"Yeah," said Steve, "you're Midwest. Pittsburgh is only two hours away and we're Eastern. Totally arbitrary."

"Steve, growing up did you get a chance to visit Frank Lloyd Wright's Fallingwater? It's only an hour outside Pittsburgh."

Rebecca looked at her watch. "Wow, we've gone a whole thirty seconds since last discussing Frank Lloyd Wright."

"Well, it is a rather remarkable house. Probably the most famous in America. Outside of the White House, anyway."

Steve turned to look at David. "To answer your question, I went on a field trip in high school. I'm five-ten and I thought the ceilings were a bit low."

"Yeah, replied David, Wright was only five-seven, and he put in low ceilings in many of his houses, mainly in the entrances, so people would bend down, then be awed when they entered the main room."

"If we sit here long enough," said Rebecca, "I can probably get my degree in architecture."

David threw a kiss to Rebecca. "My girlfriend is funny, is she not?"

"Moving on," Rebecca replied, "Amanda, if I may ask, are you of the Bahá'í faith also?"

"Oh, no. I was actually raised Catholic, but that didn't last long."

"What do you mean?"

"My parents weren't strong Catholics. I went to public schools, and in high school had a revelation of sorts about religion. Just had a hard time accepting a lot of the Catholic dogma. Hanging out with some classmates, I came upon Unitarian. Went to their church a few times, liked what I saw, so I changed over."

"Does that mean 'converted?'" asked Rebecca.

"We don't call it converted. It's more like adherence. A belief system. Jesus is not God, and we don't believe in the Trinity."

"Well, a Jew and Catholic meet in a bar," said Steve.

"Go on," said David, "what's the rest of the joke?"

"Give me a minute. Sounds like a great opening line, doesn't it?"

"Well, too bad," said Michael. "We didn't meet in a bar, but in the Free Thinkers Club."

"That's a new one for me," replied Rebecca, "but I'm only a freshman. What is it?"

"A club for people open to new ideas. Professors and sometimes students give talks on a variety of subjects, based on solid research. I met her at a talk on artificial intelligence."

"Isn't that your specialty?"

"Yeah, I've done work in the field. But this was more about predicting how AI can take over the world if we're not careful.

Less technical, more about the possibilities going forward. Very interesting."

"Amanda, what brought you there?" asked Rebecca.

"I went because AI is creeping into architectural design. So naturally some architects are worried about being replaced by a machine. I don't see it happening, personally. Michael and I got to talking after the lecture, and well, you know, two converts. We clicked, and here we are."

"Bottom line," said Michael, "she's attracted to Jewish geeks."

"But you're not Jewish," replied Rebecca, "Bahá'í I thought. Or am I confused?"

"Jewish physically, Bahá'í mentally," said Michael.

"Physically?"

"Do you want me to spell it out?"

Amanda looked toward Michael, then back at the others. "Of course, he's joking."

During this riposte, David noted how Steve continued to stare at Amanda. *I need to change the tone.* "Amanda, did you know Frank Lloyd Wright was Unitarian?"

"So he was not circumcised?" asked Steve.

"Yes, his whole family was of the Unitarian faith" replied Amanda, ignoring Steve's question. "Though he personally wasn't very religious."

"But he got the commission to design Unity Temple in Oak Park" offered David.

Amanda nodded. "A magnificent structure. You've been?"

"Oh, yeah, a couple of times."

"Amanda, I'm new to this subject," chimed in Rebecca. "A couple of months ago David took me to Taliesin. I learned about the murders there in1914. Do they teach that in architecture school?"

"No, we all read about it, in various books, but lectures and workshops are all about design. Lots of sordid histories in every profession, I think."

"What are the basic beliefs of Unitarians?" asked Steve. To David, the tone of his question seemed a bit out of place after his bouncy intros. Not conversational, but more like 'time for a new topic.'

Amanda did not seem put off. "Oh, Unitarians believe in what they call the seven principles. The inherent worth of every person, justice and compassion in human relations, search for truth and meaning, several others."

"Sounds like Bahá'í to me," said David.

"There are some similarities," offered Michael. "But Bahá'í is more inclusive, aspects of all the major religions."

Steve cleared his throat to draw attention. "All this sounds kumbaya to me."

"Boys, boys," said Rebecca, with a tone of mild rebuke. "Let's get off religion. All religions want to do good, be good, to search for truth."

"Except the ones that vow to kill all the Jews," interjected Steve.

David shook his head. *Oh, no.*

"The problem," replied Amanda, "is I think we get too hung up on the word 'religion.' This was brought home to me when I visited Israel."

"You have you been to Israel?" asked Steve, in a tone now sounding more conversational.

"Yes, as a senior in high school."

"How does a Christian girl end up in Israel her senior year?"

"After I was accepted to architecture school, I learned that the school was sponsoring a tour of Tel Aviv's White City. As an incoming student, I was allowed on the tour. It was me and ten other students. A great experience."

"I'm impressed," said David, "that you toured the White City."

"The what?" asked Rebecca. "Wasn't White City the Chicago Exposition in the nineteenth century?"

"Another White City" replied Steve.

"How many are there?"

"Dozens," said Michael, a smirk on his face.

"Stop, stop!" interrupted David. "Let Amanda clarify. As architectural historian of record, at least here in Luigi's, I'll give the preface. The Chicago exposition in 1893 was called the White City because all the temporary buildings were white. They were all torn down after the Exposition. Now Amanda, tell the assembled parishioners what you toured in Tel Aviv."

"Okay," she said. "Tel Aviv's White City is a large collection of apartment buildings built in the 1930s, called the Bauhaus style, created in Germany. They were white, hence the name. The architects were German Jewish architects who fled the Nazis. As a result, Tel Aviv has the largest number of these Bauhaus buildings in the world. Architects come from all over to study them."

"Yeah," said David, "there are hundreds throughout Tel Aviv. Most people don't appreciate the history of these buildings."

"Amanda, how do you spell bow house?" asked Rebecca.

"B-a-u-h-a-u-s."

Rebecca took out her phone. "I'll pull up the website, just to get a view of some of them."

"Too bad the British didn't let in more Jewish refugees," said Steve. "The bastards had their quotas, condemning millions to the gas chambers."

"The Americans didn't help either," offered Amanda. "Just when the Jews needed rescue the most, they clamped down on immigration. The United States could have saved millions, but anti-Semitism held sway in the Roosevelt administration."

Rebecca turned toward Steve. "Have you been tutoring

Amanda? She sounds like you. I admit to ignorance on the subject, so don't jump on me."

"The whole world shit on the Jews in the nineteen thirties," replied Steve. "And you know what? It hasn't changed much. The only difference is that now there is a homeland for them to go to. Had it existed before the war, we would not have lost millions. You know my refrain: 'don't get me started.'"

Two servers came to the table carrying dishes. "Here's the food," said David. *Thank goodness. Perfect timing.*

For the next few minutes everyone ate; no comments, except about the food. Midway through the meal a middle-aged man, wearing a Capello-style hat and Italian vest, and carrying a guitar, entered the dining room. He began strumming and singing, several tables away from the five college students.

"I was enjoying the quiet," quipped Steve. "I find these traveling singers annoying when you're trying to carry on a conversation."

"I guess it's a tradition in Italian restaurants," offered Rebecca. "We go to a place in Palo Alto that has them. Not bad, if they don't linger at your table."

David cringed, careful not to show his discomfort. He had been to Luigi's before, and knew the singer favors serenading couples with some love ditty. His table had two couples, plus one other. The singer was bellowing a crowd favorite, "That's Amore."

"A cute song," said Michael. "The tune is familiar. I think I heard it growing up in Brooklyn. Italian for 'That's Amore. Italian for 'That's love.'" He placed one hand behind Amanda's neck and gently rubbed her hair, in a gesture of affection. This move caught the singer's attention, as he ambled past several tables to approach Michael and Amanda. Siding up to them, he started the song again, smiling at the young couple; they seemed pleased with the attention.

David noticed a sour look on Steve, hoped others didn't see it.

For the last part of the song, the singer turned to face David and Rebecca. David faked a smile at the singer. *Hope he leaves soon. This is so awkward for Steve.* Without acknowledging Steve, the singer finished and moved on.

"Well, that was nice," said Michael. "It's a beautiful song, catchy lyrics. Wonder when it was written."

"I just looked it up on my phone," said Rebecca. "It's from 1953, believe it or not. Made popular by a singer named Dean Martin. Apparently very popular back in the day."

"That would be your grandparents' generation," said Steve. "You could ask them."

"They're not around," Rebecca replied, without elaboration. She then turned to Amanda. "Earlier you made a comment about religion. As I recall, something about getting too hung up on the term, which you realized after going to Israel. What did you mean?"

"Oh, I don't know if you want me to get into all that. It's not really about architecture."

"We'd love you to," said Steve. "You are a bright and shining light at this table."

David stared briefly at Steve, whose eyes still seemed fixed on Amanda. *Does he mean we're all dull? Don't ask.*

"Well," she replied, "on the White City tour we learned about the German Jewish architects as well as their buildings. That's really what opened my eyes to the plight of the European Jews during the thirties, and how German nationalism led to the Holocaust."

Steve nodded, encouraging her to continue.

"The Nazis were fanatics. Hitler was *their* religion. They didn't have to pray to God or Jesus, but it was the same. In the name of their religion – Nazism – they felt justified in mass murder. No different than people who kill in the name of traditional religions, whether its Islam or Christianity, or Hinduism. All the same. Nazism, communism, fascism – godless religions, if you will. Followers in a belief system that justifies killing innocent people."

"Amazing," mumbled Steve, barely audible to others.

* * *

From Luigi's, David took Rebecca to his apartment. She brought a small suitcase, for a one-night stay. As soon as they entered and closed the door, he put his arms around her and kissed her. She did not resist.

"Rebecca, you taunt me so. I can't stand being apart."

"Do you want to just stand here, or maybe express yourself in the prone position?"

"Don't be cruel," he replied, drawing out "cruel" in Elvis fashion. "Let me go to the bathroom."

"I've got to go, too."

A few minutes later, as they lay in bed, he asked: "Did you notice Steve staring at Amanda throughout most of the dinner?"

"Yeah, I thought it a little odd. I think that part about the circumcision turned him on a bit."

"More than a bit. I think he covets Michael's girlfriend."

"That is strange, since he's so focused on Judaism and Israel."

"I guess love makes strange bedfellows."

"I have to shut you up," she said, reaching her hand down below his waist.

* * *

The next morning they sat at his small kitchen table, eating breakfast. "Rebecca, times like this I feel like we're married. I love it."

"Do you want to just skip the intermediate steps? Medical

school and residency, law school and maybe a clerkship. Why am I the only practical one?"

"Lots of medical students are married. And law students."

"I'm still just eighteen. Birthday next month."

"Okay, I'll wait. Nineteen will do."

"You're impossible."

"I just got an email from Adele at Hillel. They missed me last Friday, asked that I come this Friday for Shabat dinner. They have a guest speaker from journalism school. A talk about media bias against Israel. Will you come with me?"

"On that topic, yes. It sounds interesting."

# FORTY

# Contact

Michael could get no information from Attorney Zimmerman about the FBI's investigation. Were they able to decipher the downloads he gave them? What software are they using?

The replies from the attorney were generic. "I just don't have any more information. All I can do is assure you the FBI is working diligently on the case, and they are very much appreciative of your efforts."

Who are "they" Michael asked in his email reply. "Can you give me names, people I can contact?"

"Michael, we very much appreciate your efforts, but I don't have any additional information. I can only promise that when I learn of anything I can share, you will be among the first to be notified."

Michael remained skeptical. *Too much bureaucracy.*

He continued to work with his AI programs, which he monitored for updates. Then a message came late Friday afternoon: "New file update," from one of his AI programs. He signed on. Files heretofore unreadable now showed up, revealed.

Revealed!

A previous jumble of code now showed a picture of a teenager, along with his student ID card. A Great Lakes University Student ID card. *He looks Middle Eastern, possibly Arabic.*

Why this student? Something about the card is not right, he thought. What is it? Michael pulled out his own ID card. It showed his head shot, with identifying information below: "Michael Solomon, Student ID #876544, Great Lakes University, Valid until -----."

The revealed ID card read "[Name], Students ID #433670, Great Lake University, Valid until -----."

Typos! *There would be no typos if legitimate. Must be a fake.*

There was more. Another uncovered document showed the first-floor plan of Hillel House! Why this? And one more, now deciphered. A date – today!

Today! Michael's head swirled. *Is this kid going to shoot up Hillel? I've got to call Mr. Zimmerman.* He punched in the number, received only a "please leave message" reply.

*Call 911? They don't have the picture. By the time I make contact, send the file, explain the situation…*

It was 4:30. Almost getting dark. *Wish I had a gun.* He grabbed his coat, left the dorm and headed toward Hillel, first at a fast-walking pace, then running. Students were just entering Hillel, with a line formed at the entrance to get through the metal detector.

*How would the kid get in with a gun? Maybe he's going to shoot outside?*

Once through the detector, Michael ran from room to room, but saw no one who even remotely looked Arabic or like the picture in the ID. Dinner was to start at 5:30.

He returned outside, found the sun setting. He looked up and down the street. *Maybe a false alarm? I wonder if David and Rebecca are coming.*

More students arrived, Jewish kids. One asked him, why are you standing outside?

"Oh, I needed to get some fresh air. A little stuffy inside. I'll go in when dinner's served."

Now almost dark, he did not see the police car across the street. It was there, but in shadows. He did see, walking toward Hillel on the sidewalk across the street, a young man. Yes! he said to himself. The one in the fake ID. He was wearing a heavy coat, of course; it's chilly. Is there a semi-automatic hidden inside his coat? How will he get past the metal detector? Maybe he doesn't plan to. Maybe he'll just unleash on the steps. He's got to be stopped.

Michael walked toward the approaching figure, stopping in front of him about fifty yards from Hillel House, "Excuse me, Hillel security here," he announced, with deep authority. "We'll need you to just unzip the front of your coat so we can confirm there is no hidden contraband."

The teen – for that's what he was – gave Michael a puzzled look and did not respond.

*Does he understand English?*

Michael quickly unzipped his own coat to show what he demanded. "Unzip, see?"

Again no response. Then the teen started to walk around Michael, toward Hillel House. Michael blocked his path, yelled "Unzip!"

Still no response.

Michael put his hands on the boy's coat and proceeded to do the task. The young man jumped back, shouted, *Atrukni wahdi!* [Leave me alone!], then proceeded to run around Michael, toward the Hillel entrance. Fast!

Michael caught up from behind, dived for his legs, just catching the right ankle. The teen fell face first. Michael climbed on top, pinning him to the ground. But the resistance was strong, and soon they were entangled, rolling over on the grass. The thick coats they wore made it difficult for him to grasp the resisting teen around the trunk, so he aimed for the neck. One arm around his neck, the other hand to unzip the coat.

The teen pulled Michael's hand away and did his own unzipping, part way. Then he slipped one hand inside and down toward his belt, and yelled *Allahu akbar!*

BOOM!

The explosion sent a shockwave in all directions, to students walking toward Hillel, to Hillel's front porch, to the police car down the street. And something else. At the foot of the stairs leading up to the Hillel porch landed an arm, severed at the humerus, oozing blood.

Students ran toward the pile of two bodies, now a jumble of parts. The police officer, now out of the car, was right behind them. "Get back!" he yelled. He shined a flashlight on the tangled mass while calling for help.

The students stood back. One vomited. Others cried or yelled questions. By now all the students inside were outside. More flashlights. Chaos.

The officer yelled: "Everyone, please go inside." Sirens wailed. Two police cars pulled up, roof lights flashing. "Please go inside, and leave the scene. That's an order!" yelled the cop.

Slowly, the students obeyed. In the main dining room, the food that had been prepared was brought out, placed on tables buffet-style, for anyone who cared to eat. Few did. Most left, went home. Among them were David and Rebecca, with more questions than answers. They did not yet know Michael was one of the two young men whose flesh and body parts lay strewn on the ground.

FORTY-ONE

# Steve's Wish Fulfilled

Michael's parents arrived to the campus the day after the bombing and met with the FBI. They refused an invitation to meet with President Hightower, or any school official. Instead, they accepted those body parts that could be attributed to their son – based mainly on artifacts of clothing – and have them cremated. Two days later they departed.

The campus reaction to the explosion that killed two young people, distinct from the one after Geddy's murder, was muted. No posters asking for donations, and no letters to the campus newspaper, or if there were, they weren't printed. It was all over the national news, and of course covered in the campus daily as another horrible tragedy, but the existential threat to GLU's Hillel was minimized. "Motive [of bomber] unclear," and "origin [of bomber] unknown" were frequent buzz words, followed by "active FBI investigation." The students could read any and all theories online, but no campus club promulgated a pro-Israel position in public. Hillel stayed mute, allowing the tragedy to speak for itself.

* * *

A memorial service for Michael was held a week after the bombing, in Hillel House. Notwithstanding his conversion to Bahá'í, Michael was still considered Jewish. And he died defending Hillel.

Steve sought out Amanda after the service. "How are you doing?" he asked.

"As well as can be expected," she replied. "This probably makes you even more determined to join the IDF."

"Michael's the first victim of terrorism I actually knew. I've read about hundreds of others, and always wondered what their families went through, after they learned a terrorist killed their son or daughter, brother or sister. Now I have a keener sense. It's some combination of rage and the desire for revenge. Do you feel that?"

"No, not really. It's more like pity for these lost souls, who just want to kill and maim. How do you revenge an entire culture?"

"Make them know there will be repercussions. I don't believe the entire Arab population is interested in martyrdom. Enough of them to cause havoc, but I bet the majority of Palestinians just want to live peacefully, if only their terrorist leaders would let them."

"Maybe so."

"Amanda, I hope you don't think this is inappropriate, so soon after Michael's death, but would you join me in a cup of coffee? I'd really like to talk to you some more, about Israel and your experience there."

"No, it's not inappropriate. And yes, I'd like that."

* * *

Steve and Amanda found an open booth in Mona's Coffee Bistro, ordered coffee and a slice of the bistro's always-favorite cream pie.

"I don't know if you noticed, that night at Luigi's, I couldn't take my eyes off of you."

"Yes, it was obvious. It bothered Michael, but I told him not to worry, that I was used to boys – guys – staring. Said he should be flattered."

"Was he?

"After we made love that night, he felt better."

"I don't get you. You're Christian, but seem to have a Jewish sense about you. Not just falling for someone like Michael, who was Jewish no matter how much he claimed to be Bahá'í. It's like, I feel you're Jewish, but then I see your blond hair and blue eyes. What attracts you to Jewish men?"

"Men? Plural?"

"Sorry. Wishful thinking." She laughed.

"I've had non-Jewish boyfriends. Well, one at least. I'm attracted to what I'm attracted to. No explanation I can offer. Your commitment to Israel attracts me, for example. Don't ask me to explain it."

"Yeah, and I held back at Luigis. David and Rebecca are two good friends, but in my world view they are naïve about Israel, Well, David not so much. But Rebecca for sure. I mean, she joined BDS, can you believe it?"

"I'm not up on the BDS club here, except that I sense it's just another anti-Semitic organization."

"Of course. That makes you more 'up on it' than the vast majority of willfully ignorant Jews. Tell me about your family."

"Liberal Catholics. Liberal enough that when I changed over to Unitarian, they didn't scream or holler."

"You mean your parents?"

"Yeah, there was some questioning at first, then resignation about my decision. Basically, they assume I'll come to my senses later and come back to the faith. I have two younger sisters who still attend mass. What about your parents?"

"Dad died when I was ten. Cancer. My mom remarried, fortunately to someone with money, or I don't think I'd be here talking to you right now. But I don't have what you might call a close family dynamic."

"Brothers? Sisters?"

"A younger brother, just about to graduate high school."

"So, your plan is to move to Israel and join the IDF?"

"Yes, it's called making Aliya, meaning to go up. That's the moving part. Joining IDF is separate and most people who make Aliya don't join the military. Only the younger crowd."

"And when is this taking place?"

"June, after graduation. Actually, me, David and Rebecca are flying to Israel together. They are touring the country for about two weeks, then going to Europe for another two weeks. Paris, I think. Anyway, I'm moving there. Do you want to come with us? That would be great."

"You're inviting me to Israel, after a fifteen-minute coffee date?"

"Why not? You'd get to revisit those Bauhaus buildings, see parts of the country you missed the first time."

"Where would I stay?"

Steve did not answer.

"Steve, I do like you. I'm in mourning now, more or less, and I appreciate your condolences. But your goal is to leave the U.S. Mine is to stay and become an architect. We're adults and can spell it out. We can't get involved. It just won't work."

"You're the smartest, most beautiful girl I've ever had the pleasure of meeting. Yeah, we have different goals. My mind is reeling, trying to see if there's a way. It's coming up empty. How about this? Another coffee klatch in a few days or a week, just to keep in touch."

"Touch?"

"Wrong word choice. Connected? No, that's no good either. How about, 'in communication?'"

"What about just email?"

"No, no, no good, Amanda. I need to see your face. No touch, just see." She laughed.

"Oh well, okay. Call me. Here," she said, pushing the half-eaten plate of pie toward him, "you can finish it. It's good."

* * *

After two more coffee dates they decided to make the best of the time left before Steve's emigration. It was a mutual decision, an affair both wanted, and one in which they knew the ending would be painful. Amanda went back on the pill, which she had stopped after Michael's death.

Steve's new relationship came up in mid-March, when he next met with David about Professor Shapiro's book. Aaron Peretz had sent in some queries about a few items. When they were done, Steve said, "I've been getting together with Amanda."

"That's nice. I'm not surprised. When we had that dinner at Luigi's, I noticed you couldn't take your eyes off of her."

"I admit. Something about the girl attracted me. Should I feel guilty that Michael had to die to realize my wish?"

"Your wish?"

"To have her."

"Should you feel guilty? Only if you believe in a manipulative God. One that would have Michael killed so his more righteous subject – you – can have the girl, who does seem attracted to circumcised men."

"Do I kill you now or wait until we get to Israel? Then it won't be murder but justifiable homicide."

"Steve, I'm happy for you, I really am. And if she likes your bed, and what you have to offer, good for both of you. In all

243

honesty, I do think it a bit unusual how she seems so attracted to Jewish guys."

"Just lucky, I guess. Her beautiful looks hide a deep-well of understanding. Hard to explain."

"'Deep well of understanding' BS. Let me translate. S-e-x."

"That, too, I admit. I imagine you and Rebecca do a bit more than just hold hands."

"So, are you abandoning Israel and the IDF, staying in the states, getting married?"

"No."

"Is she giving up architecture school, converting to Judaism, and moving to Israel?"

"No."

"I give up. What's the answer?"

"We'll string it out, see what happens. I've invited her to come with us to Israel in June, to stay for a while before I have to report to the Army. But she has a summer internship at a prestigious Chicago architecture firm, and can't leave the country, even for a week. So it will end – physically, at least – when I fly to Israel."

"I sense a titanic battle looming in Steve Mandelbaum's brain. Your love for Israel and your apparent love for this *shiksa*. Which is going to win?"

Steve did not respond.

"I'm not trying to be cruel, really, I'm not. I'm in love with Rebecca, and have asked her to marry me too many times to count. Can't imagine that I would give her up to join the IDF."

"That's because you don't give a shit about Israel."

"Right, right. In your warped mind only Americans who give up everything to join the IDF care about the country. The truth is, Rebecca's Jewish, and would move there with me if we both felt that strongly. I don't see Amanda ever having that passion. You're in a pickle, Steve. I don't know what else to say."

"David, I'll work it out. Let's get this damn book published."

# FORTY-TWO

# Good and Bad News

Two months after the Hillel bombing, Lester Zimmerman bounded into President Hightower's office.

"Richard, is it true what I just heard?"

"That I'm retiring this year?"

"Yes."

"It's true. Better retire now than be fired."

"Fired?"

"Without a doubt. Have a seat." Zimmerman grabbed a nearby chair.

"By announcing my retirement for the end of this academic year, I can preserve some dignity."

"Are you sure the Board wants you out?"

"Lester, I've spared you the hate mail, the letters, the slander. Even if the Board has confidence in my leadership, there is no way they can keep me as president. A man who presided over not one but two student murders. Think about that."

"Awful, bad luck."

"Maybe so, but my going is inevitable. Now they can appoint

a new president, who will be able to take over as early as this June."

"But they know you're not responsible. I mean firing you would be for optics, not because you are in any way responsible."

"I originally thought so also, but now I have some doubt."

"Doubt?"

"One professor wrote me, a friend actually, a long letter in which he outlined his perception. That I have allowed anti-Semitism to fester on campus. He points out BDS as just one example. There was that incident five years ago with Professor Moussa."

"Yes, the FBI's prime suspect. Still in Egypt, as far as we know."

"And other instances that never reached the legal office. None of which I had anything to do with, but as my friend pointed out, I never spoke publicly about them either, never made my position clear. In the name of 'free speech,' he wrote, I allowed 'hate speech' to fester."

"Your friend thinks you should have canceled free speech?"

"No, no. He thinks I should have been more vocal in condemning anti-Semitic events that kept popping up on campus. So, in that sense, I have failed."

"I doubt you're any different from other university presidents."

"Probably not. It's a national problem."

"You're how old?"

"Sixty."

"Kind of young to retire. Financially, okay?"

"We're fine. Ruth has a good medical practice, and she doesn't plan to retire for at least another five years. And here's the irony. I've received several enquiries from other colleges about their own BDS activity, and been asked to come in to help advise them. As a paid consultant, no less. So, I may end up being busy in that regard. All in all, retirement is not going to be a difficult period for us."

"Actually, I came in to give you the latest news. Some good and some bad."

"Give me the good news first."

"The FBI found Geddy's murderer and his accomplice, the driver of the car."

"That's great. How'd they do it?"

"Long story short. They had surveillance video of the Muslim-cultural Students Association house, and in week prior to Geddy's murder it showed the same black Honda SUV outside. Still no readable ID on the license plate, but the top of the SUV showed some luxury design feature that Honda had manufactured in only a few hundred cars of that year's model. They tracked everyone sold in this area, which came to only a handful. From those registrations, they got the license plates, which were then filed to police precincts nationwide."

"It sounds like amazing detective work."

"Yeah, it gets even better. They found the car in California. The guy driving it had bought it from a local dealer only the week before. They got the name of the person who sold it to the dealer, and turns out he had bought it from *another* guy, at a local Marriott Hotel."

"And so they found the original seller?"

"Yes, from the Marriott Hotel's credit card information, and surveillance footage in the Marriott parking lot. They found him, but he was only the driver. I don't know how they did it, but they got him to id the actual shooter, who was promptly arrested. They are both in jail in San Diego."

"That is good news. So that's four arrests, the first two from the Muslim-cultural Students Association, and now these two."

"Yes, and a bit of good news is that none of them are students or faculty or have anything to do with Great Lakes University. The two arrested in the Students Association were out-of-staters, supposedly doing a survey of our Muslim students, but really PLO operatives. The FBI thinks that was all arranged by Moussa. They think they hid the suicide bomber in one of the Township's hotels. Anyway, none of this was known to anyone associated with the school. So, it's all beginning to make sense.

"The FBI is certain the Arab kid was not from the States, but came from the West Bank, one of the PLO-controlled territories. Area A, as they call it. There was a plot to bring in these young suicide bombers, whose families would be willing accomplices. Now, you ready for this? The FBI could find no entry point into the US for this kid. No name on any passenger manifest, no profile that fit at any official entry points."

"So, how'd he get in?"

"Guess."

"The southern border?"

"Bingo. Hundreds of illegal immigrants from the middle east have entered the U.S. over that border. The ones with connections are immediately picked up and transported to safe places. There may be dozens more like this kid."

"And you said the families are willing accomplices?"

"Yes, the kid's family was no doubt paid by the PLO. Do you know how much money the PLO spends on 'pay to slay'?"

"No idea"

"I looked it up. Over three hundred million dollars a year. Two categories of payment. For prisoners who are incarcerated, and for families of martyrs. You kill a Jew in Israel, and if you are caught and imprisoned, or killed by the IDF, your family gets a bundle of dough. It works over there, but obviously would not work well in this country."

"God, I hope not."

"So, the plan was to import these suicide bombers, and perhaps the Hillel bomber was the first. The plot unraveled a bit when our student Michael Solomon hacked Geddy's computer. We think Geddy was killed because the masterminds figured he might be a double agent, so to speak. First, he communicates with Michael on that Zoom call, which reveals Abu Moussa as a possible operative. Then his computer is hacked, exposing correspondence no one is ever supposed to see. Perhaps there were other things that made the overlords suspicious. From my perspective Geddy was always a loyal terrorist, but they didn't want to take a chance."

"Okay, that's good news. And the bad news?"

"We've just been served with a ten-million-dollar lawsuit by Michael Solomon's parents."

"Did you say ten million?"

"Yes, a nice round number. The lawsuit blames the University for his death, claiming gross negligence in shutting down the BDS plot to blow up Hillel. They've hired Sullivan and Cromwell, a top New York law firm. Obviously, my office is not equipped to fight this lawsuit, so we'll need to hire our own law firm. I have one in mind, but need your permission to go ahead. It'll cost a bundle, of course."

"What chance does the lawsuit have?"

"Excellent, I'm afraid. I anticipate we'll end up settling for less than ten mill. But we first have to reply, and go through all the motions. I wasn't thinking this when I walked in, but what you told me about all the hate mail and letters you received, and the board's anticipated firing if you didn't resign, that will come out in any deposition you give. It will just confirm the lawsuit's contention that our university was negligent. It's the kind of testimony that sways juries."

"So I will be deposed?"

"Most definitely. And you'll have to disclose everything. Then there's the pictures of Michael's body parts on the lawn near Hillel. If the trial proceeds, a single large picture of them will sit on an easel in the front of the courtroom. What jury is going to deny our culpability? And you can be sure each selected juror will have one or more children."

"How much do you think the family will settle for?"

"My hunch, if I had to guess. Five million."

"Ouch."

## FORTY-THREE

# April Warming

Spring brought warmer weather, with the last vestiges of snow melted. David and Steve arranged their trip to Israel, but would not depart from Great Lakes together. The plan was for David and Rebecca to fly to New York, where she would meet his brother and see some sites. While there they also planned a trip to meet Michael's parents in Brooklyn. Through the lawsuit, Michael's parents had learned the names of his college friends, and contacted David. They had something to give him.

Steve planned to meet David and Rebecca in the United Airlines boarding area at Newark International, for flight 942 to Ben-Gurion Airport.

Toward the end of the month Steve called David with "some good news."

"David, do you remember the last time you flew to Israel?"

"Sure, in high school."

"Do you remember the airport?"

"No, not really."

"Well, it's busy and crowded. You can enter the country

either as an international traveler, with long line at Foreign Passport Control, or with an Israeli passport, and no line."

"So, what's the big deal, Steve?"

"My commitment to make Aliyah gives me a special visa. I'll be met at the airport and taken through Israel passport control."

"That's great. We'll meet you in baggage claim."

"That may not be necessary."

"What?"

"If I was traveling with family, they could come with me through Israeli Passport Control. So I asked, what about good friends, who are Jewish and are considering making Aliya?"

"You did? We are not considering Aliyah."

"Yes, you are. So is Rebecca. It's just a consideration, no commitment. When we exit the plane, an Israeli agent will meet me. He will take me through Israeli Passport Control. That agent may or may not allow you and Rebecca to come with me. I was told it's up to the agent who meets me. However, for you and Rebecca to even be considered, before the flight they need your passport numbers and a photo ID. This is a brand-new program, and it may not last, but for now it's worth a try. With your passport information, they run a check, and if you pass they give what's called a 'companion visa.' Without that, the Ben-Gurion agent can't even consider letting you come along with me. With the companion visa, he may. So, it's worth a chance."

"I see. Then what do we need to do?"

"Just photograph your passport page with the picture, and send it in via email. That's all. Yours and Rebecca's."

"No obligation to make Aliyah?"

"Hell, no. It's a lot more complicated than that, I assure you."

"Okay, I'll ask Rebecca."

FORTY-FOUR

# In Defense of Great Lakes University

Great Lakes University hired the Chicago firm of Kincaid and
Wolinsky to defend against the Solomons' lawsuit, which was
filed in the Illinois State Court. Before any depositions, the firm
filed a motion to dismiss, on the following grounds.

- The FBI knew about the risk of a terrorist attack
  based on foreign intelligence, and informed the
  school administration. The school administration
  could not possibly know about the risk before the FBI.
- The school administration, including the office of the
  president and the legal office, worked hand in hand
  with the FBI from the very beginning.
- "BDS for Justice" is a school-sanctioned club, similar
  to BDS clubs in many other U.S. colleges and
  universities. The school is impartial in its sanctioning,
  and also supports the Jewish organization Hillel and
  clubs with various political agendas.
- Mr. Geddy participated in open discussions on
  campus about the Israeli-Palestinian conflict, and

until his contact with student Michael Solomon, gave no suspicion of a plot to inflict physical harm on any students.

- Mr. Solomon turned over information found on Mr. Geddy's computer to the school's legal office, which then sent it to the FBI.
- At all times, the school administration acted in a responsible manner and relied on the FBI to pursue the possibility of a terrorist attack.
- The lawsuit is without merit, and should be dismissed.

A rebuttal to the dismissal petition was then filed by the plaintiffs' firm, Sullivan and Cromwell.

- The defendant's motion to dismiss is premature and without merit. Depositions have not yet been taken, evidence not yet presented. We affirm that discovery will reveal that Great Lakes University fostered a culture of anti-Semitism, and made it a welcome location for foreign operatives to plot a terrorist attack.
- The school administration had numerous opportunities to speak out against hate speech, right wing extremists marching with their students, and other activities that allowed a plot to fester.
- Two students of the school have been murdered. Dismissal of the plaintiffs' claim would send a message that such murders, while not routine, are "no one's fault," and just the everyday risk of attending an elite university. The court should allow this case to proceed, so the evidence can be presented to an impartial jury and justice be rendered.

It took the presiding state judge three days to respond: "The request for dismissal is denied. The case of Solomons vs. Great Lakes University may proceed."

## FORTY-FIVE

# Preparation for Israel

"Why do you get so involved with Steve?" asked Rebecca, while visiting David in his apartment. "We're not making Aliyah, so it's crazy to go for these special visas. I agreed to go with you for a couple of weeks after graduation, not to risk being drafted into the Israeli army."

"Rebecca, now you're acting a little nutso. Steve says there's a chance we could all go through Israeli Passport Control together, with Companion Visas. You sign nothing, no obligation. What's so bad about that?"

"Well, first things first. I told you my parents agreed to support me on this trip. Two weeks in Israel and two weeks in Europe is not cheap."

"Very smart, very good parents."

"And they will, but they want to meet you."

"Meet me? Where?"

"Here. They're coming for a visit next week, since I won't be going home before we leave for Israel."

"I'm getting two messages. They agree on the trip, but they want to meet me before committing?"

"My Mom didn't say that, exactly. It's just that they want to meet you before I leave. I can do what I want, but I won't go if for some reason they back out about covering the trip. I need their blessing."

"Rebecca, do they know we've been sleeping together?"

"Of course. I told them. It's no secret. They just want to meet the guy who's taking their daughter overseas for a month. Sounds perfectly reasonable. Don't forget, I haven't yet met your parents."

"But you will. I told you they're coming for graduation."

"And what if they don't like me?"

"Zero chance. It's probably not zero with your parents."

"I'm not concerned."

"What about the visas?"

"Promise I won't be drafted?"

"Promise."

"Okay, we can send in the passport info after their visit. We'll have plenty of time."

The visit went well. David impressed Rebecca's parents as a man with a future, a good fit should their daughter marry him. Three weeks after their visit, David's parents arrived for his graduation. Delighted he was hooking up with a Jewish girl, their only request was to "be careful" in Israel.

David's brother could not attend the graduation, but sent his congratulations, and a gift of stock – ten shares of a company he had researched for his mutual fund. David estimated the worth of the stock at about $500.

On June sixth David and Rebecca flew to New York, where they spent a few days. There was a dinner visit to his brother in Manhattan, a trip to Brooklyn to meet Michael's parents, and some sightseeing, plus one Broadway play.

On June tenth they took an Uber to Newark International, for the flight to Israel.

# FORTY-SIX

# Newark International

David and Rebecca exited the cab at Newark's International Terminal, pulled two large suitcases inside and waited in line at the United check-in desk.

"Steve should already be checked in, waiting for us. His Chicago flight was supposed to arrive half an hour ago."

"It's amazing how crowded this place is. They can't all be going to Israel."

"Hardly. Newark is one of the top airports for international departures. I flew from Newark when I went to Israel during high school."

A half hour later, their luggage checked and with boarding passes in hand, they stood in the TSA line; this took another twenty minutes to get through. Then a quarter-mile walk to the UA departure lounge for Ben-Gurion airport, which had its own security check. Finally, an hour and fifteen minutes after reaching the airport they entered the UA lounge, already filled with people for a flight that would not start boarding for another hour.

"I don't see Steve," said David, surveying the crowd.

"Well, let's get a seat. I'm sure he'll show up soon."

Just then, David felt a tap on his back, and a verbal order in a basso voice: "Your passport, please."

He turned around. "Steve! We wondered where the hell you were."

"This place is like a zoo," Steve said. "Do you know how many security checkpoints I've gone through?"

"Same as us. Israel is super careful. Let's go find some seats." They found three at the far

end of the lounge.

"I'm amazed at all the orthodox Jews on this flight," said Rebecca. "I've never seen more

than one or two in Palo Alto, and here there are dozens. All those fur hats and long coats."

"They are Haredim," said Steve.

"Haredim?"

"Yeah, the ultra-orthodox in Israel. All the men do is study the Talmud, and the women have

babies. Don't get me started."

"I'm new to this," said Rebecca. "I should learn about Israeli culture as much as possible. David, do you know about the Haredim?"

"Of course. I'm just not passionate about them like Steve."

"Passionate is not the right word," replied Steve. He looked around, as if to ensure no one could hear him but David and Rebecca. "They make up about thirteen percent of the Jewish population. They are exempt from the draft. The men study nothing in school except the Talmud. No math, no science, no vocational skills. As a result, they are virtually unemployable. Most are on welfare. Women marry early, and have an average six and a half kids, whereas the secular Israeli women have an average of two and a half. Do I need to go on?"

"I'm a little bit confused," replied Rebecca. "I thought the military was mandatory for Israeli men and women."

"Nope," said Steve. "When Ben-Gurion instituted mandatory draft after the War of Independence, there were only about 400 Talmudic students. They petitioned to be exempt from the draft and he said, 'sure, why not.' Big mistake, probably his biggest. Now it's a disaster. A huge portion of the Jewish population is uneducated, unemployable, and mostly on welfare."

"Steve," replied David, "in all honesty it's not that bad. Many of the women do work outside the home, and some of the Haredim do join the military in non-combat positions. Also, many secular Jews are supportive of the Haredim culture, and consider the study of Talmud a worthwhile activity, one that's fully in line with the Zionist ideal."

"Ah, the progressive justification. David, pardon me while I ask your girlfriend a single, simple question."

"Sure."

"Rebecca, based on what you now know about the Haredim, if they constituted ninety percent of Israel's population instead of thirteen percent, how long would the country last?"

"You mean only ten percent of the population would be serving in the military?"

"Precisely."

"Not long."

"Case closed. We're heading there."

"Okay, change of subject," said David. "What's the latest with Amanda? She's not coming over?"

"No, she can't. We'll stay I touch. She might have an opportunity at the end of the summer, when her internship ends. The problem is, I don't know where I'll be then."

"Do you have a schedule? How does one make Aliya and join the military?"

"It's a bit complicated. I have my Aliyah documents, and after settling in I'll have to visit a couple of agencies, have a physical and written test, and then they decide. The process could take a month or longer. We'll see."

"But your lodging is all secure?"

"Yeah, for a nominal rent they are putting me up with an IDF soldier who is stationed in Tel Aviv. I won't be too far from where you and Rebecca are staying. I think you said your Air B&B was on Bialik Street?"

"Yes."

"And I'm not too far away, near the intersection of Dizenghoff and Khisin St." Steve pulled out a Tel Aviv map, pointed to the locations. "I see you're a bit closer to the beach."

"Yeah, that'll be my first walk with Rebecca, to Tel Aviv beach. But I've planned some day trips for us. A tour around Tel Aviv, and one day to the Old City in Jerusalem. There's a train now, that wasn't running when I was last here. And of course, Haifa. Then go south. A guy I met at the Muss High School in Israel later made Aliyah, and now is in Ben-Gurion University in Beersheba. We'll go visit him, stay in Beersheba a couple of days, and see some sites in the Negev. So we have a lot planned."

"Good," replied Steve. "Maybe while in Israel you and Rebecca will consider making Aliyah."

"Not happening," snapped Rebecca. "I have a better chance converting to Haredim."

"Sorry, Rebecca, you can't convert," said Steve. "You have to be born into it. And if you could convert, you'd have to start having children yesterday. No more pills."

David raised his hand, a sign to stop. "Okay, enough of this trash talk."

"Speaking of trash talk," replied Steve, "How'd it go with your brother in New York? I remember you said he has some issues with Israel."

"Fine. We had dinner with him and his wife two nights ago. Did not talk politics. He's making a ton on Wall Street. Seems happy. When his kids get to school age, I'm sure they'll move to the suburbs. Probably Westchester County."

"Actually, he's a nice guy," chimed in Rebecca. "All I heard before we came here is how he's narrow-minded and ignorant about Israel."

"I never said he wasn't a nice guy. Narrow-minded people can be nice."

"I got your email about meeting the Solomons," said Steve. "Did they mention the lawsuit?"

"Actually, no. We're not part of it, thankfully. Maybe on the advice of their lawyers they were mum about it."

"Rebecca, is this your first transatlantic flight?"

"Yeah, and I'm not looking forward to it. Ten hours cramped. Ugh!"

"Well, David gave you the window seat, and I have the aisle. So, the one to suffer will be David."

"David *and* you," she replied, "when I have to go the bathroom, and jump over both seats."

"I'll be sleeping," said Steve. "Don't wake me."

# FORTY-SEVEN

# Ben-Gurion Airport

The Aliya agent, a young man wearing a kippah, met the trio just as they departed the plane. As requested, they handed over their passports, along with Steve's Aliyah visa, and David's and Rebecca's companion visas.

"Can we all go together through Israeli Passport?" asked Steve. "We were told that's possible."

"Come with me," he replied, in heavily-accented English, holding on to the passports and visas. They followed him down two long hallways, past a "No Return" sign, then to another long corridor, ending in the large hall designated "Entry for Israeli Passports."

"Looks promising," said Steve.

In front of one of the Israeli Passport Control booths the agent told them, "Wait here." He then approached a young woman sitting inside the booth and handed her the documents. Their conversation was in Hebrew.

"He could be telling her we're potential terrorists," joked David.

"Yeah, you have that reputation," responded Steve.

Just then the agent turned toward them and commanded, "Come with me." They walked past the booth and came before a large sign on the far wall, with a message in Hebrew, Arabic and English. They only understood the greeting in English.

## Welcome Home

While the agent walked ahead, David stopped, stared at the sign.

"What's the matter?" asked Rebecca.

He grabbed her hand, pulled her close to his side.

"Are you okay?" She looked up to his face, saw tears.

"Oh, David."

"Hey buddy," said Steve. "I understand. You're home. We all cry when we get here."

"I'm okay," said David, taking a tissue offered by Rebecca.

"Several yards ahead, the agent turned around and motioned to the trio. "Come, come." He led them to the designated baggage claim area for their flight, then spoke to David.

"When Mr. Mandelbaum's bag arrives, I will take him to an office to process some paperwork. It will take a while, so you and…" he paused to open Rebecca's passport, "Ms. Goldman should proceed on your own to Tel Aviv. Taxis outside can get you there in half an hour." He then handed over their passports, adding "I will keep the companion visas."

David and Rebecca thanked him, and he left the baggage area. Their suitcases arrived ten minutes later. They said goodbye to Steve, agreeing to meet in a day or two after they all got settled.

## FORTY-EIGHT

# Tel Aviv
---

Their apartment was small, a one-bedroom, 800-square foot unit on the second floor of an old Bauhaus building. The bathroom had a shower, no tub.

"This place is smaller than my dorm room," said Rebecca.

"These Bauhaus buildings are almost a hundred years old," replied David, as they unpacked. "My hunch is, they've been subdivided since the original construction. And of course, they had to add some special room."

"What's that?"

"We passed it just at the head of the stairs. Come with me."

He led Rebecca out of their apartment, past two others, to a door marked only in Hebrew. He opened the door and they entered., a ten-by-ten room with bare white walls, no furniture.

"What is this, a storage room?"

"A safe room. Every floor of every building, every home, has one. Bomb proof, or as bomb proof as it's possible to make."

"How do you possibly live in here? No toilet even."

"The bomb threats only last a few minutes. Until the iron

dome takes out the missiles. When the sirens sound, you go to the safe room. It's rarely more than fifteen minutes."

"How often does that happen?"

"Often enough. No schedule. They come from Gaza. Hamas and Islamic Jihad."

"Are you sure it's safe to walk outside?"

"Yes. There are bomb shelters anywhere. If you hear the siren warning, just duck into any building. In towns close to Gaza, every bus stop is also a bomb shelter."

"I'm getting the picture," said Rebecca.

"Good. That's why I really wanted you to come with me on this trip."

They returned to the apartment. "I wonder if Amanda got to see the insides of the buildings," said Rebecca. "Her fascination with Bauhaus seems to be more with the original design."

"Probably so. I imagine architects love to see how things are rebuilt or modified. Foundations have spent millions remodeling many of Wright's structures. Sometimes they had to change things to bring them up to code."

Rebecca sat on the bed as David finished unpacking."

"How's the mattress?"

"Squishy. Not firm like yours."

"We'll get used to it. We're both jet-lagged, but it's only one o'clock, and it'll be good to get out for a while before going to sleep. I want to show you the beach, which is only a few blocks from here."

"Good idea. Let's walk a bit. It's finally dawning on me that I'm going to be living with you for the next several weeks."

"And?"

"I mean, we've never spent more than two consecutive nights together. Now it's going to be every night."

"Sounds good to me," said David. "You want to formalize it? How do visitors get married in Israel? Is it legal?"

"I read somewhere married Jewish women can't get a divorce in Israel."

"Who's talking about divorce? First, you have to get married."

"David, I'm exhausted. Let's go for that walk."

*  *  *

They walked a few blocks and entered the Tel Aviv beach area south of the Sheraton Hotel.

"Wow!" exclaimed Rebecca, "I had no idea the beach was so nice. And look at all those people playing volleyball, surfing, sailing. This is more inviting than any beach I've been to in California."

"Yeah, Tel Aviv is a big tourist destination for Europeans. A short plane ride and you can stay in a five-star hotel, eat in great restaurants, and enjoy the beach." He pointed south. "See those buildings jutting out into the sea? With the clock tower? Know what that area is?"

"No."

"Jaffa. An ancient Arab port, here thousands of years before Tel Aviv was founded in the early twentieth century. It's now an artists' colony, and a neighborhood of Tel Aviv. We'll walk through there tomorrow. Now, let's go north on the boardwalk for a bit, then head back to the hotel and get some sleep."

"David, I just realized something."

"What?"

"There's no food in the apartment. Not even coffee or anything for breakfast. And very little toilet paper. We'll need to stop and pick up a few things."

"Good catch. You can see I'm clueless about domestic affairs. Reminds me of a famous quote by Jane Austen."

"I know this one," she said. "*Pride and Prejudice*. Go ahead. I have the perfect rejoinder."

"Oh, never mind."

"No, *mind*. Let's hear it."

"Okay, if you insist." He raised his voice as if giving a public speech. 'It is a truth universally acknowledged, that a single man in possession of a good fortune, must be in want of a wife.'"

"Right. So let me know when you have a good fortune."

"Okay, you win this one. There should be a couple of grocery places on the way back to our apartment. I have shekels. We'll carry as much as we can."

* * *

They fell asleep in the late afternoon, slept most of the night and awakened before the sun rose. After taking showers, Rebecca cooked some eggs and toast.

"So, for our first full day in Israel," said David, "a private tour, led by yours truly, mostly on foot. We'll walk south to Jaffa, then to the Florentin neighborhood where we'll see some amazing graffiti on building walls, then, up to Sarona Market for lunch. From there to Rabin Square, where Prime Minister Rabin was assassinated in 1995. Then on to the Ben Gurion House, which we should get to before it closes. Finally, a walk over to Independence Park, a great little park by the Hilton. It will be all-day tour. We'll use taxis when needed."

"Sounds exciting. And the next day? That's planned as well?"

"A train ride to Jerusalem, where we'll tour the Old City and visit the Western Wall. Again, your same excellent guide."

"You remember all this from your high school trip here? How to get around?"

"Full disclosure. I've been studying guidebooks, and I have a city map. It's easy. When I was last here just about everyone in all these tourist places spoke English. We shouldn't have any problem."

* * *

After touring Jaffa and Florentin, they took a taxi to the Sarona Market.

"I see why this place is so popular," said Rebecca. "So many little food stalls and restaurants to choose from."

"Yeah," replied David. "The guidebook says over ninety. Let's walk this way. I have my eye on a place that serves falafels."

"Okay, just make sure there are tables nearby where we can sit."

"There are, no problem."

He found the stall advertising falafels and they waited in a short line to order. The large menu on the wall was in Hebrew, with the prices in Shekels. "I order mine plain," he told Rebecca. "I never was a fan of hummus or the other stuff they put in, which I know you like. Should I just order the combo for you?"

"Yes, that'll be good. Can you read any of the menu?"

"Not a word."

Behind the counter one young man was taking orders, and another three young men were busy cooking. All wore kippahs. When David's turn came, the counter man said, in Hebrew: "Your order?" David assumed the question and gave his response in English: two falafels, one plain, one with everything, plus cokes.

"Herzog!" yelled the counter man. "English."

Herzog stepped over, asked David to repeat the order, then translated it into Hebrew. The order placed, David inserted his credit card into the reader. The whole transaction took less than two minutes. "This must happen a lot," said David. "They don't miss a beat."

A few minutes later they had their food and sat at a small table. "It *is* good," said Rebecca. "Nice to sit for a while. Where to next?"

"Rabin Square, just a short walk, maybe twenty minutes."

A few minutes later Rebecca's phone beeped. "I have an email. Let me check."

She pulled out her phone, read the email, then handed it over to David. "Read this. From attorney Zimmerman."

He read the message. "Well, I'm not surprised they want your deposition. They'll probably depose all of Michael's friends, to get a full picture of what went down. I'm surprised I haven't been notified." Just then his phone beeped. The email was the same.

"Zimmerman's been busy," said Rebecca. "Do you think he sent the same message to Amanda?"

"Without a doubt. Well, there's no hurry. I'll schedule mine for when we return to the states. You should, too."

"Where do you think this case is headed? How can the school be responsible?"

"A good legal question. When you join the plaintiff's bar, you'll have some insight."

"Defense bar. Defense."

"Whatever," sighed David, as he finished the last of his plain felafel.

## FORTY-NINE

# Jerusalem

The train from Tel Aviv to Jerusalem took only forty minutes. En route David gave Rebecca a map of the Old City, and pointed out the four quarters, and how they differed. From the Jerusalem station they took a cab to Jaffa gate, the most visited entrance to the Old City.

"This is where most tourists enter," said David, as they exited the cab.

"How many entrances are there?"

"I think seven or eight. We'll walk from here to the Jewish Quarter."

Past the gate, David stopped and asked her to look at the map. "So, tell me which quarter we're now in."

She scanned the colored map, found the Jaffa Gate. "Looks like we're between the Armenian and Christian Quarters."

"Right. And which direction should we walk to get to the Jewish Quarter?"

She pointed straight ahead.

"Right again. Lead the way."

"I see why you wanted to enter this way," she said.

"Why?"

"We're going to walk on David Street."

"Really? Let me see."

She handed him the map. "Well, I never checked the names of these streets. Just a coincidence. I thought you'd be intrigued by the colorful passageway to the Western Wall."

He handed back the map and they continued walking down the, narrow street, crowded with tourists. On either side were dozens of kiosks selling souvenirs. She stopped at one to look at the merchandise, more out of curiosity than intending to buy anything.

"Rebecca, there's nothing here you need, trust me. It's mostly drek."

"David you're too jaded. The scenery is amazing. There's nothing like this street where we live. Let me take a selfie." She took out her iPhone and snapped a picture of herself and David with the street as backdrop.

"I think you'll find the Western Wall a better place to take pictures."

They continued walking, Rebecca resisting the urge to stop and explore racks of souvenirs. In another ten minutes the street ended at a large plaza, and before them was the Temple Mount, one of its walls being the Western Wall, a scared Jewish site.

"Wow," she commented. "There it is. Didn't know it is so large."

"Just one wall of the ancient Jewish Temple," said David. "The gold dome you see above it is the Dome of the Rock, said to be the third most religious Arab site in the world. Jews can't go there."

"I read the Western Wall is segregated, so we can't walk up to it together?"

"True See the division?" He pointed to a fence perpendicular to the wall. "The small area to the right is for women; the larger area to the left is for men. We'll split up there. The custom is to write a request for God, stuff it in the cracks, and trust that it will be read. When you get up close, you'll see hundreds of pieces of paper stuffed in cracks. I brought a pen and some paper for you." He handed her the items.

"You've been here before. Was your last request answered?"

"I don't remember. I was in high school. May have been something stupid. Probably was."

They walked to the dividing point and David entered the men's section, Rebecca the women's section. David took out his phone to get a wide-angle picture of orthodox Jews praying, and tourists writing notes – wishes – to place in the crevices. Then he wrote his note, stuffed it in a crack between stones.

After a few minutes David and Rebecca met in the common area.

"What did you write?" he asked.

"You first."

"Okay. That you and I will live happily ever after, together."

"Do you think God will grant that wish?"

"If there is a God."

"I've never heard such doubt before."

"Never mind. What did you write?"

"That Israel should thrive, and the Palestinians should work to live in peace with the Jews."

"What will God do with that wish?"

"If there is a God?"

"Rebecca, my brain is reeling from hunger. Let's go have lunch. There's lots more to see after we eat." He took her hand and led her back to the Armenia quarter, to a restaurant his guidebook recommended.

FIFTY

# Some Important News

While David and Rebecca were returning from Jerusalem, Steve received a text message on his phone.

> Please call. Something important. It's 10 am here, so 5 pm there? Love, Amanda

He replied,

> I'm just leaving American consulate office. Some routine paperwork. Will call within the hour. Love, Steve

\* \* \*

Back in his apartment bedroom, Steve called.

"Hi" she answered. "What time is it there?"

"Quarter to six. I miss you. What's important?"

"I'm pregnant."

"What? Are you sure? How'd that happen?"

"I'm sure. The test is positive, and I skipped my last period. As to the second question, how do you think?"

"I…I thought you were on the pill."

"I quit after Michael's death. Didn't restart until that first night with you. Don't you remember, you used a condom? Then you didn't, the next time. The pill doesn't take full effect right away."

"How many weeks are you?"

"Five, best guess."

"What are you going to do?"

"Do you mean, have an abortion?"

"Uh, yeah."

"What do you want me to do?"

"Me?"

"Yes, the baby's yours. What do you think I should do?"

"On, God, Amanda. I'm thousands of miles away, about to join the Israeli military. You're training to become an architect. We didn't plan on this happening. So…"

"So? So what? Are you saying I should have an abortion?"

"You're busting my balls. Yes, that seems the logical thing to do."

He heard soft crying on the phone.

"Amanda?"

"I can't kill my baby."

*I can't believe this is happening.* "At five weeks the fetus is not viable. It's not killing." *What am I thinking? She was brought up Catholic.*

"I want you to come home. We'll get married, have the baby, then we can decide if we are really meant for each other. First, the baby needs a father."

"What about your architecture career?"

"I'll finish. It's been done before. My parents will help."

"Have you told them?"

"Not yet."

"Amanda, what if I can't return?"

"Why can't you?"

"I don't know. This Aliyah and IDF process is more complicated than I realized. I've signed lots of documents. I don't honestly know what my immigration status is at this moment, or whether I've fully committed to the IDF. It's a bit complicated."

"Steve, you're an American citizen, for God sakes. They can't lock you up. It's your decision."

"Are you committed to not having an abortion, then? There's still plenty of time. Up until the second trimester, is my understanding."

"Yes."

"Yes?"

"Yes, no abortion."

"Let me check with immigration to get things clarified. I will get back to you soon."

"When?"

"Just give me at least a day."

"Steve, do you remember how much we said we loved each other?"

"Yes."

"Do you still feel that way?"

"Yes"

"Or do you love Israel more?"

"Not a fair question. I'll call you sometime tomorrow."

"Okay." More audible tears. "Bye."

Steve clicked off. *Shit.*

# FIFTY-ONE

# Meetup with Steve

On the train back to Tel Aviv David received a text message from Steve: "Where are you guys? Can we meet sometime tomorrow?" He showed the message to Rebecca.

"It's okay with me," she said. "What else did you have planned?"

"A couple of more places I want to take you to see in Tel Aviv. One of them is the Bullet Factory. If we meet him for lunch, we can still go there. The others we can skip. I'll text him. We're going to Haifa the following day."

"Do you know of a quiet place for lunch?"

"What about that café down the street from our apartment? I noticed they have outdoor tables on the side. Very little street traffic so should be quiet. We can eat there."

"Sounds good."

"Okay, I'll text him."

\* \* \*

Steve walked over from his apartment to the Bialik Street Café. He found Rebecca and David seated outside, at one of several tables beside the restaurant, some distance from the street. Three menus were spread on the table.

"Long time, no see," said David. "Have a seat. How's Aliya going?"

"Lot of paperwork. What have you guys been up to?"

David recounted their excursions over the previous two days.

"Ah, tourists, what a nice life," said Steve, picking up his menu. "What's the food situation here? Let's see. Okay, pizza. That's good. This meal, by the way, is on me."

"What's the occasion?" asked David. "Are you now officially in the IDF, on salary?"

"No. The occasion is, I'm going to bend your ear, take advantage of your wisdom and expertise. Yours and Rebecca's."

"Oh, some intrigue," said Rebecca. "About the IDF?"

The waiter came and they ordered pizzas all around.

"So, what's the story?" asked David.

"Amanda's pregnant."

Reflexively, Rebecca and David turned to look at each other, then back at Steve.

"How far along?" asked Rebecca.

"Five weeks, maybe six. No more."

"So, yours?"

"Yes. Apparently so."

"And I assume," said David, "totally not planned. So, I am seeing a conundrum."

"Call it what you will," replied Steve. "She does not want an abortion. She wants to have the child. She wants the child's father to return to the U.S. She is not flexible."

"I can see pregnant women are like that," said Rebecca. "Sorry, just had to throw that in. Are you locked into the IDF? Can you leave?"

"Rebecca, that's not the question," said David. "The question is, does he want to leave." David opened his palms toward Steve, imploring an answer.

"At this moment, I am not locked into the IDF. I've signed a bunch of immigration papers, and if I left it might create a mess if I ever tried to again make Aliya, but legally I'm not locked in."

"So why don't you go home and take care of domestic affairs?" offered Rebecca. "I'm not grasping the conflict."

"I grasp it," said David. "He feels strongly about his commitment to Israel, maybe even more than his commitment to Amanda and their child."

"If true, David, do you condemn that feeling?"

"Hey, I'm not making value judgments. Just trying to clarify your situation. I don't see how Rebecca and I can help, though. It's a decision you have to make on your own."

"No opinion? No support? No advice?"

He's getting angry, thought David. "I don't know what you want us to say. I appreciate that you feel Israel needs you, and that Amanda needs you as well. What do you want from us?"

Rebecca nodded in agreement.

"You know," replied Steve, now with some anger in his tone, "you two sit here in judgment. You fuck every night, traipse around all the tourist sites during the day, and have no concern about safety because the IDF is there, protecting you. I don't think you give a shit about the country. You'll be gone tomorrow. Who's going to defend it? You aren't," he said with a finger jabbed at David, "and you're not," the same finger jabbed at Rebecca.

"Steve, calm down," pleaded Rebecca. "We're trying to help. We're your friends. You don't need to use that kind of language, or accuse us of things that aren't true. I have a great passion for Israel, much more so after meeting David and coming here, if only for a couple of days so far. Just because we're not making Aliya —"

"Fuck Aliya," interrupted Steve. "I am so sick of these

goddamn justifications for this, for that. You were in BDS, for God sakes. If Michael hadn't rescued you, you could have been killed. What about all the Israelis here, who can be attacked anytime by terrorists? Do you give a shit about them?"

David stood. "Steve, you've got to quit this tirade. Stop picking on Rebecca. You're acting a little bit irrational. Please calm down." Other diners looked over at their table.

"Steve, people are hearing you," said Rebecca. "Please stop."

Steve stood opposite David, only the small table between them. Just then the waiter arrived with the pizzas, placed them on the table and left.

"Let's sit, Steve, have some lunch. We can resume this afterwards."

"You know what? I'm suddenly not hungry. I've lost my appetite. I'leaving. Sorry about the lunch. I had good intentions." Steve walked away, toward Bialik Street.

David sat, staring at three small pizzas. "We've lost him."

"He's crazy. Attacking me like that."

"He's always had an irrational streak, like a messianic passion. How he ever got hooked up with Amanda, I don't understand. And to get her pregnant – do you think she planned that?"

Rebecca shook her head. "Definitely not. Not with her career goals, and knowing he was going overseas. Probably she wasn't on the pill long enough. What do you think he'll do?"

"I honestly don't know. And to think he was my college roommate and at one time a good friend. Now I'm done with him, that's for sure. If he comes calling again, I won't discuss the issue. You shouldn't either."

"David, I don't want to be within 100 feet of him. He scares me."

## FIFTY-TWO

# Bahá'í Gardens

The next day Rebecca and David boarded the intercity bus for a ninety-minute ride to Haifa. David chose a bus over the train, as he thought it would afford a better view of the countryside, with stops in Netanya and Caesarea. Once in Haifa they would take a guided tour of Bahá'í Gardens, which he had signed up for online.

After leaving the station Rebecca reflected on recent events. "Sometimes I feel like this is a movie, and we're in the middle. How's it going to end?"

"You mean with Steve?"

"Not just Steve. The lawsuit by Michael's parents. The trial of Geddy's murderers. Professor Shapiro's book, when it comes out – will anyone read it? The future of Great Lakes University under the new president. And us."

"Glad you added that last bit."

"No, I mean us, our careers. You a doctor, me a lawyer. Where will we end up?"

"Together, I hope."

\* \* \*

After leaving Netanya, they rode to Caesarea, site of ancient Roman ruins, now a national park on the Mediterranean. Though not visible from the bus. David showed her some pictures on his phone. "If we have time one day, we'll come back here to tour the ruins. I did that in high school. Actually, quite interesting."

"Can you rent a car in Israel?"

"Of course, but at my age, I don't think so. I think you have to be twenty-five. Why?"

"Just curious. If we were driving, we could take a quick stop now."

"Well, maybe. But it's not a quick stop. There's actually quite a bit to see. I have a different idea, one that takes advantage of the fact we're not driving."

"What?"

"All those questions you asked before, about how things are going to end. Let's write our own answers for one year from now. Best guesses. Then compare our answers."

"If you want."

"I have paper and a couple of pens in my backpack." David opened his small backpack and pulled out a notebook, plus two pens.

"You always carry those things?"

"On campus, yes. Never know when they might come in handy." He tore off two pages, placed them top of his backpack and on each wrote identical headings.

Prediction at 1 yr.
Steve – where? with Amanda?
Lawsuit – settled? Won? amount?
Murder trial – Outcome?
Shapiro book? – Reviews? Reception.

New GLU pres. – good? Bad?

Us - ???? (be specific)

He handed one sheet and a pen to Rebeca. "Use the notebook for a flat surface. I'll use part of my backpack."

"Give me some time to think."

"No problem. We don't stop for another half hour. Let's compare notes in about ten minutes."

Rebecca, sitting by the window, occasionally glanced outside, then returned to her scribbling. David, for his part, kept eyes glued on his writing.

After ten minutes he said, "Okay, let's compare. First category, Steve. Your prediction?"

"He returned home and married Amanda. However, the marriage is rocky, and he's considering leaving and coming back to Israel."

"I predicted he stays in Israel, and she has the baby anyway. He lives with guilt and volunteers for every dangerous mission. Soon he will be killed fighting terrorists, and declared a national hero."

"You're not writing a novel, David. Basically, we disagree on this one. What about the lawsuit. I predict the parents settle for several million."

"Bingo, on that one. I wrote five million. See?" He shows her his number. "What about the murder trial. I predict they each get fifteen years to life."

"A year from now," said Rebecca, there is still no trial. There are all sorts of legal complications, including the fact that two of the defendants are not from the U.S. They are still in prison, though."

"Plausible, I guess," said David. "What about the book?"

"A dud., Ignored by mainstream media. A few obscure reviews in some far-right publications. The campus newspaper calls it a 'hit job,' a sad commentary on the life of a popular professor."

"Look what I wrote." He shows her his scribble. "NYT bestseller. Rocks on campus nationwide."

"You really believe that?"

"Why not? It's a great book."

"So far, we agree on two, disagree on two. The new president?"

"Positive," said David. "Restoring the campus reputation through civility and hard work."

"Okay, I agree. I wrote 'doing good job, respected.'"

"Which brings us to…*us*. What did you write?"

She pointed to her written comment: "Not married. Not pregnant."

"Two negatives? No positives?"

"Considering Amanda's situation, that's pretty positive. Let's see what you wrote."

He showed her his one-word response: "Engaged."

"Well," she replied, "that's more realistic than married."

"This was fun. I'm going to keep these pages, refer to them in a year."

Most tourists only see the Bahá'í Gardens from a lookout on Yefe Nof Street. Buses daily park on the street, disgorge their tourists who can then easily view the garden terraces far below, surrounding the Shrine of the Bab. After pictures taken of the scenery – and selfies – they reboard their bus to continue their tour.

To walk the gardens, see them up close, you have to take a guided tour. It's free, but you must sign up, as David did. They joined seventeen other tourists and their guide, a young woman who explained the restrictions. "No walking on the grass or touching the flowers. Please stay on the paths. You make take pictures, of course. Follow me."

David carried a light backpack, and Rebecca had a fanny pack around her waist. They had rehearsed their plan, but how it would work out on the actual ground was unpredictable.

About twenty minutes into the tour, they stood at the back of the group, on a gravel path, furthest from the guide. Next to the path lay a beautiful flower bed. David nodded to Rebecca. She reached into his backpack and pulled out a small urn, eight inches tall, with a screw-on cap and handed it to David. He walked beside the flowers, unseen by the guide, Rebecca took out her phone and began to video his movements. David unscrewed the cap and spread its contents among the flowers: fine grain black dust. Back and forth he waved the upended urn, until all the dust lay on the ground.

He screwed the cap back on the urn, walked up toward Rebecca's phone, acting like just another tourist taking a video of their trip. He spoke into the phone, ending a two-minute clip he would soon email to Michael's parents.

"Goodbye, Michael. You're home now."

# FIFTY-THREE

# Beersheba

Beersheba
Beer-Sheba
Be'er Sheva
Beer Sheva

You'll find several different spellings of the largest city in the Negev Desert, seventy-five miles southwest of Jerusalem. Often referred to "Capital of the Negev," Beersheba is Israel's fourth most populous metro area, after Tel Aviv, Jerusalem, and Haifa.

Beersheba is not a top tourist destination, and likely not on the itinerary for first time visitors to Israel. David had visited the city following his semester at Alexander Muss highs school. It was one stop on a wide-ranging tour of the country, undertaken with his buddy Gerald Fishman, another Muss student. Gerald wanted to investigate Beersheba's Ben Gurion University, telling David, "I might apply there for college."

After Muss, both students returned to the US, to finish their senior year of high school. Gerald decided to make Aliya and become an Israeli citizen. That meant serving in the IDF before college. David, though passionate about Israel, had no desire to move to Israel, and applied to Great Lakes University.

* * *

The day after their Haifa trip, David and Rebecca boarded a Tel Aviv bus to Beersheba, where they would spend two nights in a hotel. On the day of arrival they would tour Beersheba with Gerald, now a student in Ben Gurion. The next day, Gerald planned a day trip to Sderot, a town twenty-five miles west of Beersheba, very near the Gaza border.

On the bus Rebecca noted many Arabs, and remarked. "I can't get over how Israel is so *not* apartheid. Nowhere in Tel Aviv or Jerusalem was there any evidence. In fact, the only place of discrimination was the Western Wall. The orthodox keep the women and men separate. But that's not apartheid."

"Israel's not a lot of things you hear back in the states," David replied. "We've pretty much covered that, but it's always nice to hear your revelations. Maybe when we get back you can rejoin BDS and tell them the truth."

"And be killed," she said, without a trace of irony.

"Yeah, I guess not a good idea."

"I know you told me your friend's in medical school, but if you went to high school together, and you're just going to enter med school…I guess the math doesn't compute."

"I thought I explained it. Maybe you were sleeping. Gerald made Aliya after high school, and joined the IDF for two years. All Israeli Jews – at least all but the ultra-orthodox – have to join the military out of high school. Usually women do two years, men three years. However, Gerald was able to shorten his IDF obligation when he got into medical school. The confusion is that Israel's medical schools are six years, and combine undergraduate with formal medical education in those six years."

"I see. So when you entered your junior year at Great Lakes, he was just entering college. So now he's just finished his sopho-more year of the combined program."

"Right. He's likely had no formal medical school lectures. They will begin his third year, while I'm in my first year of the four-year medical school in the states."

"So you two will have a lot more in common than just high school."

"Yeah, we'll both get our medical degree the same time. I don't know what he plans to train for. Maybe surgery, I think."

"And where's he from?"

"Georgia."

"Atlanta?"

"No, Savannah."

"Savannah? That's interesting. I've never been there. Nor Charleston. But I read about them. Civil War history."

"I've not been there either. I'll put it on our travel list. It's apparently very popular now with tourists."

"There are a lot of Jews in Savannah?"

"I asked him once. He said about three thousand. Three synagogues, and one of them goes back to the nineteenth century. An old city, apparently very beautiful."

"Does he have a Geogia accent?"

"He did. Though now he speaks Hebrew, so don't know how that will come across accent-wise."

"What do his parents do? Oh, let me guess. Doctor-lawyer. Or, lawyer-doctor."

"Try again. Not even close."

"I'm lost. Are there other careers for parents?"

"Yeah, it's called the business world."

"Owns a store?"

"Nope. Runs an import-export business out of the Savannah port, called Fishman Brothers. His mother works for the company, though I don't know her job there."

"So, they have money?"

"I assume so. But Gerald will have no part of it, I mean the business. He's committed to stay in Israel."

The bus trip was two hours, and with stops they arrived at noon. The hotel was only a block from the station, so with suitcases on wheels, they were able to walk there.

After getting settled David called Gerald. He would meet them in the lobby and begin their tour of Beersheba.

\* \* \*

David and Rebecca were in the hotel lobby when Gerald bounced in, a slim young man wearing a kippah and sporting a short beard. The two guys met and immediately hugged. Then, holding David at arm's length, Gerald drawled, "Well, look at you, you finally made it home." Looking toward Rebecca: "And this must be your lovely wife."

"Not yet, Gerald. Not yet."

Gerald grabbed Rebecca's hand. "David's told me all about you. So glad to meet you."

"Nice to meet you, too," she replied.

"Well, ready for the tour? My car's right outside. It's a small Hyundai."

\* \* \*

David sat in front and Rebecca in the back seat. Gerald proved to be an able guide, knowledgeable about the history of the region. "I've given this tour before," he said, "just so you know. To my parents, and a cousin who visited last year. If I talk too much, tell me to shut up."

"Do you like living in Beersheba?" asked Rebecca.

"Love it. Much quieter than Tel Aviv or Jerusalem. And cheaper, also. I live in a dorm, but next year I'm going to look for a flat."

"Are you worried about the missiles from Gaza?" she asked. "I know you're close to the border."

"We've never been hit. We trust the iron dome to take out any that come close. But of course it's always a concern. Any that could hit us could also reach Jerusalem or Tel Aviv. One thing you can say. Hamas is not stupid. A direct hit on any of the cities would bring severe retribution."

"How close have you been to Gaza?" she asked.

"As close as we're going to get tomorrow. Sderot and the surrounding area, about a mile away. You'll see. Safe rooms everywhere, including in the indoor children's playground. My friend works there and will give us a tour. For now, though, let me show you Beersheba and Ben Gurion University."

* * *

The tour lasted several hours, with stops at Ben Gurion University, the Old Turkish Town, and Beersheba River Park. While each had its interesting aspects, none excited her like Jerusalem's Old City, Tel Aviv's intricate layer of busy streets and shops, or Haifa's Bahá'í Gardens. As Gerald made clear, though, the cost of living and the topflight Ben Gurion University made it a great place to live and study.

She looked forward to a quiet evening meal, where they could discuss non-touristy stuff. Around 5 pm Gerald asked, "anyone hungry?"

Starved, said Rebecca, more so out of developing boredom than real hunger.

"I have just the place. Dinner's on me."

"Not so fast," said David. I'll cover dinner, as long as it's not McDonalds or Burger King."

He took them to Saba Jebeto, a top-rated Mediterranean restaurant. Once seated, they ordered from a wide-ranging menu.

"So, Rebecca, do you like Beersheba?" asked Gerald.

"Very interesting. It's an old city, as you explained, but seems very modern."

"Yeah, after the 1948 war, it changed dramatically as more Jews started moving in. And when the university started in nineteen sixty-nine, we had a building boom. And then came River Park, a huge investment by JNF."

"JNF?"

"Jewish National Fund," answered David. "It's a century-old charity that helps build facilities for Israelis, from playgrounds to rehab centers to hospitals. I contribute every year. Anyway the goal has been to take some of the population pressure off Jerusalem and Tel Aviv, and have people move down south. Tomorrow Gerald's taking us to Sderot, a town smack dab against the Gaza border.

"Actually about a mile away," corrected Gerald.

"Your accent is interesting," said Rebecca. "What was it like growing up in Savannah?"

"Not much different than growing up in Palo Alto., A lot more humidity. More African Americans. Not an academic hot spot, for sure, like Palo alto. But we had a fairly strong Jewish community for a small city."

"So you never applied to college in the U.S.?"

"No. Moved to Israel right after high school graduation."

"Was that a public school?"

"No. Country Day, a snobby private school."

"So you *were* a snob" exclaimed David. "I knew it all along."

"Did David tell you about our friend – our used-to-be friend – Steve Mandelbaum?"

"No, what's that about?"

David recounted the story, emphasizing Steve's wish to join the IDF. Just as he finished, the food arrived.

As they started eating, Rebecca asked Gerald, "Given that story, do you think Steve can ever join the IDF?"

"Sure," said Gerald. "We have lots of assholes in the army. He would fit right in."

Rebecca looked at David, who just shrugged, and continued eating. When done eating she claimed exhaustion. "If you guys want to keep talking, I'm fine with that, just drop me off at the hotel. I've had it for today."

"Actually, me too," said David.

"Of course," said Gerald. I'll pick you guys up at nine tomorrow for our trip to Sderot."

The waitress brought the bill, and handed it to David. Gerald snatched it away.

"Too late," said David. "It's already been paid. Tip included. On my brief trip to the bathroom break."

"Sneaky you are," said Gerald.

# FIFTY-FOUR

# Sderot

The next morning Gerald picked up his guests at their hotel. As Rebecca opened the car's back door, David grabbed the handle. "No, for this trip you get to ride in the front." He then opened the front door and motioned for her to get in the passenger seat. She complied. David then closed the door and went in the back.

"Good mornin' Rebecca," said Gerald, handing her a single sheet of paper. "David wants you in front, so we can talk on the way. He asked me to give a little history of the area we're going to visit, and thought it would be easier than having to raise my voice for the back seat. I prepared this one-page handout just for reference."

"Is there a test at the end? Will this affect my college grades?"

"Be careful, Gerald." David warned from the back seat. "She's smart as a whip, and will walk out of a lecture if bored."

"Well, of that I'm not worried. Not at fifty miles an hour."

"Actually," said Rebecca, scanning the sheet full of one-line bullet points, "I read much of this history last night, in preparation for the trip. On Wikipedia."

"Great," said Gerald, as he started the car and drove toward

Sderot. "So you know that Israel pulled out of Gaza totally in 2005, and that Hamas won an election for control the following year. And that there hasn't been an election since then."

"Yeah, I get it. A total dictatorship, and a recognized as a terrorist organization by both the U.S. and European nations."

"And so you know that Egypt controls Gaza's southern border, and has had to destroy tunnels to keep Hamas from invading the Sinai. So it's not just Israel that controls the Gaza border."

"Yes, I read that, too. What I don't get is why there are Israeli towns and villages so close to the border, so vulnerable to missiles fired from Gaza."

"Told you she was smart," said David.

"Good question, for sure," said Gerald. "Towns along Gaza were originally camps for the wave of Jewish immigrants from the middle east. The idea was to have a chain of settlements to block infiltration from Gaza, which at the time was controlled by Egypt. Many Moroccan Jews settled there, and later Jews from Romania, Ethiopia, and Russia. They had the full support of the government, and of course there were no missile threats until Hamas took over this century. So Sderot grew, and now has 30,000 inhabitants. It's one of the closest communities to Gaza."

"So when the missile attacks began, there was no mass exodus?"

"No. Instead the government built thousands of bomb shelters, both inside buildings and homes, and also at every bus stop. Israel's Iron Dome missile defense gave a sense of security as well. Still, there's no doubt the missile attacks have taken a toll, psychologically for sure. Our first stop will be an indoor playground, where we'll see bomb shelters for the kids and staff."

After some more talk about Gaza, Rebecca felt the need to change the discussion. "David said your parents run an import-export business in Savannah. Do they do business with Israel?"

"No. Savannah's a deep-sea port, so we get container ships

from all over the world, but mainly from Asia. I would say most of their business deals with China, Japan, and some from Europe."

Rebecca then asked about his college career, the medical program he was about to enter, and his career goals.

"You haven't asked him about girlfriends," said David, from the back seat.

"None of my business," she replied.

"It's okay," said Gerald. "She's back in the states this month. Otherwise, you would have met her."

"A southerner?" asked Rebecca.

"From New York. Brooklyn."

His answer made her think of Michael.

As they entered Sderot, Gerald pointed out bomb shelters at every bus stop. "The closer you get to the Gaza border, the more shelters you'll see."

"When you say bomb proof, you don't mean a direct hit, do you?"

"No. I suppose if a missile landed directly on top, it would be toast. But in the neighborhood, the shelter will protect you from shock waves and flying debris. So everyone knows to get into one when the sirens go off. We're going to stop at the indoor playground, for a private tour. As I explained yesterday, my friend is one of the directors, Gideon Levy."

They pulled up to a large one-story building with a sign out front stating, "JNF Indoor Playground."

"I see JNF has been busy in this area," said Rebecca.

"They parked and entered the building.

The guard at the entrance took their names, made a call, and within a minute Mr. Levy appeared, greeted them with "Welcome, welcome."

Gerald introduced his guests.

"Come in. Come in," said Levy. Inside, he pointed to kids playing in a large room, about an acre in size. Swing sets, climbing ladders, slides, batting cages – all sorts of activities. "The facility is open throughout the day, but most of our activity is right after school. Kids come here while their parents are working, stay for an hour or two until picked up."

"And if a siren goes off?" asked Gerald. "Gideon, tell them."

"If a siren goes off," replied Levy, "meaning missiles have been launched from Gaza, people inside have fifteen seconds to get into a safe room."

"Did you say fifteen seconds?" asked Rebecca.

"Yes, the border is only a mile from here, and God knows where in Gaza the missiles come from, but once detected by the Iron Dome, fifteen seconds. So all the kids are trained. We have five safe rooms in the perimeter. Come, I'll show you one."

He led them to a room in a corner of the play area, 20 by 20 feet, with several mattresses stacked against one wall.

"Are all the kids musical?" asked Rebecca. "I see a keyboard, ukulele, guitar, a sound system. But no toilet or food. How long are the students supposed to stay here?"

"We keep the instruments here for the teachers to entertain the kids," replied Levy. "As to no toilet or food, the time spent in these rooms is always short, maybe a half hour at most. We've always received the all-clear signal by then."

"So these rooms are much more reinforced than the rest of the building?"

"Yes. Anything other than a direct hit, these rooms will protect our kids and staff from blast effects that might crumble regular construction. And we have regular training exercises, so the kids know just what to do. No coaxing needed."

"How does that affect the kids psychologically?" she asked.

"It's an issue, no doubt, there's a high incidence of PTSD among all the residents of Sderot."

"So why do people stay here?"

"That's a complicated answer," said Gerald. "There are financial incentives, much cheaper cost of housing, lots of community support. So people stay in towns near the border and live with the missile threat."

"Just missiles? What about Gaza army crossing the border and invading Sderot?"

"Oh, that's not a concern. There's a huge wall on the border, and if they tried to breach it, the IDF would mow them down."

"I didn't see any IDF driving in here. Where are the soldiers?"

"Close by, not stationed here. But they could no doubt arrive within minutes."

* * *

After leaving the Indoor Playground Gerald drove to the Black Arrow Memorial, a small park which commemorates Israeli Paratroopers who fought Egyptian terrorist in the early 1950s. For tourists, Black Arrow is as close to Gaza you can get; from there you can see the Israeli-Gaza border fence just a half mile away. Visible a mile or so beyond the fence is the town Beit Hanun, closest Gaza city to the northern border with Israel.

Gerald led them around the walking paths, gave them time to read the various memorial inscriptions, and answered Rebecca's several questions.

"Scary," she said, "how close Gaza is. I understand the wall can prevent stragglers from wandering into Israel. But would it prevent a full-scale assault? Wasn't the Great Wall of China a colossal failure? What's to prevent the Gaza army from tearing it down, and marching in?"

"Rebecca, there is no Gaza army," replied David. "Just a bunch of terrorists. They have missiles for sure, but they don't have anything like an organized army. When Israel was attacked by Syria and Egypt in 1973, it was by their armies. Israel was caught by surprise, but mobilized quickly and defeated both. So a bunch of random terrorists aren't going to breach this wall and do much harm, not without instant retaliation. No, the threat is the missiles, not an invasion."

"People in Sderot and surrounding communities, they go about their business like anyone else," added Gerald, "except when the sirens go off. So that's the real threat.

"I hope you're right," said Rebecca. "This part of Israel gives me the jitters. A whole population of Arabs who want you dead, just a few miles away. Scary."

# Epilogue

October 7, 2023, changed everything. The summer of '23, and into the early fall, Rebecca still harbored misgivings about how the Palestinians were treated by the Israelis, and what Israel could do to make things better. She no longer had illusions about BDS, but her passion for Israel was nowhere near David's. She gauged the situation as similar to that between her own mother and father; two people in love, and compatible, with just some different political and social views.

As reports came in of the October 7 massacres committed by Hamas —the mass murder of 260 young people at a music festival, the killing of children and elderly women in the Kibbutz, the rapes — her anger boiled. Some of it was directed toward herself, for her naivete of the situation leading up to the invasion.

But then David was also naïve, as was his good friend Gerald Fishman. The questions she asked near the Gaza border, about an invasion, were poo-pooed. Only threat is the missiles? Obviously not.

So David was right about the overall existential threat. But like the Israeli government itself, he misunderstood the risk of a cross-border invasion, and its singular goal to simply murder innocent civilians She had no basis for saying, "I told you so," for she had merely asked the question.

In one year Rebecca had undergone a remarkable transformation, from a naïve high school girl, living in a bubble, to a mature young woman, out of the bubble and cognizant of the culture that wanted her and her boyfriend and her family dead. She pondered the arc of this transformation: meeting David; the attack in the BDS march; her research on links about BDS; her mother's advice during Thanksgiving break; Weisel's book *Night*; Michael's murder; her summer trip to Israel. And now, the October 2023 war.

\* \* \*

Steve's last words to Amanda, that day in June when she told him of her pregnancy, were:

"I'll call you sometime tomorrow."

He did not. Instead, he texted that he was still working on his status and would get back to her "shortly."

Amanda would have none of it. She wrote a letter to the Israel Defense Force, addressed "To whom it may concern." In the letter she pointed out that the father of her unborn child was "stuck in Israel," and that all their plans – "I was to join him but on the advice of my doctor am told not to travel overseas" – were in disarray. She needed him home, not in Israel, and she asked the IDF to "please release him so he can return to help me raise his child."

Not knowing where to actually send such a letter, she traveled to the Israeli Consulate in downtown Chicago, met with a representative and presented her story. She showed a record from her obstetrician, affirming pregnancy, and also a note advising – written at her insistence – that she should not travel overseas while pregnant.

The Israeli rep stated he would forward her letter to the "appropriate channel," and it would find its way to the IDF recruitment office.

Two days later Steve had an intake interview with the IDF. To his total surprise, the interviewer brought up his girlfriend's pregnancy. After a few embarrassing moments – for Steve – the interviewer explained that IDF could not accept him "at this point," adding: "We need fully-committed volunteers, not young men from overseas who have deep personal conflicts, as you have. First, you must take care of your personal situation."

After rejection by the IDF, Steve no longer had reason to stay in Israel. He returned home and to Amanda. There was anger on both sides: his, over her letter the IDF; hers, over his vacillation on making the right decision. They agreed to seek counseling. Several weeks later, with Amanda now approaching her second trimester, they married.

Steve entered the graduate engineering program in Great Lakes University. She entered her third year of architecture school. They had a healthy baby boy the following May. Her parents funded a full-time nanny so she could continue her training. In the year following his return, Steve had no further contact with David or Rebecca.

* * *

The prosecution against the four defendants in the Geddy murder case was only partially resolved after one year. The driver of the SUV claimed he had no idea his passenger intended to kill Mr. Geddy; he was told to simply drive by the house for "surveillance" purposes. Immediately after the shooting, he was offered ten thousand dollars to drive out of state and sell the car; this act made him an accomplice to the crime.

Once caught in California, and realizing he faced potentially years in prison, the driver identified the shooter, who was then quickly apprehended. The killer had received an unknown amount, in crypto, for the hit, but he refused to identify anyone who hired him.

At trial the driver had to rely on a public defender, who did her best to show he was an innocent man. The jury found him guilty, and the judge sentenced him to three years in prison.

The killer had a private attorney, but given his refusal to name names, or state a motive for the killing, his attorney had no reasonable defense. The shooter was found guilty and received a fifteen-year sentence.

The other two defendants were foreign nationals, from middle eastern countries, both in the U.S. with what turned out to be fake passports. Their trial was delayed over issues of immigration, and who exactly had arranged for them to come to the Muslim-cultural Students Association at Great Lakes University. Working with the Justice Dept., the FBI tried in vain to find the source of their funding. Their attorney – a public defender – also could not get them to reveal sources, and after one year their case had yet to go to trial.

Geddy's girlfriend was never charged with any crime. After her boyfriend's murder, she left campus and moved back to her parents' home in Minneapolis, where she enrolled in the state university.

One byproduct of the investigation was that the FBI designated GLU's BDS club an unindicted co-conspirator, which allowed the school to remove its charter and close it down. When the national BDS organization heard about this move it cried foul, and sent an angry letter to the campus newspaper, which published it. In response, Attorney Zimmerman replied, pointing out that once a campus club is implicated in any illegal activity, the university has no choice but to remove its charter.

\* \* \*

Regarding the Solomons' lawsuit against Great Lakes University, President Hightower's deposition did not go well. During discovery all the negative correspondence he had received was turned over to the plaintiff lawyers. Using this information, he was grilled incessantly on his "failures, his lack of concern for rising anti-Semitism on campus." He denied as much as possible but, as Attorney Zimmerman explained afterwards, a lay jury would likely not be sympathetic.

The university was insured for this type of lawsuit, which meant the insurance company would decide what to do once there was a choice between settlement and trial. After the discovery phase and depositions, it came down to heated negotiations between Sullivan and Cromwell, plaintiff's firm, and Kincaid and Wolinsky, the defense firm.

If S&C stood its ground on their $10M demand, K&W insisted they would go to trial, and pointed out the Solomons *could* lose. After all, despite the obvious tragedy, it's a thin legal argument that the campus culture of anti-Semitism was the *fault* of the university. K&W was prepared to have several university presidents testify on behalf of GLU, pointing out a similar culture across many elite campuses.

K&W offered the plaintiffs $5M. S&C countered with $7M, and they settled on $6M, an amount close to what Attorney Zimmerman figured when the claim was filed. The insurance company agreed, and paid.

* * *

David was right about Professor Shapiro's book, *Useful Idiots*. The title brought attention, and it was reviewed in *The New York Times* and other left-leaning media such as *The Atlantic* and *The Washington Post*. The reviews echoed Rebecca's pre-publication comments about the book being only a series of selective anecdotes. This criticism did not surprise David Applebaum, as he told Rebecca, "They were all written by college professors. What do you expect?" What most upset him were negative reviews by progressive Jewish organizations, like J Street and Jewish Voice for Peace. They took the Professor's argument and somehow managed to twist it into a rant about the West Bank, implying that the anti-Semitism on campus was understandable, if not totally justified, as long as Israel continued its unlawful occupation.

The most positive reviews appeared in newsletters by Zionist Organization of America and Jewish News Syndicate, two organizations that unequivocally support Israel. "It's astounding how all the other Jewish organizations seem to want to ignore reality," David told Rebecca. "ZOA and JNS get it. None of the others seem to."

The publicity, negative or not, did increase sales, especially on college campuses, and for several weeks the book was on the NYT's nonfiction bestseller list. Since it came out after the settlement of Solomon vs. Great Lakes University, its content had no bearing on the case.

Steve, being ensconced in the graduate engineering program when *Useful Idiots* was published, avoided having to answer questions about his Forward to the book. Neither his professors nor fellow graduate fellow students had much interest in what they deemed "political" topics.

* * *

An interim president was appointed for Great Lakes University, the former Dean of the School of Arts and Sciences. While she served, a search committee went looking for a new president. The publicity of the Solomons' lawsuit, and of Professor Shapiro's book, made the interim tenure a bit difficult, but there was no noticeable drop in application quality or numbers. So, a year later, the school stood as before, one of the top ten, its recent horror show receding into the background.

\* \* \*

David entered GLU's medical school in downtown Chicago, and Rebecca entered her second year of pre-law on the main campus. She lived in the same dorm as her freshman year. David rented a small one-bedroom apartment in one of the skyscrapers adjacent to the medical school. "Larger than what we had in Tel Aviv, and cheaper," he told her.

After one year, she remained unmarried and unpregnant, but as close to David as ever. On weekends, when unencumbered with work, she took the train downtown and stayed in his apartment. In another two years she would enter law school, and David would be a senior, applying for a residency position in internal medicine. That would be decision time: where should both apply to end up in the same city. It was doable, they discussed it, and the assumption was, at that point, they would get married.

# Sources Cited or Referred To

Book titles attributed to fictional characters are also fictional, i.e., Aaron Peretz's *The Israeli-Palestinian Conflict, Why It's Not Resolvable Anytime Soon*, and Professor Shapiro's *Useful Idiots – How Academia Fosters Anti-Semitism*. Thus, "reviews" or commentary on these works are also fictional. All other sources mentioned – organizations, books, articles, and documentaries– are real. They are listed below, along with internet links.

## **Organizations (in alphabetical order)**

Algemeiner
www.algemeiner.com

Amnesty International
www.amnesty.org/

American Jewish Committee
https://www.ajc.org/

Anti-Defamation League
https://www.adl.org/

Boycott, Divestment, Sanction
https://bdsmovement.net/what-is-bds

Committee for Accuracy in Middle East Reporting and Analysis
www.camera.org

Hamas Covenant 1988
https://avalon.law.yale.edu/20th_century/hamas.asp

Human Rights Watch
www.hrw.org/

J Street
www.jstreet.org

Jewish News Syndicate
www.JNS.org

Jewish Virtual Library
www.jewishvirtuallibrary.org/

Jewish Voice for Peace
www.jvp.org

Middle East Media Research Institute
www.memri.org

## Books (in order of publication)
Elie Wiesel, *Night*, 1960
Amazon

Alan Dershowitz, *The Case for Israel*, 2004
Amazon

Ben-Dror Yemini, *Industry of Lies*, 2017
Amazon

Jasbir K. Puar, *The Right to Maim*, 2017
Amazon

Andrew Pessin and Doron S. Ben-Atar, *Anti-Zionism on Campus: The University, Free Speech, and BDS*, 2018
Amazon

Alan Dershowitz, *The Case Against BDS*, 2018
Amazon

Ronen Bergman, *Rise and Kill First*, 2018
Amazon

Alan Dershowitz, *Defending Israel*, 2019
Amazon

Charles Jacobs and Avi Goldwasser, *Betrayal: The Failure of American Jewish Leadership*, 2023
Amazon

## Articles

Benny Steve, "The Liar as Hero," *The New Republic*, March 16, 2011
https://newrepublic.com/article/85344/ilan-pappe-sloppy-dishonest-historian/

Peter Beinart, "You Can't Save Democracy in a Jewish State," *The New York Times*,
    February 19, 2023.
https://www.nytimes.com/2023/02/19/opinion/israel-democracy-protests.html/

## Documentaries

"Boycott This!" (2016)
IMDB: https://www.imdb.com/title/tt5937592/
Amazon Prime Video: Link

"Boycott" (2021)
IMDB: https://www.imdb.com/title/tt15721106/
Amazon Prime Video: Link

www.ingramcontent.com/pod-product-compliance
Lightning Source LLC
Chambersburg PA
CBHW061934170626
46813CB00006B/2390